DUAL
INNOCENCE

DUAL INNOCENCE

An ESI Novel

CEARA NOBLES

Riverside
PRESS

ALSO BY

CEARA NOBLES

.

THE ESI SERIES

COUNTERPLAY

LEGACY EXPOSED

TRUTH REVEALED

SIGN UP FOR MY MONTHLY NEWSLETTER

TO RECEIVE SPECIAL OFFERS, GIVEAWAYS, DISCOUNTS, BONUS CONTENT, UPDATES FROM THE AUTHOR, INFO ON NEW RELEASES AND OTHER GREAT READS:

WWW.CEARANOBLES.COM/SUBSCRIBE

For my husband Grady, who always encourages me to chase my dreams.

CHAPTER 1

THE CAMERA'S SHUTTER SNAPPED, loud as gunfire in the late afternoon stillness.

Bellamy straightened, examining the photo she'd just taken. The lighting looked good, and the street sign was clearly visible in the background. Her client couldn't mistake the area she'd intended, which covered her in case something went wrong.

In the two weeks she'd been scouting this area, she hadn't seen a homeless presence and only a handful of cars had driven by. The abandoned warehouses on either side of the narrow street would provide perfect cover.

It was an excellent location for a black-market exchange.

Bellamy slid her phone out of her pocket and hit '2' on her speed dial.

It only rang once.

"Yes?"

"I've got it. I'll meet you at the usual place in ten." Bellamy didn't wait for him to respond. She dropped her phone and her camera into the backpack at her feet, then swung it over her shoulder.

It was a short walk to her usual meeting place, so Bellamy took her time.

This wasn't her usual gig, but she didn't mind the change of pace. It was kind of fun to scope out new locations and use her camera for something besides taking pictures with Sam. Usually her buyers had locations pre-chosen and she had to trust that they'd done their homework - and trust was not something she liked to give.

It was nice to do the legwork herself this time. She could have peace of mind knowing that there wouldn't be any random police patrols or nosey homeless people poking around the area on the night of the exchange, which was scheduled for tomorrow.

Her contact was waiting for her when she arrived, seated at a corner booth in the back of the shop. Bellamy nodded at Bob, the shop owner, as she passed. He waved a hand, his grumpy expression never changing, and returned his attention to his customer.

"Officer Ruiz," Bellamy said, sliding into the booth across from him. She shrugged off her black leather jacket and dropped it onto the seat next to her.

Ruiz was dressed in plainclothes - his preference during their meetings, so as not to draw attention to himself. He glanced up and his eyebrows drew together over dark eyes. "I told you not to call me that."

Bellamy smiled. "How many times have we had this

conversation? This is a safe space. One of the only ones in the city." She drew the polaroid photo out of her backpack and slid it across the table. "This is the location for tomorrow night. The area's completely abandoned; as long as you make sure there isn't a police presence in the area, we should be clear."

Ruiz examined the photo, then slid it into his pocket. "All right. I'll make sure you're paid once the deal goes through successfully."

"I expect nothing less." Bellamy leaned back in her seat. "Aren't you going to ask me how I found this spot? It's a good one."

Ruiz snorted. "You're the best fence in the city. I'm sure you've had an exchange there before."

"I don't recycle my locations. But I did have one a block away." Bellamy grinned. "Went off without a hitch, and I expect this one will too."

"All right. I'll pass this on to the buyer." He stood and dropped a couple dollars onto the table next to his still-full coffee cup. "I'll be in touch."

"Adios, muchacho," Bellamy called after him.

He raised a hand and flipped her off over his shoulder.

Bellamy grinned and called the waitress over. She ordered a slice of apple pie and a pot of fresh coffee.

Once she was sure Ruiz had left, she pulled out a small notebook and set it on the table. Flipping it open to the first blank page, she scrawled two lines.

Governor Ronald Powell.

NE Marx St.

* * * * * *

It was late evening by the time Bellamy made it back to the studio. The lights were on and the dented blue Subaru sat out front, so Sam was still working.

Bellamy pasted a smile on her face as she opened the studio door.

As she'd expected, Sam stood in the middle of the room, hands on hips, expression petulant. "I've been calling you for hours, you jerk."

"Sorry, sorry." Bellamy dropped her backpack on the chair just inside the door and sidestepped Sam's pile of junk littering the entryway. "Really, could you at least drop your stuff off to the side? I'm going to trip over it one of these days and break my neck."

"Serves you right," Sam sniffed. "That's not important right now. Why are you keeping secrets from me?"

Bellamy froze. A thousand scenarios whipped through her brain at lightspeed, along with a thousand pre-planned excuses she could use to explain them away. "What are you talking about?"

Sam gestured wildly at Bellamy's laptop, which sat open on the counter. "The funeral," she said. "I read your emails from Sarah. Why didn't you tell me?"

"Oh, that." Bellamy waved a hand. "I'm not going."

"Why not? They're like family to you. You haven't seen them in ages."

"I have stuff to do here. Besides, you said it yourself. I haven't seen them in ten years. All that crap happened a long time ago and I don't really want to relive it. I'm not the cute girl-next-door I was when I left there." Bellamy gestured at herself, as if the nose ring, leather jacket, and spunky short brown hair emphasized her point.

Sam wrinkled her nose. "You may not wear ribbons in your hair anymore, but you're still Bellamy, and they're still important to you. If they weren't, you wouldn't still be talking to Sarah, and you wouldn't be Googling the family all the time."

"I do not Google them."

"Your search history doesn't lie."

Bellamy snapped her laptop closed. "How many times have I told you to stay off my computer?"

"Then pick a password I can't guess. As usual, I've been forced to take matters into my own hands. Here." She pulled a folded piece of paper out of her back pocket and handed it to Bellamy. Before Bellamy could unfold it, Sam said, "It's a plane ticket. You leave tomorrow morning and come back tomorrow night. You won't even be gone twenty-four hours."

"Sam, I'm not -"

"You're welcome." Sam grinned and kissed Bellamy on the cheek. "I've gotta go. There's an important story calling my name, and I've got a lot of work to do before you get back tomorrow night."

Bellamy scowled and shoved the plane ticket into her pocket. "What story? It's not about Powell, is it? Because we've talked about that, Sam."

"Can't tell you yet. I'm still nailing down the details." Sam scooped up her bag from the pile in front of the door. "You'd better be on that plane tomorrow morning, Bellamy

Burke. I paid good money for that ticket, and you know you need to be there."

"Ugh, fine. I'll go to the stupid funeral."

"That's what I like to hear. Toodle-oo!" Sam blew her another kiss and left, closing the door behind her.

Bellamy blew out a sigh. Just how she wanted to spend her Friday.

CHAPTER 2

IT WOULD BE A COLD DAY IN HELL before Bellamy set foot in the state of Washington again.

That's what she'd always told herself.

Yet here she was, driving through her childhood home of La Conner, because Sam had bought her a plane ticket. After three years working together, Bellamy should've learned how to say no. But once Sam had her mind set on something, there was no changing it.

Between that and the fact that she was the nosiest person on the planet, Bellamy never stood a chance.

The picturesque little town hadn't changed much in the last ten years. Waterfront shops facing the Swinomish Channel sported colorful facades and darkened windows. Boats bumped gently against the docks. Rainbow Bridge, the red monstrosity that connected La Conner to the Swinomish Reservation, stood sentinel at the south end of the channel.

Bellamy pulled into the small gravel area that served as parking lot for La Conner's only funeral home. The packed pebbles crunched under the weight of the rental car's tires and dust kicked up around the vehicle, prompting Bellamy to roll up her windows before the inside of the car was covered.

Judging by the crowded parking lot, this was the biggest turnout for a funeral in La Conner's history. Bellamy eased through the rows, cursing her midsize rental. It was a lot longer than her '94 Honda.

If only she was driving the beat-up Civic now. Not only was it easier to park, but the musty smell of age and cigarette smoke brought a sense of comfort she could really use right now.

That smell always calmed her down when she was on her way to an exchange for one of her clients. In fact, the old girl was more well-known in Portland's black market than Bellamy herself. She liked to use it to her advantage. When she rolled up in a car that looked like it was about to fall apart, her first-time clients laughed.

How could a fence move such high-ticket items when she couldn't afford to buy a decent car?

They always changed their tune once they worked with her, though. She was efficient and discreet, and none of her clients had ever been caught by the authorities.

Bellamy maneuvered into a tiny space between a minivan and a hedge, cursing the stupid midsize rental car she was stuck with.

She stared up at the oak trees that towered over the

one-story brick building. The funeral home was just down the street from the bus station. The surrounding trees were so tall that she could see them from where she'd sat ten years before, waiting for the bus that had taken her away from La Conner forever.

Or so she'd thought.

Bellamy shook off the memory and sat up in her seat. She met her own blue eyes in the rearview mirror and lifted her chin.

"You're not fifteen anymore," she told her reflection. "Time to put on your big girl panties and get this over with."

She almost wished someone was around to witness her talking to herself. Maybe word would spread that she was crazy, and nobody would talk to her when she went inside. She'd started the habit years ago, when she first started working with Sam. Sam often rambled on about things. It didn't matter if they were developing photos or staking out a possible subject. Sam just liked to chatter; she'd often tell the same stories over and over again. At first it drove Bellamy crazy, but she'd gotten so used to it that now she hated silence. Next thing she knew, she was talking to herself when she was alone. Sometimes it eased the ache of loneliness that hit her in the middle of the night.

Bellamy turned off the ignition and pulled out the key. "Why are you so nervous? It's been ten years. Nobody's going to recognize you." She nodded at her reflection. Her heavily lined and shadowed eyes didn't hold the same confidence that her voice did. Her dark hair, once artfully arranged in a just-got-out-of-bed pixie cut, was now flat on one side and sticking straight up on the other.

What the hell. It's not like she was here to impress.

Bellamy shoved the door open. It bounced off the hedge and immediately slammed closed. Muttering under her breath, she shouldered it open again and shimmied through the small gap. Branches scratched her bare arms and legs as she slid down the length of the car and out into the open.

Well, this day was starting out just great.

Bellamy straightened her pencil skirt as she approached the funeral home. It wasn't exactly traditional, but she couldn't bring herself to leave her leather jacket at home, so she wore it over her black blouse. Without it, she just didn't feel like herself.

An easel sat outside the front door. A large sign rested upon it, displaying beautiful scripted lettering.

Paul Erickson, 1960-2018. Beloved Father and Friend.

Next to the sign was a portrait of an aged man with graying brown hair and a kind smile. His dark brown eyes twinkled at the camera like he was laughing at one of his own jokes.

He probably was.

Memories drifted into Bellamy's mind, misty with age. At dinner, Paul had always cracked jokes to his family. He'd follow it up - when he actually finished the joke - with uproarious laughter. The rest of the family would laugh with him, but his snorting belly laugh was always funnier than the joke itself.

Bellamy sucked in a breath at the unexpected stab of pain in her chest.

All that shit she'd spent years trying to forget came

rushing back.

Paul looked older now, but she could still see the same man she'd idolized as a child. A man who had put his business and his family on the line to help her, who had treated her as one of his own children, even though she never thanked him for it.

If only he could see her now. If only he could see the path her life had taken.

He'd roll over in his grave.

Shaking the tension out of her hands, Bellamy repeated her mantra under her breath one more time. "I'm not fifteen anymore."

Cold air blasted her as she stepped into the building, a stark contrast to the early September heat outside. The low murmur of voices drew her toward the viewing room.

Every inhabitant of La Conner had somehow found a way to cram into the tiny room. In a town this small, a death like Paul's was a big event. People stood shoulder-to-shoulder, filling the room way past capacity. A harried funeral worker with a bad perm and coffee-stained teeth wove through the crowd, ushering everyone through the line to view the casket. The procession meandered out the door on the other side of the room, exiting at the rear of the building.

How quaint. All these people had shunned Paul and his family when he tried to help Bellamy ten years ago, and now they had come to pay their respects. It made Bellamy want to puke. She hated La Conner and all the two-faced, backstabbing people in it.

There were many faces she recognized in the crowd.

Mrs. Sparks stood hunched over her walker halfway up the line. Bellamy wasn't sure how the old bat was still alive. She had to be a hundred years old by now. In front of her, Bellamy's childhood neighbor Mr. Harris held a phone to his ear. His booming voice overpowered the din of conversation in the room and his right hand made wild gestures in the air while he talked.

The room was so full that nobody took notice of Bellamy when she slipped inside. She slid to a corner and slouched against the wall where she could observe things. Through the shifting shoulders, she caught sight of the familiar faces she'd been most dreading to see.

The Ericksons stood in the family line next to the casket.

Their family had always been big fish in the small pond of La Conner. They were everything a family was supposed to be. Mary, the matriarch and Paul's wife, was a powerhouse in the kitchen. She was known for spontaneously delivering freshly baked cookies and bread to other families in town. Sarah, the only daughter and Bellamy's childhood best friend, was beauty and brains all rolled into one. She was a cheerleader and graduated high school at the top of her class. Owen, Sarah's twin brother, was the class clown and teenage womanizer. Emmett, the oldest, was the strong silent type, a star football player and the second man of the house.

From her vantage point, Bellamy allowed her gaze to travel from face to face. It was strange to reconcile her memory of each person with the version standing there.

Her slow perusal came to a stuttering stop on the last

Erickson in line, the most familiar face of all.

Chance Erickson.

The years had been good to him. She could still see a bit of the tall, lanky boy she remembered, but he was all man now. Dark hair, long and unruly in childhood, was cut short and neat. His square jaw was more defined than she remembered and covered in a shadow of stubble.

Chance stood closest to the casket. His expression was sober, hands shoved deep in his pockets, as he nodded at the neighbors giving their condolences. The tension lines around his eyes and mouth made Bellamy's heart ache.

Fifteen-year-old Bellamy would already be running across the room and throwing herself into his arms. She would be kissing him and squeezing his hand, comforting him the best way she knew how.

Twenty-five-year-old Bellamy had too many aches, resentments, and grudges to be so forward. She'd thought that urge had been squashed inside her forever, so she was surprised when she had to tap her foot to keep herself from running across the room to him.

Her retreat to the corner didn't last long, however. The funeral worker with the bad perm soon found her and ushered her toward the crowd. She found herself standing in line to offer condolences to the family, pinned on both sides by other well-wishers.

There was no escape route in sight.

Bellamy cursed herself and Sam as she inched closer and closer to the Erickson family. It pissed her off that she was here in the first place, and even worse, that the scared little girl from ten years ago was still inside her somewhere.

Sure, she could wheel and deal with the worst of Portland's black market with no problem, but the people she used to call family scared the hell out of her.

If this was happening to anyone else, she'd think it was hilarious. But since it was her own suffering, it was definitely not funny.

One by one, the people in front of her greeted the grieving family with hugs and kisses. Some chatted for a few moments, reminiscing about memories with Paul. Others approached the casket with sad smiles on their faces.

By the time she reached Emmett, who was first in line, Bellamy had composed herself. He greeted the person in front of her, nodding as the woman offered a soft word of condolence.

Then his eyes turned to her.

His expression was blank for a moment and his eyes narrowed, as if trying to place her face in his memory.

Bellamy let out a small breath of relief. She didn't look anything like the teenager she'd been when she left La Conner. Her 'preacher's daughter' vibe was gone forever. Long, wavy brown hair had been replaced by a punk-rock pixie cut, her bare face now covered in heavy makeup. A small silver hoop glinted from the right side of her nose.

There's no way anyone would recognize -

"Bellamy?"

Her polite smile froze. Damn.

"Bellamy Burke?"

The dull buzz of conversation in the room went silent at Emmett's exclamation. She felt the weight of hundreds of pairs of eyes drilling into the back of her head.

All right. Not what she'd expected, but she could handle this.

Bellamy schooled her features into a cool smile and clasped her hands together so they'd stop shaking. "Hello, Emmett."

Up close, Emmett was huge. There was a reason he'd been a football star in high school; he was wide as an ox and equally intimidating. Bellamy had heard he joined the military; it showed in the set of his shoulders. He could probably snap her neck with those gigantic biceps of his.

Could everyone hear her heart trying to burst out of her chest?

Bellamy couldn't help it. She glanced down to the end of the line.

Chance stood frozen, like the rest of the crowd around her. His dark brown eyes were wide on her face - he looked like he'd seen a ghost. In a way, she guessed he had.

"Bellamy!"

She turned as Sarah threw her arms around her neck in a tight hug. Her long blond ponytail tickled Bellamy's nose.

"I can't believe you came," Sarah said. She drew back, her hands resting on Bellamy's shoulders, and flashed her a megawatt smile. Her makeup, although smudged, was applied with an expert hand. It was a far cry from their cartoonish attempts at using her mother's cosmetics when they were twelve years old.

Chance was still staring at her. Bellamy could see him out of the corner of her eye. She kept her gaze on Sarah and felt a genuine smile stretch across her face. "I wouldn't miss it," she lied. "I'm so sorry, Sarah."

Sarah's expression sobered at the reminder of why they were there. She stepped back, but her gaze was still warm. "Thanks. It's so good to see you."

Owen stepped up next to Sarah and leaned forward, tilting his head to peer at Bellamy's face. His green eyes had the same twinkle that Paul's always had. He looked every bit Sarah's twin, with the same tall, slender frame and blond hair.

"Wow, look at you." Owen let out a long whistle. "We thought you were dead."

Sarah smacked him in the chest with a loud "thwack."

"What? It's true!" Owen said, rubbing his chest. He winked at Bellamy, lightening the sting of his comment. "You look pretty good, for a ghost. We even have the same haircut."

Bellamy eyed his perfectly gelled blond spikes. He was wrong; he had much better hair than she did, especially after two hours on an airplane. "I learned from the best," she said lightly. "Good to see you, Owen."

Chance's eyes hadn't left her face since he'd seen her. Even worse, he hadn't said a word. He hadn't even moved.

Mary stepped forward next. Her expression was gentle as she gave Bellamy her signature mom-hug. "It's been so long," she said into Bellamy's ear. "I'm so glad you came. Paul would be so glad you came."

If only that were true.

Bellamy was raised as a Christian, but it had been a long time since she felt sure of her beliefs. Either way, Paul was staring at her from the afterlife, and he probably knew every sin she carried in her soul. There was no way he'd be happy to see her there, a black mark on his otherwise beautiful funeral day.

Bellamy swallowed hard, ducking her head as she stepped back. "Thanks. I'm so sorry for your loss."

Then, clenching her hands into fists, she turned her attention to the last member of the Erickson family. "Chance."

"Bellamy." His voice was hoarse. He still didn't move, but his gaze swept her from the top of her head down to her toes. She couldn't read his expression; was he happy to see her? Surprised? Disappointed? "It's... good to see you."

"You too."

They stared at each other for a long moment. The weight of a million unspoken questions hung in the air between them. Bellamy opened her mouth, but what could she say? Nothing could make up for the past, and it was ages behind them now.

So she didn't say anything. Instead she gave him a small nod and stepped past him.

The people in line behind Bellamy stepped forward to greet Emmett. The tension in the room eased as the sounds of conversation filtered back into the air, banishing the suffocating silence.

Bellamy laid a shaking hand on the edge of the open casket. Paul Erickson's expression was peaceful as could be, even in death. It was jarring to see him like this. In her mind, he was still the fit, middle-aged man who played kickball with the kids in the backyard. He ran the Boston marathon three times and had the energy of ten men, but the cancer had eaten away his muscle and the chemotherapy had rendered him bald.

Flashes of memory flipped through her mind like an old, grainy slideshow. Family dinners. Late night talks on the front porch. Iced tea in the backyard. Gentle smiles, welcoming arms.

Her throat ached. She swallowed hard, biting the inside of her lip, and forced composure she certainly didn't feel.

This was why she hadn't wanted to come here. This stupid town was full of memories and people she never wanted to revisit.

Sam was going to get an earful when Bellamy got back to Portland.

After a moment, the terrible tightness in her chest eased and she was able to take a full breath. Straightening, she followed the line toward the door and exited into the parking lot.

She couldn't resist one last glance over her shoulder as she left.

Through the crowd, Chance was still looking her way. He took a step forward as if to follow her, but Emmett put a hand on his shoulder and murmured something in his ear.

Bellamy let out a breath of relief. One awkward encounter with him was enough for the rest of her lifetime, thank you.

She'd vowed a long time ago to let the past remain there. Coming home had unlocked the door in a closet that held enough skeletons to bury her. If she wasn't careful, that door would blow open and she might never be able to close it again.

CHAPTER 3

"CHANCE!" THE WOODEN GATE slammed against the fence, echoing in the late afternoon quiet. A small girl flew through the opening, dark pigtails bouncing against her back as she chased after a boy a head taller than she was. "Chance, give it back. It's mine!"

Chance cackled as he leaped onto the front porch. He swung around and stuck his tongue out at the little girl who was still only halfway across the yard. "Catch me if you can!" he yelled, using the advantage of his long legs to run around the corner toward the back of the house.

The little girl stopped at the porch stairs, breathing hard, fat tears falling down her rosy cheeks. She plopped down on the top step and crossed her arms over her chest. "That's not fair," she whined. "I'm gonna tell your mom on you."

After a moment, Chance poked his head around the

corner, brow furrowed. "Hey, you're not following me."

"I'm tired. Just give it back."

"No. Finders, keepers. Losers, weepers."

The little girl puffed out her lower lip and wiped noisily at her eyes. "I hate you."

Chance stomped back over to where she sat and dropped down next to her. "You're such a crybaby. Here." He thrust out a fist. The little girl's favorite doll dangled from his grip.

She snatched the doll from him and hugged it to her chest.

"I don't even know why you like that thing. It's so old and dirty."

"It is not."

"Is too."

"Is not!"

Chance snorted and stood up. "Come on, let's go play cowboys in the backyard."

"You always want to play that game." She pouted. "I can't. I have to go home."

"Come on, just for a little while."

She frowned at him. "I said I can't."

"Pleeease, Bella. Just for a little while!"

Bella considered him for a moment before she nodded. "Fine. But just for a little while. And leave Lucy alone. Promise?"

A big grin spread across Chance's face. "Promise."

* * * * * *

Paul Erickson's burial took place at the only cemetery in La Conner.

A crowd gathered around the casket. One of the men from town stepped forward, a set of bagpipes in his arms, and a haunting tune filled the air. Birds stopped singing and the ever-persistent breeze slowed to a standstill. The world seemed to hold its breath in respect for the man's burial.

While the bagpiper played, seven uniformed men marched to the front of the crowd, rifles shining in the afternoon sunlight.

Bellamy stood near the back of the crowd. When the uniformed men fired their rifles, the first shot startled most of the crowd; many flinched at the report. A smirk tugged at her lips. If there was one thing she was used to, it was the sound of gunfire. She'd moved a lot of guns over the years; it was only natural that she learned to fire one herself.

The soldiers fired three times in a twenty-one gun salute for Paul. Afterwards, the lead soldier performed the flag ceremony and gave it to Mary, who clutched it in her lap.

The bagpiper finished his somber tune and the minister spoke, but Bellamy was too far away to hear anything except the low, deep cadence of his voice. Chance and his family stood next to the casket; she caught glimpses of them through the shoulders of the people in front of her. None of them glanced in her direction. After the debacle at the funeral home, she was happy to remain inconspicuous.

"You're Bellamy Burke, aren't you?"

Bellamy stifled a groan. So much for her changed appearance acting as a disguise. Word must have spread about her presence at the funeral. The La Conner gossip mill sure worked fast; at least that hadn't changed.

Glancing over her shoulder, she met the eyes of an elderly man standing just behind her. He leaned on a cane, his blue eyes sharp on her face. She remembered a slightly less wrinkly version of him standing on a porch and waving his cane in the air, yelling at the kids on his lawn.

"I was so sorry to hear about your mama," the old man said, a tinge of sadness in his voice. "She did my grocery shopping for years. Wonderful lady."

Bellamy rubbed her suddenly cold hands on her skirt. "Thank you."

"People still talk about your family, you know. A God-fearing woman like your mama didn't deserve what she got."

Bellamy almost scoffed. God hadn't saved her mother, nor had He saved Bellamy herself. Bellamy wasn't even sure that He was up there; if He was, He certainly didn't care about her or her family. "Is she buried here?"

If the old man was surprised, he didn't show it. But he wouldn't be; her family's history was about as common knowledge as the Kardashians' current drama. He pointed his cane to the other side of the cemetery, a shady area where the headstones were crammed together in a disorganized mess. "Everyone in town raised the money to have her buried. It was the respectful thing to do."

Bellamy tried to form some semblance of a smile and spared one last glance at Paul's casket. She stepped away from the crowd and smoothed her skirt for the millionth time as she weaved through the headstones. The past was done and over with; she'd buried it years ago and left it to rot. It was the only way she could survive. But she couldn't fight the invisible string pulling her toward her mother's grave, even as every step dredged up memories she'd fought too hard to bury.

* * * * * *

Bellamy. Bellamy frickin' Burke.

Chance stood under the awning at the cemetery with his family. As the minister quoted a few of his father's favorite passages from the Bible, Chance couldn't stop his gaze from wandering back to the ghost of the girl he'd thought was dead.

How was she even there?

He couldn't wrap his brain around it. His thoughts were running a million miles a minute. Why did she return now? Where had she been? How could she look more beautiful than he remembered? What the hell happened ten years ago?

He'd been wondering that last part every day since she disappeared.

In ten years, she hadn't changed much. Sure, her hair was shorter and she had a nose ring now - one that he found very sexy. But she hadn't grown an inch, still barely over five feet tall if he had to guess. She still looked like she was fifteen years old, but in the brief moment that their gazes met, he'd seen the age in her eyes. Dark blue eyes that were almost too big for her face, and skin that was still that beautiful porcelain he remembered. She looked like a punk rock version of a damn china doll.

His gut tightened as he watched her across the crowd. She stood at the very back, almost out of his line of sight. Was that on purpose? Probably.

Her appearance at the viewing had about knocked him out. And then she'd spoken to him and all he could do was stare at her, trying not to faint like some damsel in distress. While she stared at him expectantly, conflicting emotions had torn apart his insides until there was nothing left. He couldn't decide whether to hug her or shake her.

Then the moment had passed, and she'd stepped past him without a backward glance.

After some contemplation, anger won out over relief. Damn right, he was angry with her. It still kept him up at night, wondering why she left without an explanation or even a goodbye. Worrying that she was a cold case somewhere and he'd never know what happened to her.

Chance frowned and jerked his attention back to the minister. It wasn't the time for ghosts from the past. Next to him, his mother's petite frame shook. Swallowing past the lump in his throat, he rested his arm around her shoulders and gave them a reassuring squeeze. Mary looked up at him and smiled through her tears, as if trying to comfort him instead of the other way around.

Chance gritted his teeth. Give him an enemy base to infiltrate, a kidnapping victim to rescue, or literally any other military scenario... No problem. But he'd rather be shot in the leg than listen to his mother grieve. He didn't know how to handle the helpless frustration burning a hole in his gut.

As the grave dedication ended, the crowd stood in

silence as Sean O'Connor played another sorrowful tune on his bagpipes. Soldiers from the closest army base fired off a twenty-one gun salute, and they presented the flag to Chance's mother. Her hands shook as she accepted it from him.

The final note from the bagpipes faded into the cooling late afternoon air and the crowd began to dissipate.

Chance stared hard at the casket, every muscle strung tight, and fought to keep his expressionless mask in place. A hard elbow jabbed him in the side and he blinked down at his sister. Sarah's eyes were red-rimmed, but she glared up at him and pointed toward the crowd.

At Bellamy's retreating form.

She wasn't going back to the parking lot with everyone else. Instead, she was heading deeper into the cemetery.

Chance hesitated. Did he really want to open this can of worms right now? He had his own shit to deal with. But damn if his heartstrings weren't tugging, urging him to follow her.

"Chance, go." Sarah gave him a little push. It was about as effective as moving a brick wall. He had sixty pounds on her and she knew it. "You haven't seen her in ages. Go say something."

Chance grimaced, but took a few steps after Bellamy. What was he supposed to say? He had a thousand questions, but one burned more brightly than the others.

Why did you leave?

Behind him, Emmett cleared his throat.

Chance looked over his shoulder to see that his brother's expression was troubled.

"Ten minutes," Emmett said gruffly, frowning at Bellamy's retreating figure. "We need to get home to receive guests."

Sarah shot her oldest brother an exasperated look and gestured at Chance to go on. For his younger sister, she was quite bossy. If it had been any other time, he would've denied her out of spite alone.

Behind Sarah, Owen made a wisecrack and their mother chuckled softly as she accompanied him toward the parking lot.

The knot in his stomach eased a bit. Owen could handle things for a few minutes. It was his specialty to distract people, especially their mother, and she needed it now more than ever.

Chance nodded at Emmett and turned to follow Bellamy.

Her head was on a swivel, scanning every headstone, as Chance shortened the distance between them. She stopped next to a newer one. Unlike many of the other headstones in the area, this one was free of adornment. No flowers or trinkets sat next to it; it was indistinguishable from the surrounding graves, but Chance knew whose it was.

He'd visited it several times himself.

A breeze drifted by, rustling Bellamy's black leather jacket against her thin frame. Chance was again struck by how small she was.

He took a few steps forward, careful to shuffle his feet so she could hear his approach, and stood next to her.

His heart pounded too fast and too loud in his chest.

They both stared down at the headstone.

Emma Burke, 1975-2012. Wife, Mother, and Friend.

"Seven years. I can't believe it's been that long." The words were soft, so soft that Chance wasn't even sure they'd come from her. She looked up at him, and the terrible sadness in her blue eyes gutted him. Memories flooded back, memories that were too old and too painful to remember.

Lightning. A knock on his window. A beautiful girl on his bed next to him. Gut-wrenching sobs. More helpless than he'd ever felt in his entire life.

Chance shoved his hands in his pockets to hide their trembling and cleared his throat. "Is this the first time you've seen it?"

Bellamy didn't answer. Instead, she mimicked his movement and shoved her hands in the pockets of her jacket. "How did it happen?"

Chance didn't want to tell her. The brief glimpse of sorrow he'd seen in her eyes was almost enough to convince him not to. But her expression was hard now. She could probably handle it.

Wait, why was he trying to protect her? Obviously she was capable of taking care of herself. She'd been doing it this long.

"She was beaten to death. The police said it was a robbery gone wrong."

Bellamy snorted. Her expression vanished, hardened, contorted into steel. "Right. And my father?"

Chance felt his own face twist into a scowl. "Nobody has seen him in years."

Judging from her expression, Chance suspected she'd drawn the same conclusion the rest of town had. Her mother's death and Pastor Burke's disappearance at the same time was too much of a coincidence.

Chance stared at her, trying to remember the anger he'd felt all these years. Anger at her for leaving him. For never reaching out. For never coming back.

"Bella..." he said. He couldn't help it. "Where have you been?"

It didn't come out as a demand like he'd intended. More like a plea, which pissed him off.

Her shoulders stiffened at the use of her old nickname. "Does it matter?"

"Yeah. To me it does." He took a step toward her. They were only a breath apart. The top of her head barely reached his shoulders and she had to crane her neck to meet his eyes. "It's been ten years. Ten years."

She regarded him coolly. He wanted to grab her shoulders and shake her.

"I was staying with family."

"Staying with...? Why didn't you ever contact me? You could've at least let me know you were okay."

Bellamy shifted. Her blue eyes didn't stray from his. That age he'd seen before was back, but this time it wasn't sad. It was... hard. That was not an adjective he ever would've associated with her before. "I'm sorry about your dad, Chance. I came as soon as I heard."

"You owe me an explanation, Bella. What happened that night?"

Bellamy took a step back, lengthening the unbearable

distance between them. She straightened her shoulders and her chin notched higher. "I don't have to explain anything to you."

"The hell you don't. You can't show up after ten years and expect me to accept it with no questions asked." His body moved before he could stop it. He closed the distance between them, fast, and grabbed her shoulders, bringing her face close to his.

She stiffened under his grip. "Take. Your hands. Off. Me."

The words were quiet, but they bit the air like a whip. Chance dropped his hands as if he'd been burned. Stepping back, he shoved them into his hair. He was the world's biggest asshole.

"Look, Chance, we may have a history, but you don't know me anymore. I don't owe you anything. I left La Conner and the past behind me a long time ago. I suggest you do the same."

She eyed him up and down, her expression coldly furious, turned and stomped away.

Chance stood frozen, watching her leave. A sense of deja vu flooded him, and he wondered if it would be another ten years before he saw her again.

CHAPTER 4

"**WELCOME TO PORTLAND**, ladies and gentlemen. The current weather is..." The pilot's voice crackled over the speakers as the seatbelt signs turned off with a melodic sound. Passengers moved to gather their bags.

Bellamy breathed a sigh of relief as she pulled her backpack out from under the seat and shuffled off the plane. Her stomach hadn't stopped roiling since her encounter with Chance in the cemetery, and being enclosed in such a small space with so many people didn't help.

The unbearable weight on her shoulders lifted slightly as she entered the Portland airport. She may have grown up in La Conner, but Portland had become home over the past seven years. This was where she was comfortable; she knew the lay of the land, and the people that lived in it. She had dirt on every significant criminal in the city. Here she was important; here she had power.

Bellamy pulled out her phone and turned off airplane mode, smiling when it vibrated in her hand. Five missed calls and a voicemail from Sam. For anyone else, that would signal an emergency. For Sam, it was a typical Friday.

She was still going to give Sam an earful about forcing her to go to the funeral, but it was nice to know she'd been missed.

Before Bellamy could dial voicemail to find out what Sam's urgent "news" was, her phone rang. After a moment's debate, she hit the green button.

"Hi, Sarah," she said.

"Bellamy Ann Burke, I can't believe you left without saying goodbye. Again."

"Sorry." Bellamy smiled at the indignation in Sarah's voice. "I had to get back for work and Sam needed me for - "

"Bull. You were running, and you know it."

"I don't run from my problems. I really did have something tonight that I had to be back for." Bellamy paused and sighed. "But being back there was harder than I expected."

"I know." Sarah's voice softened. "I get it. I just missed you. I wanted to hang out. Are you back home already?"

"Yeah, my plane just landed." Bellamy shifted her bag on her shoulder and followed the signs to the parking garage. She already regretted the fifty dollars she was about to spend on parking. She'd been running late that morning, so she had to park in short-term parking since it was closest to the terminal. Another thing Sam would hear about, since it was entirely her fault. "It was good to see you though."

Sarah chuckled. "Yeah, right. You blew into town, went all *ghost of Christmas pas*t on everyone, then disappeared without a trace. Will you at least have lunch with me next time you're here?"

"Sure, but La Conner isn't exactly high on my priority list. How about you come visit me instead? Maybe on your next school break. I know some fun places to party."

"Yeah, maybe." Sarah's voice wobbled a little.

Bellamy grimaced as a pang of guilt struck her. She was such a jerk. Sarah was dealing with the loss of her father and here Bellamy was, inviting her to party. That was Bellamy's self-medication of choice, but maybe it wasn't Sarah's.

Despite the circumstances, it had been good to see Sarah. Before today, she was the only one that had known Bellamy was still alive. Over the years, they'd kept in touch with letters and infrequent phone calls. Last year, Bellamy even stopped to have lunch with her when she and Sam were in New York for a story.

Sarah cleared her throat. "You caused quite an uproar, you know. Chance has been storming around all day. I don't know what happened between the two of you, but he's in a mood. And Mom... Well, you know her. She was really hoping to see you for refreshments after the funeral. She's been cooking up a frenzy all week."

Bellamy couldn't help her smile. Mary hadn't changed. The kids always knew when something was amiss because an enormous array of baked goods would line the counters.

That's how Mary had become known for delivering them to other families in town. She ended up making too much and needed to get rid of it, so she decided to pay it forward. "I'm sorry. I didn't mean to cause so much trouble." She snorted a sardonic laugh. "I guess that's my M.O. where your family is concerned."

"Hey, knock it off. You know you're always welcome. Seriously. All that stuff happened so long ago, nobody even remembers it. No matter what Chance says, no matter what you may think... La Conner is your home. You're always welcome back here."

Bellamy's heart warmed. She wouldn't be taking Sarah up on that offer, but she appreciated it nonetheless. "Thanks, Sarah."

She clicked off. As usual, Sarah had a way of saying just the right thing.

Bellamy wished she could be a better friend in return, but secrets were always holding her back. Sarah probably wouldn't be so friendly if she knew how Bellamy made most of her money these days.

Bellamy shook herself and flipped her phone open again to dial her voicemail.

"Hey girl." Sam's voice was bright as always. "I hope you're having fun down there in La... whatever it's called. As much fun as you can have at a funeral, anyway. Don't be mad at me. You know you needed to be there. I'll pay for your parking or whatever else you're going to yell at me about later. Anyway, that's not why I'm calling. I have the best news. My story took an interesting turn and you'll never believe what I found." Sam's voice came out in a breathy rush. "This is going to make my entire career."

Sam was equal parts optimistic and plucky. She'd been Bellamy's savior since day one, when she took Bellamy under her wing and trained her to be an investigative photographer. They spent the last three years traveling all over the world together, chasing the next big story that would "make Sam's career." Even when Sam annoyed her to death, Bellamy couldn't help but love her.

She'd been in a bad place when Sam found her; living on the streets of Portland, dealing in underhanded gigs that were likely to get her killed. It was the only way she'd known how to survive while she was on the run.

Because of Sam's influence, she'd been able to get out.

Well, sort of. More like she'd upgraded. She dealt mostly with white collar crime these days, fencing between high profile clients that were a lot more careful than the thugs she used to hang out with.

Sam's voice chattered away in Bellamy's ear. "You know that story I've been working on? I know you told me to leave it alone, but you know that's not my style. My gut is screaming that something big is going on and with the evidence I've found already, it's a sure thing. I can't believe we stumbled into this one, Bells, I mean, come on. It's like something out of a movie. Secret identities and affairs and even murder."

Bellamy's blood turned to ice in her veins.

Sam couldn't be talking about Powell. Bellamy had warned her off; he was not a guy to mess around with. Every reporter, investigator, or regular Joe that poked into Powell's affairs ended up dead. Every single one.

Why didn't Sam ever listen to her?

An older couple stumbled into Bellamy from behind. She looked up, not really seeing them, her phone clenched in her white fingers. The husband grumbled something under his breath in her direction before his wife pulled him away.

"Anyways, I'll tell you all about it when you get home. Love ya."

Click.

Bellamy shoved her phone into her pocket and ran out the doors.

* * * * * *

Bellamy threw open the door to the photography studio she and Sam shared. "Sam," she called. "Sammy?"

No answer.

Bellamy fumbled for the light switch next to the door and flipped it on. Her sharp intake of breath was the only sound in the room.

Their studio had been torn apart.

Sam wasn't a clean person; she never had been. Over their years together, she drove Bellamy crazy more times than she could count with her constant messes. She was the type of person who walked into her apartment at the end of the day and left a trail of clothing from the front door to the bedroom. She never rinsed her dishes out in the sink, she never cleaned up spills when she made them, and she never put her laundry away. Bellamy couldn't even walk into Sam's apartment without feeling the urge to disinfect everything. Things were no different at the studio. Sam left her camera equipment on the floor, in the walkway, so Bellamy always tripped over it. She spilled chemicals on the floor in the darkroom and never cleaned them up, leading to stains and a permanent odor.

But this... this was different.

Photos and equipment were strewn all over the floor, but not in a logical manner like Sam's messes. This was haphazard. Cupboard doors hung open, half-ripped off their hinges. Drawers had been yanked from their cabinets and thrown to the floor, their contents scattered over the scratched hardwood. The door to the darkroom stood open and light spilled into the main studio area, bathing the room in a blood red glow.

Bellamy's gaze darted around. "Sammy?"

Silence met her call.

The hairs on the back of her neck prickled. Whoever did this might still be around.

She hoped the bastard was, because she was going to kill him.

Bellamy grabbed a bent piece of metal from a broken tripod lying nearby and hefted it like a baseball bat. She should have stopped by her apartment to pick up her gun on the way over, but panic had made her clumsy. The one she usually kept in a drawer next to the door was nowhere to be seen in the mess on the floor.

Bellamy crept through the studio, into the darkroom, and checked the bathroom.

The studio was empty.

Chest tight, Bellamy yanked out her cell phone and

dialed Sam's number.

Ring, ring, ring.

No answer.

She tried again. And again. And yet again. But still, no response from her friend.

"Shit shit shit," she snarled as she made her way back to the main room. "Where are you, you idiot?"

The studio's destruction yawned back at her, threatening to swallow her whole, but Bellamy wasn't the type to panic in a crisis. If there was one thing her past had taught her, it was to keep her mind crystal clear.

Her time as a fence in Portland had one perk; she had connections.

She may not know where Sam was, but she knew somebody who did.

Pulling out her phone, she dialed 911.

* * * * * *

Lieutenant Governor Ronald Powell yanked his desk phone off its receiver when it rang. The caller ID told him it was the chief of police.

"Governor Powell speaking."

"Governor, this is Chief Simon."

Ronald rolled his eyes. He barely kept the annoyance from his tone when he responded, "I know. I have caller ID. What can I do for you?"

"You requested that I call if anything came through the pipeline for that photographer's address." Chief Simon's voice was brisk. He'd been working with Governor Powell for too long to suffer hesitation at the governor's special requests.

"Well?"

"We received a 911 call from one of the addresses you gave us. She says her name is Bellamy Burke, sir."

"All right. What did she call for?"

"To report a missing person."

"Ah, I see." Governor Powell fiddled with the pen on his desk, spinning it in circles on the smooth wood surface. "Have you dispatched an officer yet?"

"Yes, sir. She requested Officer Ruiz specifically."

"Good. Send Ruiz to me once he's finished. I shouldn't need to tell you to make sure this is reported as nothing more than a burglary."

There was a brief hesitation on the line. "Understood."

He hung up without a goodbye.

Ronald scowled at the headset as he returned it to the receiver. Was Chief Simon going soft on him? It couldn't be. Ronald had a good deal of leverage over the police chief that he could use to press his advantage. But he would let that insubordination slide for now. He had bigger things to worry about. Nervous flutters began in his stomach, but he forced them to silence with sheer force of will.

There was no way they'd find anything that linked back to him.

* * * * * *

Bellamy paced back and forth in front of the door,

picking her way through debris, until Ruiz arrived. The red and blue flashes on her wall through the blinds signaled that he'd finally made it.

Bellamy pulled the door open before the officer even made it up the stairs.

"Thanks for coming," she said as he approached.

Ruiz nodded. "Mind if I come in?"

Bellamy motioned him inside. Ruiz was average height, with dark skin and black hair that was trimmed neatly against his head. His dark eyes were friendly as he stepped into the studio and looked around. He let out a low whistle. "Looks like a burglary," he said. "Find anything missing?"

Bellamy closed the front door. "Cut the act, Ruiz. Sam's missing. Do you know anything about it?"

He frowned, the picture of innocence. "I don't know what you're talking about. Are you sure she didn't run off?"

Bellamy slammed a hand down on the nearest table. "You and I have been working together for years. Are you really going to pull that shit on me? I'm not an idiot."

"You work with a lot of shady people, that's all I'm saying. I'm hurt that you think I'd have anything to do with your friend's disappearance. I thought we were friends."

Bellamy snorted. "Sure, we're friends. As friends, let me warn you that Governor Powell has gone too far, and I'm going to nail him to the wall for this."

Ruiz's friendly expression immediately hardened. "Isn't it against the fence code to know the identity of your clients?"

"Yeah, well I'm not stupid like most fences. I cover my own ass, which means I have dirt on everyone I work with.

Including you, and including him."

Ruiz took a step closer, his right hand resting on the butt of his holstered gun. "I'd be careful with my words if I were you, sweetheart."

Bellamy tipped her chin up, meeting his eyes. "Do I look like I'm messing around? If you know anything about Sam, now would be the time to tell me. Believe it or not, I do consider you a friend. I'd rather not destroy your life if I don't have to."

After a long moment of silence, Ruiz finally stepped away from her. He let his arm relax, dropping it to his side. "I don't know anything about your friend," he said. "But you're playing with fire here. Watch your back, okay?"

"Noted." Bellamy opened the door and watched Ruiz exit into the hallway. "Tell Maria and the kids I said hi."

Ruiz lifted a hand in a wave over his shoulder as he left, and Bellamy locked the door behind him.

Once she was alone, she let her shoulders droop. Her head fell back against the door with a thud.

Now what?

She had resources in the city, but Powell was no joke. He'd been around for a long time, and he had contacts in higher places than she did. All of her fence contacts were probably burned. Powell was known to have contacts in the police force, even above Ruiz's head, so she couldn't count on the authorities to help her either.

Sure, she could release all the dirt she'd gathered on him. It would destroy his career and his life, but it would also guarantee that she'd never see Sam again.

She was well and truly hosed.

Who could she turn to when she had no resources?

She lifted her head and let it fall back to the door with a loud thump. The answer was staring at her straight in the face, but she didn't want to acknowledge it.

She knew someone outside of Portland with the resources to help.

The problem was, she'd vowed never to speak to him again.

* * * * * *

"You are a grade-A moron."

Chance rolled his eyes and ducked as his sister flicked her dish towel at him, spraying water droplets into the air. They stood opposite each other in the kitchen, a granite island countertop between them, drying the dishes as their mother washed them. The last of the well-wishers had left only a few minutes before, but Mary wasn't going to relax until the house was spotless again. Mostly the kitchen, since she'd cooked up a storm in the past few days in preparation for the funeral.

Sarah had been glaring at Chance all day. He figured it was about Bellamy, so he'd been avoiding her. Now that everyone was gone, though, he had no choice but to let her get it all out.

Emmett and Owen sat at the kitchen table nearby, each holding two playing cards. Owen was on a poker kick. He'd spent hours playing blackjack and Texas Hold 'Em with their father in the hospital. Paul was the only one who could beat Owen's insanely good luck. Since Paul's death, everyone had been forced to play cards with Owen every spare moment they had. It was irritating, but mostly they didn't mind. Everyone was dealing with his death in their own way.

It was also a convenient excuse to get out of cleaning up.

"You shouldn't speak to your brother like that," Mary said over her shoulder from the sink. Her tone was light, even though she'd buried her husband just eight hours earlier. But she'd never been the type to mope around. Chance loved that about her. He knew she would mourn later, in private. She and his dad had been deeply in love even after forty years of marriage. Though the cancer had progressed quickly, they'd known his time was coming. It brought some level of comfort that everyone had gotten a chance to say goodbye.

"Well, he is a moron," Sarah said, shooting him another glare. "He's the reason Bellamy got out of dodge so fast after Dad's funeral."

"It's too bad," Mary replied. "I was hoping she'd stay for dinner. It's been so long."

"Well, you can blame Mr. Grumpy Pants over there."

"Mr. Grumpy Pants? What are you, twelve?"

Sarah flicked more water at him. "I may be younger than you, but I'm way more mature."

"When are you going back to New York again?"

Sarah stuck her tongue out at him.

Chance opened his mouth to fire another insult, but he caught his mother grinning at them. It had been a long time since they'd all gathered under one roof. His heart hurt when sudden moisture gathered in her eyes. She was alone in this big house now, and he had a feeling it was still sinking in.

"I'm not even sure why she came," Emmett said from his position at the table. His eyes never left the cards in his hand, but Chance could see him frowning in disapproval.

"Bellamy was a part of this family for years," Mary replied. "She loved your father. I'm sure that's why she wanted to be here today."

"Funny. She didn't look real pleased to see any of us."

"Well, lover-boy sure chased her off fast," Owen drawled. "Real smooth, bro."

"I didn't chase her anywhere, thank you."

Owen laughed. He laid down his cards and let out a whoop when Emmett did the same. "I win again," he said, reaching around the pile of Hershey's kisses on the table acting as poker chips. He pulled the stash toward him, a huge grin splitting his face.

Emmett glowered and shuffled the cards for another round.

Sarah sighed. "I really wanted to hang out with her today, too. I wish she hadn't left."

"You're better off," Emmett said, cutting the deck and dealing Owen and himself another hand.

Chance slid a couple baking sheets into the cupboard. He didn't know what to think anymore. Ever since Bellamy left, again, he'd been a complete mess. He hadn't handled her return in the most graceful way, but what did everyone expect? It was a freaking sucker punch to the gut to see her again. To say that her disappearance ten years ago was hard for him would be a massive understatement. It took him years to accept that she was gone. He didn't truly move on until he joined the Marines.

Hell, even then, he thought about her every day.

Chance shook himself and pulled his thoughts back to the present. He folded his damp towel and left it on the kitchen island, crossing to lean his hip against the counter next to his mother. "Mom, what are you going to do with the house?"

Mary glanced up at him, brow furrowed. "What do you mean?"

"I know you might not want to hear this, but this house is big. And old. You can't stay here by yourself."

Mary smiled softly and patted his arm. "I'm not by myself. Owen's here. This is my home; I'm not going anywhere else."

"Owen's hardly good company. I mean, look at him."

Owen's head snapped up, the end of a Hershey's kiss sticking out of his mouth. He inhaled it and swallowed. "What's that supposed to mean?"

Chance shot him a look. "It means that you keep odd hours and you're always at the office. When you are home, you don't ever leave your room." He looked back at his mother. "You can stay with me. ESI is really taking off and my house just finished a few months ago. It's safe and I've got plenty of room - "

"I'm not moving in with you, son," Mary chided. "I'm perfectly fine where I am."

"As long as offers are on the table," Sarah chimed in, leaning against the kitchen island and shooting Chance a big smile. "Can I stay with you?"

"Why?" Chance asked, raising an eyebrow. "Don't you usually stay here when you're in town?"

"Mom makes me do chores."

Mary sputtered out a laugh.

"Aren't you going back to New York soon?" Emmett asked with a pointed look.

Sarah shrugged. "I'm taking a little break from school. Since I've got my EMT license, I thought I could help around here. ESI could use a medical professional like myself."

"Hell no," Emmett growled from the table.

Chance met Emmett's eyes and nodded his agreement. Erickson Security, Inc. was Chance's baby. After leaving the military, he knew he'd never be able to hack it at a desk job. So the year before, he'd started the company. Emmett joined up not long after and he now ran operations while Chance monitored the business side. Owen had recently joined as well, lending his computer expertise to the team. Together, the three brothers and their team were a powerhouse in the private security world. They specialized in both government and private contracts and though their firm was young, their contacts at the military had landed them some large contracts already. A lot of them were dangerous - it was part of the job - and had already resulted in too many close calls.

There was no way the brothers would allow their little sister to be involved in their work.

Before Chance could find a gentle way to tell Sarah that, the sound of "Eye of the Tiger" pierced the air. Sarah grabbed her purse off the kitchen table by Owen's elbow and rustled through it.

"Nice ringtone, Rocky Balboa," Owen said with a chuckle.

Sarah shot him a look and pressed the phone to her ear. "Hello?"

Owen laid down his cards and grinned in triumph at Emmett. "Royal flush," he announced with a flourish.

Emmett dropped his cards onto the table in disgust. "I think you're cheating."

Owen grinned and popped another Hershey's kiss in his mouth. "Nope, I'm just good at what I do." He threw the wrapper at Emmett. It bounced off his forehead and landed on the table.

Emmett's expression turned murderous, and he stood up to tower over his youngest brother.

"Bellamy, slow down. I can't follow you when you talk that fast."

Chance's head whipped in Sarah's direction, the smile falling off his face. Everyone else did the same. "Bellamy?" he repeated, dumbfounded. "Is that Bellamy?"

Sarah glanced at him. "Okay, okay, yeah. I'll put Chance on the phone. Hold on." She used her hand to cover the phone speaker and held it out to Chance. "She wants to talk to you. Sounds like there's trouble."

Chance grabbed the phone and held it to his ear. "Bella, what's going on?"

"Chance. Hey."

The world spun for a second and Chance found himself gripping the counter in front of him. Her voice was steady, but something about her tone brought memories rushing back. It was higher-pitched than normal, the same one she used to use when they were kids. The one that said she was scared but didn't want him to know.

He wanted to annihilate whoever had caused it.

"Look, I'm sorry for the way I acted today. Coming back to La Conner brought a lot of things up for me and I didn't handle it as well as I should have. I know it's been a long time. We've both moved on and you don't owe me anything, but -"

"Bellamy." He glanced up to see four sets of eyes intent on his face. He turned his back to them and lowered his voice. "What's wrong?"

"I want to hire you. More specifically, I want to hire ESI."

"What is it?" Sarah whispered, appearing at his elbow.

Chance waved her away. "How do you know about ESI?"

"I... heard people talking at the funeral. I don't know what exactly you do, but something about private security? I'll hire you. I can pay you. Just... I need your help." Each word sounded like it was dragged from her throat.

An emotion that Chance hadn't felt in years ripped through him.

Something had scared Bellamy. What had caused her to put aside her pride - especially after the way she had left things that afternoon - and reach out to him for help? Had she really heard about ESI at the funeral? It was old news, so Chance couldn't imagine why anyone would be talking about it.

Come to think of it, how had Bellamy gotten Sarah's number?

Chance glanced at his younger sister. Her expression

reflected nothing but concern, but her fingers worried at the end of her blouse, twisting it into agitated knots.

Now wasn't the time to ask Bellamy any of those questions. There were more important tasks at hand.

"Tell me what happened," Chance said. He allowed his voice to settle into what Sarah called "military mode," the calming demeanor he used when dealing with civilians in crisis situations. Sarah had accused him of being in military mode for the past few months since his father's diagnosis. It was the best way he knew how to handle his grieving family, specifically his mother, and it worked on Bellamy like a charm.

The words came rushing out of her like a broken dam. "It's my friend Sam. Our studio is trashed and she's missing. The situation is kind of complicated. I don't really want to discuss it over the phone, but-"

"Bellamy." Chance waited for her to take a breath. "I'll be there in three hours. Lock the doors and stay put. Understand?"

"... Yeah."

"Good. I'll see you soon."

Chance clicked off the call and shoved the phone back into Sarah's hand. "Text me her phone number."

Everyone in his family talked over each other, asking him questions and demanding answers. Chance brushed past all of them and headed to the door. Emmett reached out to grab Chance's arm as he walked by, but Chance shot him a look. Emmett let his hand drop to the table, his eyebrows drawing together.

"I'll let you know as soon as I know something," Chance

said. He met his mother's eyes.

She nodded once and placed an arm around Sarah's shoulders. "Go. Make sure she's okay."

Chance left the house, cell phone in hand, plans already forming as he made the long drive to the airport.

CHAPTER 5

BELLA EASED THE BACK DOOR CLOSED, *sighing in relief when the sound of raised voices was finally muffled. She sat down on the back porch step and stared at the puffy clouds floating across the sky above her.*

It wouldn't be long until they realized she'd slipped out. They would come looking for her soon, and she didn't want to be around when they did.

She finished tying the laces on her worn sneakers and stood.

Slinging her backpack over her shoulder, Bellamy jogged to the trees at the edge of her backyard. It didn't take long to navigate the small stretch of forest until she reached the river. From there, she followed the water upstream toward Rainbow Bridge until her favorite house came into view.

She knew the path by heart.

The fifteen-minute walk gave her ample time to compose herself.

It was blessedly quiet when she emerged from the trees. Her sneakers slid on the wet grass as she ran through the backyard and up the porch steps. She didn't knock; she never did. Instead, she threw open the back door and walked into the small mud room just off the kitchen.

"Bellamy, is that you, sweetheart?"

Bella dropped her backpack into the basket by the door and entered the kitchen. She breathed in deep, savoring the smell of whatever sweet treat was baking in the oven. It smelled like banana bread. Goodness, she hoped it was banana bread.

Mrs. Erickson was the nicest person she'd ever met and she always had good things to eat. Bella's favorite pastime was trying to guess what was cooking before she entered the kitchen. Mrs. Erickson always experimented with new ingredients and new combinations, so meals there were never boring.

"Hi, Mrs. Erickson," she called.

Mrs. Erickson turned around from her place at the stove and beamed at Bella. "Hey there, sugar. Hungry?"

Bella nodded enthusiastically, pulling out a chair at the table. It wasn't long before Mrs. Erickson set a plate of steaming french toast in front of her.

"Your timing is perfect, as usual, my dear. Before you eat, why don't you go roundup Sarah and the boys? They're around here somewhere."

Bella obediently ran from the kitchen, mouth already watering. She found Sarah in her bedroom playing with her dolls. She wanted Bella to play with her, but once she heard breakfast was ready, she dropped her doll and followed Bella back downstairs.

They found the boys in the TV room. Emmett sat at the desk doing homework and ignoring all of them, as usual. Some kind of boy-ish cartoon played on the TV. Chance and Owen rough-housed in front of the screen, yelling something about transformers and Optimus Prime. Chance looked like he was winning, which was only fair since he was bigger than Owen and had the advantage.

Sarah and Bella yelled that breakfast was ready, and a foot race ensued. Chance and Bella tied for first place, only Chance shoved Bella out of the way just before they got to the door, so he got inside first.

"Chance, no fair. You cheated," she whined, picking herself up from the floor. Sarah helped brush her off.

"Now, now, let's not argue," Mrs. Erickson tsked. "And wash your hands before you sit down at this table, boys. You've been out playing all morning."

The boys grumbled and went to the sink while Sarah and Bella picked their favorite seats at the table. Bella's stomach growled. She and Sarah giggled as they each pulled a piece of French toast out of the stack and dropped it onto their plates.

* * * * * *

Chance wasn't kidding about his vow to make it to Portland in three hours. Two and a half hours after she hung up the phone, Bellamy peered out the window of the studio to see him unfolding his tall frame from the back of a taxi. Her stomach flipped like it had when she saw him for the first time at the funeral. She wasn't a coward, but she took advantage of her hiding spot behind the curtain to stare at him without attracting his attention.

His gray cotton t-shirt clung to his muscled chest and biceps as he leaned in to say something to the taxi driver. Bellamy had really hoped that he would be less attractive after ten years apart. It wasn't fair that he looked like he should be plastered all over a magazine somewhere, not crossing the sidewalk to her building.

His years in the Marines showed in the way he moved. His eyes scanned the area as he walked and a tell-tale bulge at his hip indicated he was armed.

How did he get that gun on the plane?

Chance approached the building and his gaze swept over the window where she was standing. His dark eyes locked on hers as if a magnet had drawn them there.

Bellamy sucked in a breath and dropped the curtain back into place, ducking out of sight. Holy hell, her heart was racing like she just ran a mile. How could he still have such an effect on her?

By the time Chance opened the door, Bellamy was standing in the middle of the room, trying her best to look unbothered.

He didn't knock; he just shoved the door open and stood in the doorway. Framed in the light from the hallway, he looked huge and dangerous. His gaze moved from her abandoned backpack just inside the door to the destruction of the studio and finally landed on her. He studied her for a moment, frowning.

"I told you to lock the door."

The authority in his voice made Bellamy's spine straighten. "I did. I unlocked it when I heard you coming."

His brows lowered and he looked away from her long enough to close the door behind him. He engaged the deadbolt, the doorknob lock, and the chain before turning to face her again. Gesturing to the bag at his feet, he said, "You haven't been home?"

"Uh, no. I've been a little busy." Plus, it hadn't been worth the hour trip to her apartment in city traffic. What would she have done there, anyway? She could pace there or she could pace here, and she'd rather be here.

Chance picked up the backpack and dropped it onto a nearby armchair, then settled down next to it. "Tell me what happened."

Bellamy hesitated. She'd asked him here, but having him in her space made her uneasy. She didn't want to tell him about her life; she didn't want him to know anything about it. The more he knew, the more he would realize that she wasn't the same girl who left La Conner. If he realized how damaged she was, and the things she had done, he wouldn't be so willing to help her.

That's why he could never know. Sam's life depended on it.

Chance leaned forward, resting his elbows on his knees. "Look, this isn't an inquisition. But I can't help you if you don't give me some information first. You said your friend is missing. Can you tell me about her?"

Bellamy perched on the edge of the armchair across from him, steeling herself. She didn't really have a choice; Sam's safety was more important than her comfort level right now.

Besides, she lied to criminals all day long. How was this any different?

She felt herself slipping into her "business" skin. Her shoulders automatically straightened; her chin rose a couple notches. "Sam is a close friend of mine. We've been working together for a few years now."

Chance studied her like he was trying to solve a puzzle. "Sam... is she... more than a friend?"

Bellamy let out a startled laugh. "No."

He smiled. "Just covering all my bases. That would have been a good excuse for leaving La Conner."

Her hackles immediately rose. "My best friend is missing. I didn't hire you to talk about La Conner."

"I'm just trying to ease some tension. I know this is awkward after, well, how our last conversation went. You were right. It's been a long time and we've both moved on and built lives since then. How about we forget everything else for the moment and be friends? It will make this a whole lot easier. Deal?" He held out a hand, smiling at her.

That was the best thing she'd heard all day. It's not like she wanted this strained relationship with Chance; in fact, she had more leftover feelings for him than she cared to admit. She just couldn't let him get too close, for her own safety and his.

Bellamy released a sigh and placed her hand in his. "Okay. Deal."

"Good." Chance settled back in his chair. "So, friend, you said you and Sam work together. Here?"

Bellamy nodded. "We're investigative photographers. So basically we poke around and take pictures of things and pitch them to newspapers so they can be developed into stories."

"Interesting. You don't write the articles yourselves?"

"Sometimes, but Sam doesn't like to spend much time behind a desk. So she usually sells her photos to a reporter or newspaper and they'll do the reporting on it."

"How did you two meet? I don't remember you being interested in photography."

"I had to make a living somehow. Look, we can be friends but I'll say it again. I'm not here to talk about the past. Does it matter how Sam and I met? The point is that she's missing."

Chance leveled her a look. "Damn, you're prickly. Okay. Tell me what happened."

"Stick to the script and I won't have a reason to be prickly. Sam has been investigating Lieutenant Governor Ronald Powell. Powell is into a lot of shady things and Sam was hoping to find some evidence of it. I got this voicemail when I got off the plane this afternoon. Then when I got to the studio, I found it like this. Here, listen." Bellamy pulled out her phone and replayed the message on speaker.

Chance listened. His posture was relaxed, but she suspected he was memorizing every word. "This story she's talking about. Are you sure it's about the lieutenant governor?"

"I'm positive. That's all she's been talking about for a

few weeks now. I told her to leave it alone, but as usual, she didn't listen to me."

"Why didn't you want her to pursue it?"

"This guy is bad news. Other people have tried to go after him, and it hasn't ended well for them. We're talking disappearances, suddenly getting fired, or unexplained accidents." Bellamy formed air quotes with her fingers around the last word.

"How do you know that?"

She shrugged. "People in the journalism community like to gossip. We're tight-knit that way."

"All right, if you think the governor is behind this, why not just go to the police?"

"I did. They're in his pocket. They're not going to do anything about it, so that's why I'm hiring you." Bellamy stood and surveyed the mess around the studio. "We need to find Sam's notebook. She keeps all her important story notes in it. If she found any evidence we can use, that's where it will be."

"Okay, where would she keep it?"

Bellamy settled her hands on her hips. "I thought it might be here, but I spent the last few hours looking with no luck. Maybe her apartment?"

Chance rose and stepped around Bellamy's armchair. His gaze swept the debris scattered around the room. "Let's head over there, then. I'll get in touch with Owen and have him start tracking Sam's phone. Emmett can also reach out to some contacts in the police force. Maybe he'll shake something loose that explains their hesitation to pursue this."

Fat chance. Governor Powell's pockets were deep enough to pay off the entire police force, but Bellamy didn't tell Chance that. He'd find out soon enough.

* * * * * *

Ruiz bounced back and forth on his toes, jingling the car keys in his hand. He was too jittery to sit down, and the floor-to-ceiling bookshelves lining the walls in Governor Powell's office felt like they were closing in on him.

He did not want to be here. That saying, 'don't shoot the messenger,' didn't apply in Governor Powell's world. Ruiz had disposed of too many messengers in his too-long career with the governor to think he was safe.

If running was an option, Ruiz would have done it a long time ago. Unfortunately, he had a family to take care of and a wife who refused to move, no matter how many times he'd asked. She loved their tiny craftsman home more than she loved her husband's life, apparently.

Not that she knew the illicit activities Ruiz took part in. He'd always been careful to keep her safe from that knowledge. If his work ever went sideways, it was the best chance he could give her to live a normal life.

Tonight might be the night that Ruiz's luck finally went south.

He wanted to hate Bellamy Burke for the role she'd played in this whole shitty situation, but he couldn't. In the years he'd worked with her, she'd always been worthy of his trust and respect. If anyone else in the city had been on the other end of this, he would've had Bellamy's back.

But Governor Powell was a powerful man, and Ruiz valued his own life more than anyone else's.

Because of that, he would throw Bellamy and anyone else to the wolves. That was the nature of their work, and he knew Bellamy would understand.

The door opened and Governor Powell strode into the room.

Ruiz straightened and quickly stepped forward to shake the man's hand. The office immediately felt smaller with the governor's presence.

"Ruiz," Governor Powell said. He positioned himself in the tall chair behind his desk and clasped his hands on the surface, the picture of calm. "Let's hear your report."

"Yes sir." Ruiz perched on the end of the armchair facing the governor's desk. "I met with Bellamy Burke this afternoon. She asked me if I knew anything about that photographer's disappearance. I told her I didn't."

"And?"

Ruiz took a deep breath. This was it. Once Governor Powell knew his identity was compromised, Bellamy was dead - and Ruiz would be lucky if he didn't follow close behind. "She said she knows you're involved. She threatened to expose your illegal activities if she doesn't get her friend back."

Governor Powell's expression didn't change. "How, pray tell, does she know who I am? You assured me that my dealings with her would remain anonymous."

"They were. They are. I keep all my clients anonymous. I don't know how she traced it back to you, but she's resourceful. If she says she has evidence against you, she probably does."

A long moment of silence passed. Ruiz felt a bead of sweat trickle down his temple.

Finally, Governor Powell smiled.

"Resourceful, indeed. It must run in the family." He slid a pen in front of him and spun it in a slow circle. "She's not as knowledgeable as she thinks she is. Proceed as planned. Ensure that there's no police investigation into that photographer's disappearance and find someone to keep tabs on Miss Burke."

Ruiz blinked. That was not the reaction he'd expected. What did the governor know that Bellamy didn't? More importantly, why didn't Ruiz know anything about it? Perhaps he wasn't as high on the totem pole as he'd always believed.

"And, Ruiz." Governor Powell slapped his hand down on the pen, forcing it to a sudden stop. He pinned Ruiz with a cold stare that promised death. "While this isn't damaging at the moment, I'm not pleased with your performance. You will ensure that any information she has about me disappears before it can see the light of day, do you understand?"

Ruiz scrambled to his feet. He felt the stupid urge to salute, but he restrained himself. "Yes, sir. I understand. Of course."

"Good. Get it done."

Without another word, Governor Powell spun his pen in a circle again.

Ruiz hurried out of the office on shaky legs before the governor could change his mind.

* * * * * *

Sam's apartment was in a run-down neighborhood on the outskirts of Portland. It was small, only three stories high, but the exterior was in decent condition, with red brick walls and white concrete window sills.

As Chance pulled into a parking spot just outside the front of the building, he raised an eyebrow at the entrance and the uniformed doorman standing there.

"A doorman?" he asked incredulously. "It's nearly midnight."

Bellamy cracked a smile. "It's odd, I know. But that's why Sam likes this place. She says it makes her feel rich, even though the rent is low."

"Does she feel like she needs a lot of security?

Bellamy shrugged. "We live in a dangerous world. People don't like it when we air their dirty laundry."

"Do you live here too?"

"No." She didn't look at him as she got out of the car.

Chance sighed and followed her lead. How was he supposed to get anything out of her - or solve his personal mystery - if she refused to reveal anything about herself? She was more secretive than the informants he'd worked with in the military. He had a feeling that nothing short of death and dismemberment would convince her to open up to him.

Good thing he liked a challenge, because Bellamy had 'challenge' written all over her.

He would have to find the right questioning tactic to

keep her guard down. Done correctly, he could glean plenty of information without Bellamy saying a thing.

The doorman smiled at Bellamy as they approached. He was an older gentleman with graying hair. Judging by his wiry frame and the easy way he balanced on the balls of his feet, he could probably hold his own in a fight.

"Hi there, Miss Burke."

"Frank." Bellamy graced him with a smile. "Have you seen Sam? I've been looking for her."

Frank frowned and shook his head. He adjusted the wrists of his white gloves, pulling them tight. "No, I haven't seen her since the day before yesterday. Is something the matter?" He eyed Chance warily. "Who's your friend?"

"This is Chance. He's an old friend, just visiting."

Chance glanced down at her in surprise. The lie rolled easily off her tongue, her gaze was steady, and no nervous tics or twitches. She seemed remarkably well-practiced. A product of her investigative photography career, perhaps?

"I wanted to introduce him to Sam, but I can't get a hold of her. I'm sure she's just in the wind on another job." Bellamy's smile remained in place, but her hands trembled slightly as she stuffed them in her pockets. She honestly thought that something bad had happened to her friend.

Chance was beginning to suspect that himself. He stepped forward, extending his hand to Frank. "Chance Erickson. Pleasure to meet you. Can you tell me about when you saw Sam last? We're trying to track her down."

Frank straightened in response to the authority in Chance's voice. "Like I said, it was the day before yesterday. I hadn't seen her in a couple days and she came by real late that night."

"How long did she stay? Do you remember when she left?"

"Well, yeah, she was only inside for a few minutes. You know how excited she gets," he added to Bellamy. "She said she found something and she was going to do a good old-fashioned stakeout."

Uh-oh. Chance's gut lurched. Had she gotten caught during her stakeout? Had Powell kidnapped her so she wouldn't release whatever she'd found? Glancing at Bellamy, it was obvious she was grappling with the same questions.

Chance turned back to Frank. "Did she say where she was going?"

"No, that's confidential."

"She likes to keep her stories private until they're in print," Bellamy said. "She's always afraid someone will scoop her story before she has a chance to sell it."

Damn it. Why couldn't she tell at least one person what she was working on? At least they'd have a trail to follow. "All right. Do you mind if we check inside?"

Frank opened the door and gestured them through. "Go for it. I hope everything's all right. Do you have a key?"

"Yeah, I've got my spare." Bellamy shot him a half-hearted smile and preceded Chance into the building.

Sam's apartment was on the top floor. Chance held out a hand for the key and signaled her to stay back. Turning the knob, Chance stepped into the room, pulling his Glock out of the holster under his shirt. He swept the area, but it was empty.

"Looks like someone broke in here too," he said quietly.

Bellamy stepped up behind him, examining their surroundings. "Nope, this is just Sam's version of lived-in."

Chance glanced at her, aghast. "Really?"

She nodded and kicked a pair of worn brown boots out of her path.

Piles of clothes, papers, and books littered every spare surface. The garbage can next to the stove was overflowing with fast food wrappers and pizza boxes. Beneath dangerously-stacked towers of books in front of the couch, a bright orange rug covered the floor in the living room. The walls were painted a matching orange and dark purple curtains hung at the windows. Tapestries and paintings adorned the walls in extravagant colors and sizes.

Sam seemed like a free spirit, all right.

"Does anything look out of place?" Chance asked.

"No. It looks the same way it always does."

"That's a good thing." He pulled a pair of stretchy black pants off a lampshade - fire hazard - and dropped them onto a nearby pile. "If both places were broken into, we'd have legitimate cause for concern. As it is, the mess at the studio might have been a random burglary."

"You think so?" Bellamy looked up, eyes full of hope.

"I don't know. But let's not jump to any conclusions until we have all the facts." He watched her pick through the debris. "Do you see her journal anywhere?"

They searched for a while. It didn't take long before Bellamy came out of the bedroom, thrusting an old leather-bound book into his arms. "I found it!"

She swept off a corner of the kitchen table, toppling a

pile of newspapers into a heap on the floor, and watched as he set it down.

"It's weird though. She never leaves this thing behind. Her laptop is sitting on the bed in there, too. She never leaves the apartment without them, especially if she's working on a story. And if Governor Powell was behind this, why wouldn't he make sure all the evidence was taken too?"

"Let's see what the book can tell us. Then we'll decide if we need to be worried."

Bellamy flipped through some pages. Most contained random scribbles and drawings. When she reached the very last page, she looked up. "This is the only one I don't recognize."

Chance leaned forward, resting his hand on the table on either side of the book, and squinted at Sam's nearly-illegible handwriting.

Motel 6, 8/8/2018. Cafe Mocha, 8/15/2018. Portland General, 9/3/2018.

"Dates and places," he said. "Do they mean anything to you?"

Bellamy shook her head, her expression thoughtful. "Maybe this is her surveillance data. I think she was out of the office for all of these dates."

"No names though." Chance frowned. "Is she always this disorganized?"

Bellamy choked on a laugh. "You don't know the half of it. Try working with her."

"I never thought you'd be the organized one."

"Tell me about it. Desperate times and all that."

Chance grinned. "I'll have Owen check these out.

Maybe he can pull some footage from these areas for these dates. That might give us a trail to follow." He pulled out his phone.

"Hey," Owen answered on the first ring.

"Any luck on Sam's phone?"

"Hey, Owen, how are you?" Owen's voice mimicked Chance's clipped, no-nonsense tone. "I'm great, Chance, thanks for asking. I've been sitting in this dark room, staring at this bright computer screen, for twelve hours. I haven't eaten. I haven't showered. Mom's threatening to pry me away from my keyboard if I don't take a break."

Chance rolled his eyes. "Stop being overdramatic. You were busy playing cards when I left a few hours ago."

"Yeah, whatever. You don't know my pain. Anyway, no luck yet, but I think I'm getting close. You can't rush art, bro."

"Uh-huh. Keep me posted. I have something else for you to check into. I'll email it to you now."

"Sure, sure. Keep throwing more work my way - "

"Goodbye, Owen."

"Hey, wait a second. Emmett said to call him. He's been trying to get a hold of you."

"... I know. Later."

Chance hung up, took a picture of the journal page, and emailed it to Owen.

Last he checked, he had fifteen missed calls from his older brother. He knew what Emmett would say. He was protective of his family and held a grudge like nobody's business. It wasn't a secret that he resented Bellamy for the hell his family went through when they were kids. None of it was her fault, but Emmett had been young and Bellamy was the easiest to blame.

The truth was, Chance's parents had tried to do a good thing and rescue Bellamy from a horrible situation. It pitted them against Pastor Burke, a well-respected and influential figure in town. As a result, their friends and neighbors turned on them and the next few years were rough. Everyone in the family suffered to some degree. Their father's business ultimately failed, Emmett was forced into the military to pay for college, and Owen dropped out of school due to bullying. Not to mention the fact that Chance went nuts trying to find Bellamy.

Chance understood why Emmett wasn't receptive to the idea of delving back into a relationship - business or otherwise - with Bellamy. While Chance was the owner of ESI, Emmett ran operations and functioned more like a partner than an employee. In their flagship year of operation, Emmett and Chance had their fair share of disagreements. Emmett could be a bore when things didn't go his way.

The problem was, he was usually right.

This time, though, Chance had to follow his gut.

Even if it meant going against his brother.

Chance shook himself from his brooding and looked up to see Bellamy standing near the window that overlooked the street. Her silhouette was dark against the dim streetlight peeking through the glass. He couldn't see her expression, but from the set of her shoulders he could tell she was deep in thought.

Stepping forward, he put a hand on her shoulder. "We'll find her, Bella."

She nodded, but her eyes were distant. "I hope so."

"If there's any pattern in those notes, Owen will find them. In the meantime, let's head back to the studio and grab a few hours of sleep. We're no good to Sam if we aren't thinking clearly." Chance dropped an arm around her shoulder and steered her toward the door. To his surprise, she leaned into him. It was so familiar, something they'd done a million times as teenagers, that Chance had to remind himself to stay cool.

It was a small thing. Bellamy probably didn't even know she'd done it, but it was an act of trust. Whether she knew it or not, she was beginning to trust him again.

As Chance escorted her to the car, he vowed that he'd never again do anything to lose it.

CHAPTER 6

THE NEXT MORNING CAME FASTER than Chance would have liked. He stood silently by the front door of the studio and watched Bellamy sleep. Her expression, all hard edges since she'd reappeared in his life, was soft and relaxed. She was curled up in a leather armchair, her legs tucked under her body. She'd folded her arms on the armrest and her cheek rested against the crook of her arm. Her cropped hair stuck up in all directions. He would have smiled, but even from the other side of the room, he could see the dark circles forming under her eyes.

As sunlight filtered through the window, she stirred. Her eyes blinked open and she sat up with a deep sigh. His coat slipped from her shoulders, sliding to her lap, and she picked it up with a blank expression.

Chance forced a bright smile despite the churning in his gut. She was damn beautiful. Ten years ago, he'd had deep feelings for her, but it had been the childhood adoration of best friends with the potential for more. Now his body reacted to her presence as only a man's could. It was uncomfortable and unwelcome, and he needed a cold shower.

He cleared his throat. "There's coffee and doughnuts on the table." He nodded to the steaming bag sitting a few feet away from her. "I set up a meeting with the governor for this afternoon."

Bellamy scowled. "Care to ask for my opinion? I'm pretty sure I hired you, which makes me the boss."

Chance raised an eyebrow. "I apologize. What's your opinion on the matter?"

"It's a horrible idea. We're not going."

"Why?"

Bellamy folded her arms over her chest. "Did you not hear anything I said last night? The guy is dangerous. If we pop up on his radar, it could get both of us killed."

"I hate to break it to you, sweetheart, but you're Sam's business partner. If she's investigating him, you're already on his radar. If you think he's involved, I need to meet him face-to-face." Chance shot her a cocky grin. "Besides, you don't need to worry. I'll protect you."

"I don't want your protection," Bellamy said through gritted teeth. "This is my turf. I know this guy, and I'm telling you it's a bad idea to meet him face-to-face. We need to find some evidence we can use against him first."

Chance grabbed a doughnut out of the bag on the table and took a bite. "You hired me, but this is my investigation. We'll run it the way I want to. If you'd rather stay here, that's fine, but my meeting is in forty-five minutes. I'm going with or without you."

Bellamy grumbled something under her breath and shrugged into her leather jacket.

Chance suppressed a smile. "Well, we need to get moving if we want to make it on time."

Bellamy snorted, but she grabbed a doughnut to go and followed him out of the studio.

* * * * * *

The lieutenant governor's mansion resided in a quiet neighborhood on the outskirts of town. Chance drove them past well-manicured lawns and luxury cars as they made their way to their destination.

Bellamy sulked in the passenger seat.

Nothing was going according to plan. She'd hoped to find something usable in Sam's notebook, but of course Sam's notes didn't make any sense. Bellamy had evidence of her own that she could use as leverage, but from what she knew of Governor Powell, he didn't take well to blackmail.

She could only hope that Chance and ESI found Sam before Powell could hurt her. Once Bellamy knew Sam was safe, she could destroy the governor's life once and for all.

They pulled into the drive and Chance spoke their names into the intercom at the gate.

After a moment, the gate slowly slid open to admit them. Chance drove up the gently sloped drive and parked the car next to the door. He whistled at the impressive mansion as they got out.

Bellamy scowled at him. The house was something else, but now was hardly the time to be impressed.

It looked like something right out of the French countryside, with cream-colored stucco and dark wood trim. The driveway looped around by the front door and reconnected with the road that led back to the gate. The house was surrounded by mature trees and boasted a small garden in front with waist-high hedges surrounding it and a beautiful statue of a Greek goddess in the middle.

Chance smiled at Bellamy and winked. "Quite the place. Let's go see what the man has to say for himself, shall we?"

Bellamy didn't answer. She didn't even glance around as they ascended the steps to the front door. This was a horrible idea. Powell might know who she was, but he didn't know Chance.

The idiot didn't even know how much danger he was putting himself in, and it's not like Bellamy could tell him.

Hey, by the way, I've been smuggling weapons for this guy for the past year, so I know exactly how dangerous he is. Also, if he associates you with me, he'll probably kill you and your whole family for even showing your face here.

Yeah. That would go over well.

Bellamy felt like she was going to crawl out of her skin. Her entire job as a fence was done on the condition of anonymity, and she'd just spilled to Ruiz that she'd broken that sacred rule. No doubt he had already passed that information along to his boss.

They were so screwed.

"Are you all right?" Chance asked in a low voice. "You

seem tense."

Bellamy barely glanced at him. "No shit, Sherlock. We're at a crime boss's house. How else am I supposed to feel?"

He rested a hand on her shoulder. "Don't worry. I've got this."

She nodded, her lips pressed into a thin line. What else could she do?

At Chance's knock, the door swung open to reveal a thin, well-dressed woman. Blond hair was arranged on top of her head in a pristine bun. Her pretty brown eyes looked them over and she inclined her head, a polite smile curving her lips. "You must be Mr. Erickson. I'm Susan Powell, the governor's wife. He's expecting you."

Bellamy eyed the woman. As far as she could tell, Susan wasn't involved in the governor's dealings. She spent most of her time out of the public eye, and only appeared at press conferences as a smiling ornament on Governor Powell's arm.

Chance smiled and extended a hand. "So nice to meet you, Susan."

Susan eyed his hand as if debating whether to take it, and finally placed her hand in his. Her fingers were thin and fragile-looking. The woman looked as if she'd fall over if he so much as breathed on her. "This way," she said.

Chance placed a hand on the small of Bellamy's back as she preceded him into the house. She rolled her shoulders at his touch and took a step forward, just out of his reach. She didn't meet his eyes as they entered the large office, too afraid he'd read the emotion on her face.

Susan gestured to a couple of large leather chairs across from an impressive desk. The office was dark, with floor-to-ceiling wooden bookshelves covering the walls and dark wood blinds covering the only window. Only a beautiful chandelier provided light for the room. The massive desk was tidy, with a few papers stacked on one side, turned over so Bellamy couldn't read what they were. A single, thin laptop sat in the middle of the desk, closed and turned off.

"Can I get you anything to drink?" Susan asked.

"We're good, thanks," Chance replied as he sat down.

Bellamy didn't sit; instead, she stood behind Chance, arms crossed over her chest.

"You have a lovely home," he added with a smile.

Susan gave him a ghost of a smile in return, fiddling with the plain gold wedding band on her left hand. She didn't sit down either. "Thank you. It is quite beautiful."

"I heard your husband's political success was quite the surprise. Was it much of an adjustment once he became governor? It's quite the change, to suddenly have everyone's eyes on you."

Susan cleared her throat. "Yes, it was. But he's wonderful at his job. He's had more financial and political success than any previous person in his position. This city is better with him as governor."

Bellamy choked out a laugh, quickly disguising it as a cough.

Chance shot her a quelling look over his shoulder.

She raised her hands as if to say, "What?"

"Well, I've certainly tried."

Bellamy dropped her hands and looked toward the doorway on the opposite side of the room. Governor Powell stood just inside it. He wasn't a powerful-looking man. His brown hair was graying at the temples and he was average height, not thin but not overweight either. Despite his lackluster frame, he was dressed in an expensive suit and he stood straight, shoulders back and chin up. His presence filled the room, as if he had some unspoken power that senses couldn't detect.

As Lieutenant Governor Powell took a few strides forward and settled into the chair at his desk, he said, "Thank you for showing them in, my dear." His gaze never left Chance's.

Susan lowered her head in a half-bow. "I'll leave you to it," she said quietly, and backed out of the room.

Once the door had clicked shut, the governor leaned forward, hand extended.

Chance shook the man's hand. "My name is Chance Erickson, sir, with Erickson Security. This is Bellamy Burke. Thanks for seeing us on such short notice."

Lieutenant Governor Powell turned his gaze to Bellamy and extended his hand. Something in his eyes was mocking. Jaw clenched, she thinned her lips in some version of a smile. She didn't move to take his hand.

There was an awkward silence.

"Sorry, sir, she's a bit of a germaphobe," Chance said, casting a look in her direction.

The governor smiled briefly and sat back in his chair. "I understand. You can't be too careful these days."

Chance cleared his throat. "I'll get right to the point.

We're looking for a missing woman. We have reason to believe she may have been in this area. Her name is Samantha Larson." He pulled out a picture and held it out for the governor to see. Bellamy recognized it from Sam's fridge. He must have pocketed it while they were looking around the night before. "Do you recognize her?"

The governor barely glanced at the photo. "No, I'm afraid I don't. What is this about?"

"She's been missing for several days. She's a journalist and we believe that she may have been investigating you, Governor Powell. You're sure you haven't seen her?"

The man's expression didn't change. "I am sure. The press already dug into mine and my wife's past quite thoroughly when I became governor. As they discovered, I simply don't have any skeletons in my closet, Mr. Erickson. Thus, there's no reason for a journalist to investigate me."

Bellamy circled around the armchairs and stepped in front of Chance. Leaning over the governor's desk, she shot him an icy smile. "That's not what I hear. Word has been floating around about your office on Marx Street. I hear it's going to close down soon."

Lieutenant Governor Powell stood. His own smile matched hers. "Ah, rumors can be a double-edged sword. I hope you find your friend, but you won't find her here."

Bellamy's eyes narrowed, but the governor's expression remained serene.

He sidestepped her to address Chance. "Unless you'd like to accuse me of something, I have important matters to attend to. You won't be admitted again without a police escort and a warrant. It was nice to meet you."

Chance's hand appeared at Bellamy's back, and he gently pushed her toward the door. "Thanks for your time."

They didn't see Susan Powell as they left the building.

"I see why Sam was investigating him," Chance said as they drove away. "Something about him seems slimy. What was that comment about his office, though?"

"Nothing. Just something I heard. I was hoping to rattle his cage." Bellamy leaned her head back against the seat.

Why hadn't her comment bothered him? It was a clear warning that she knew about his weapons trading. If she gave that information to the authorities, they could link it back to him, just like she did. His life and governorship would be over.

So why had he looked so amused?

CHAPTER 7

"HEY, BELLA."

Bella looked up from her seat just outside the front doors of La Conner Junior High. She squinted in the bright sunlight as Chance jogged up to her. "Hey, cowboy."

He shifted his backpack on his shoulder and grinned. "Stop calling me that. I'm not a kid anymore. What happened to you yesterday? I didn't see you after church."

Bella shrugged. "You'll always be a cowboy to me. We had to get home. Dad wanted to watch the game."

"Well, next time you should come over for dinner. Mom made chicken and shredded potatoes. You missed out."

Bella stood up. She winced as she lifted her backpack onto her shoulder.

Chance frowned at her. "What's wrong?"

"Nothing. I think I slept wrong last night or something."

"Is it your back?"

She shook her head. "I'm good. You taking the bus home?"

"Emmett's picking me up. Do you want a ride?"

Bella smiled. "No thanks. Mom wants me to go right home from the bus. Maybe I'll come over later tonight though."

"All right, suit yourself." He looked at her for a second more, his brows drawn low over his eyes. He opened his mouth to say something else, but the sound of a car horn blared in the afternoon air.

Chance and Bellamy both jumped and looked toward the parking lot.

Emmett's car was parked at the curb. He leaned on the horn, waving at Chance to come closer. Even at this distance, Bella could see his annoyed frown.

"You'd better go before he leaves you."

Chance laughed. "He wouldn't dare. Mom would skin him alive." He tapped Bella lightly in the shoulder with one fist. "See you around."

Bella smiled and waved as he ran to the waiting car. She sat back down to wait for the bus, taking a deep breath at the sharp pain in her ribs.

* * * * * *

Chance's phone rang when they were halfway back to the studio. He pulled it out and up to his ear as he navigated

Portland's traffic. It was Owen.

"Hey, the ping finally came through. I've got a location on your girl."

Relief slammed him hard in the gut. Thank God. He didn't want this case to have an unhappy ending. "Where?"

In the passenger seat, Bellamy perked up.

"She's at a bank by the river. The last ping was just a few minutes ago. I sent you the coordinates."

"Thanks. I'll be in touch."

"He found her? Where is she?"

Chance checked the coordinates and slid the phone back into his pocket. "She's at a bank by the river in the warehouse district. Owen pinged her cell phone."

Bellamy blew out a breath and let her head fall back against the seat. "Thank God. Maybe she really was just in investigation mode this whole time."

"Let's head to the bank and see if we can catch up to her. Any idea why she would be over there?"

"She has a safe deposit box there. That's where she keeps her valuables and her more case-sensitive information."

"Okay. We should be able to make it there before the bank closes."

Chance accelerated around a bus that was pulled over, unloading passengers. He should have been thinking about this case and the missing girl, but he was far too aware of the woman sitting next to him.

Dark strands stood out haphazardly from her head and heavy lids half-covered her blue eyes. The makeup she'd been wearing the day before had smudged, giving her the appearance of a raccoon. How long had it been since she'd gotten a good night's sleep? The few hours the night before hadn't done her any good. After his time in the Marines, Chance was accustomed to going days without sleep, but Bellamy was a civilian. Now that they knew where her friend was, she sagged against the seat, her head resting against the window. Relief was clear on her face.

When they were children, Bellamy hadn't made friends. Her strict family life and shy personality put off most children in their age group. Chance and his siblings had been the only exception to that rule.

Sam must be a special kind of person to knock down the walls that Bellamy had built around herself. Chance wondered for the millionth time what had happened during that ten-year gap, and decided to venture a question.

"How did you meet Sam?"

Bellamy's eyes remained glued to the window. She was silent for so long that he doubted she would answer. But finally, she smiled a little. "She saved my life."

"What do you mean?"

She glanced at him. "Look, I really don't want to talk about the past, if it's all the same to you."

"I don't mean to be pushy, Bella. I just want to understand your relationship with her."

She blew out a breath. "Sam is the greatest person I know. She met me at the darkest time of my life and instead of turning away, she reached out a hand and pulled me out. She's been dragging me all over the world ever since, chasing stories. She loves capturing moments that no one else can see. That's why she's good at what she does."

"So you travel together?"

"Yeah, she's teaching me. I'm nowhere as good as she is though."

Chance fell silent as he considered this new information. A surge of that old bitterness welled in him again. He'd thought she was dead, for years, and she'd been traveling to exotic places to take pictures with her best friend. Why had she never reached out to him? Had she pushed him off to her past and swept him under the rug just like everything else? Not only him, but La Conner, his family, and her own mother. Bellamy might not have had a stellar childhood, but everyone in La Conner had shaped her into the person she had become. Why would she want to forget all of that?

A few minutes later, they pulled into the parking lot of the Albina Community Bank next to the river. It was located in the warehouse district, which was a lesser part of town. Not dangerous, but not safe either. The bank was a small brick building. Chance parked next to a minivan, the only other car in the lot. Bellamy got out and, not bothering to wait for him, rushed inside.

Chance followed, shoving down the thoughts churning about Bellamy, and focused on the matter at hand. If Sam was still around, she must have walked or hitched a ride. He doubted that minivan was hers.

The more he thought about it, the more this situation didn't sit well with him. Why would a photographer have a safe deposit box on the opposite side of town? And if she had discovered evidence of murder, why didn't she go to the police instead of trying to tackle it herself?

The bank lobby was empty. Chance entered in time to see Bellamy approach a young woman at the counter. She pulled out a photo and held it up for the woman to see. "Have you seen this girl here lately?" she asked.

The girl stared hard at the picture and Chance didn't miss the recognition in her eyes. He moved to Bellamy's side and glanced at the picture. He hadn't seen her grab anything before they left.

This was a different picture than the one he'd shown the governor. That one had been a serious self-portrait, probably used for business purposes. Sam was pretty, with short blond hair in an edgy haircut like Bellamy's and sparkling brown eyes. In the photo he'd shown the governor, she'd been staring seriously at the camera.

In the photo Bellamy held out now, Sam was grinning, her arm thrown casually around Bellamy's smaller frame. Bellamy's hair was still long, so it must have been an older picture. Her expression was surprised, her face turned toward Sam, but she was laughing.

Chance's stomach flipped at the sight. Bellamy looked so happy, the opposite of the woman he'd spent the last couple days with. He could see his best friend in the photo, the younger version of Bellamy that had been seared into his brain since they were children.

He'd do anything to make her smile like that again.

"Yeah, she was just here yesterday," the bank associate was saying. "Who are you guys?"

Bellamy froze. "Y-Yesterday? But - "

Chance extended his hand to the woman. "Chance Erickson, with Erickson Security. We have reason to believe that this young woman is missing. Any information you have would be appreciated."

The woman's eyes widened. "Well, she was here last night right before we closed. She got something out of her safe deposit box and left. She was in a hurry."

Chance glanced behind him. The desk was off to the left of the bank's entrance, so the parking lot wasn't visible from where the woman stood. She wouldn't have seen what kind of vehicle Sam left in. He turned back to her. "Do you know what she took out of the box?"

The woman shook her head. "No, sorry. And before you ask, I can't open the box without a warrant or permission from the owner."

Chance nodded. He'd expected as much. He scanned the lobby again and spotted a camera in the corner of the ceiling. It had a good view of the lobby and the parking lot beyond. "Thanks for your help," he said to the woman, and started across the lobby and toward the parking lot.

"Hey, wait," Bellamy protested, hurrying after him.

Chance held up a hand, requesting patience, and pulled out his phone. "Owen," he said when his brother answered. "The teller says she hasn't been here since last night. I need you to pull security footage from the bank. Find out what she got out of that safe deposit box and where she went from here."

"I'm on it," Owen replied. "Stay put for a minute while I work my magic."

Chance hung up and looked at Bellamy, but her focus wasn't on him. She was studying the building, her eyes moving to sweep the area.

"If I was on such a high-stakes case, I would want to make sure I wasn't followed. Most banks in the city have cameras in the parking lot."

"Yeah," Chance agreed, following suit. "I wouldn't park my car out front."

"The back?"

Chance nodded and grabbed her hand, more out of instinct than anything else. Her fingers were warm in his grip, and she didn't pull away. His heartbeat quickened and he wasn't sure if it was because of her or the investigation.

A small alley ran past the back of the bank. It was just wide enough for a car to fit through. There wasn't much there besides a dumpster and a god-awful smell. No cameras in the area either, probably because there wasn't a back door to the bank that needed to be monitored. If Sam parked back here, they'd have a hard time tracking her.

Chance eyed the gravel road. "Tire tracks," he said, kneeling next to an indent in the gravel. "Maybe she - "

Wait. He knew that smell.

"Bella," he said, his voice sharper than he intended. "Go back to the car."

She gave him a flabbergasted look. "Why?"

Familiar nausea churned in his gut. He slowly rose to his feet. Memories from his time in the military came rushing back and he had to grit his teeth against the familiar ache they brought with them.

That smell in the air wasn't from old food.

* * * * * *

Bellamy scowled and crossed her arms to hide the sudden pounding of her heart. Chance's expression had gone completely blank. A prickle slid down her spine.

"Tell me."

"Bella. Please, just go back to the car and wait for me." His voice was polite, but it had a steely edge. Something was terribly wrong.

Bellamy set her jaw and widened her stance. She'd never been one to shy away from bad news, and she certainly wouldn't abandon her friend now that they were so close. "Chance. Whatever you found, just tell me. I'm not a child anymore; I can handle it. Was she kidnapped? Is that what the tire tracks are? Just...just tell me."

He stared at her in silence. A vein stuck out at his temple.

Bellamy's chest tightened. Terror clawed its way up her throat.

Chance's phone rang, startling them both. He yanked it out of his pocket and put it to his ear. "Yeah?" He listened for a moment, then his eyes closed as he let out a breath. "Yeah, I think I already know. Call over to the police department. Make sure we're in on this investigation."

He hung up and pinned her with a stare as he slid the phone back into his pocket.

Bellamy's stomach dropped. She knew that expression. She'd been on the receiving end of similar ones her entire life.

It was pity.

A cold numbness started in her heart and spread through her body, preparing her for the news her heart knew she was about to receive.

"Bella…" Chance's voice was gentle, as if he was talking to a frightened animal that might bolt at any second. "I need you to go back to the car, sweetheart, okay?"

"No." She turned her back on him and looked around the area, scanning everything, looking for what he'd already found. She meant what she'd told him. She wasn't a child anymore.

The dumpster.

Before Chance could stop her, Bellamy ran over to the dumpster and threw open the lid. The smell assaulted her before the sight did. It smelled like feces and urine and decaying flesh. She gagged, wanting to turn away, but her eyes were inexplicably drawn to the sight. She couldn't stop her blue eyes from meeting a pair of lifeless brown ones.

Brown eyes surrounded by a mangled body covered in blood.

All activity in Bellamy's brain grinded to a halt. The body was almost unrecognizable, but she knew that blond hair, those brown eyes. Pain pierced her chest where her heart had been. Now it was ripped in two; one half would forever remain here, in this dumpster, with the body of her best friend.

A red haze settled over her vision. She knew who was responsible for this.

"Powell." Her hands clenched into fists.

Hands gripped her shoulders and pulled her away from the dumpster, but the image of Sam's body was burned into her retinas. She didn't think she would ever stop seeing it.

"Bella."

Chance's deep voice barely pierced the fury roaring in her mind. It was so loud that her ears were ringing.

"Bellamy, look at me. Look at me."

Slowly, she turned her gaze up to his.

Chance let out a harsh breath. His hands went to either side of her face and he bent down so his head was level with hers. When Bellamy tried to turn her face away, he pulled her forward and crushed her to his chest, one hand on the back of her head, the other around her shoulders. Bellamy let him hold her for a moment before she shoved him away.

"Bella, baby, I'm so sorry you had to see that. We'll find out what happened, I swear to you. Everything will be okay."

Bellamy stepped away from him as the sound of sirens in the distance grew louder. She was all too familiar with this feeling. She'd felt it when she left La Conner all those years ago. She'd felt it before Sam had found her. And she felt it now.

It was despair, but there was a crucial difference this time.

This time, she knew who was responsible and she could do something about it.

Chance continued to murmur comforting things to her.

Finally, she held up a hand for him to shut up. Then she looked him squarely in the eyes, and put every ounce of the rage she was feeling into her next words.

"I'm going to destroy that bastard's life for this."

CHAPTER 8

CHANCE PERCHED ON THE TOP STEP *of the staircase, just outside his bedroom. He listened as his parents' hushed voices drifted up from where they sat at the kitchen table below.*

"Something's not right there, Paul. I can feel it, and I think it's getting worse lately. She hardly comes over here anymore and when she does, she's so withdrawn."

"I know. I've noticed it too. But he's the pastor, for crying out loud. He gives the best sermons in the state and he has most of the city in his pocket. Everyone loves him; he has all the power here, Mary. If we implicate him without any evidence, it could have consequences for us. For the business."

"I don't care about the consequences. This is Bellamy's life we're talking about. We can't stand by and let this continue to happen to her. Eventually, she'll stop coming over here completely and we won't be able to shelter her anymore."

Paul's deep sigh drifted up the stairs. "I know, love. I know. I just need to figure out the best way to handle the situation. Maybe we can ask her about it next time she's here."

"She's fourteen. Talking to adults isn't cool anymore. Last week, she hardly looked at me when she came over. She and Sarah just locked themselves in Sarah's room all night. I just feel like she's withdrawing from us, and he's the one responsible for it."

There was a lengthy silence. "I'll do some checking with the police department and see if we can file a report. Maybe we can get social services to do a welfare check. With any luck, that will shake something loose."

"Thanks, Paul. If we don't do something, no one else will. We might be the only ones Bellamy has looking out for her."

"She's part of this family. We'll protect her, just like we'd protect any of our kids."

Silence descended on the kitchen again, and Chance took the opportunity to creep away from the stairway and retreat to his bedroom. He sat on the bench underneath his window and looked outside. From his vantage point, he could see the roof of Bella's house down the street. All seemed quiet.

After a while, Chance climbed back into bed, hoping he

could ignore his churning stomach and get some sleep before his geometry test the next morning.

* * * * * *

Chance paced the small interrogation room for the millionth time. Each time he reached the wall, he about-faced and glared at the two-way mirror before he started toward the other wall.

Hours had passed since their discovery of Sam's body. They'd separated him and Bellamy upon their arrival, and Chance had suffered through inane, winding conversations with three police officers who claimed to just be "doing their jobs."

Was Bellamy all right?

She'd just seen her best friend's body. He could only imagine the thoughts going through her head; she shouldn't be stuck by herself in a police station with cops interrogating her like she was the killer.

At least that was the vibe he'd gotten from Officer Ruiz, the prick that finally came in after Chance talked circles around the first two deputies.

Chance had worked with a lot of law enforcement officers at ESI. In most cases, they were crucial to the mission's success, and he respected the hell out of the work they did.

But Officer Ruiz was dirty.

Chance knew it within the first three minutes of their conversation, when he asked why they hadn't reported Sam as missing right away and Officer Ruiz gave a smooth, well-practiced answer. Something about timeframes and holes in witness statements - a bunch of bull, really.

And he'd scurried away like a cockroach when Chance began to press him about the lieutenant governor.

The whole thing stunk to high heaven, and Chance couldn't wait to get Bellamy out of this place so he could get his team on the case. If Officer Ruiz was lead on the investigation - and he'd told Chance he was -, the police weren't going to do their damn jobs. ESI could run circles around them, sans red tape.

Now he understood why Bellamy didn't trust the police.

He'd seen a lot of horrible things during his time as a Marine, but the way Sam's body had been mutilated... He'd never forget it. It was personal. Calculated.

What had she discovered that could make Powell that angry? It hardly seemed like a run-of-the-mill scandal, or an affair, like her voicemail had implied.

Bellamy was right; Governor Powell was much more dangerous than Chance had initially thought.

Things still weren't making any sense, though, and Chance didn't feel like they were any closer to an answer. He needed time and space to clear his head and get a good view of the situation. He needed Emmett and Owen to brainstorm with and give him insight he could use to get some traction here. There were too many unknown variables and not enough clues to go on.

Chance stopped his mental tirade when the door opened behind him.

An officer entered the room. He was young, but he looked more serious and put-together than Officer Ruiz had.

"Mr. Erickson, you're free to go. And you have a phone call."
He held out a cordless phone and Chance's cell phone and
withdrew, leaving the door open behind him.

Chance put the cordless phone to his ear. "Erickson."

"Chance." It was Emmett.

Chance never thought he'd be so happy to hear his
older brother's voice. He plopped down on the hard metal
chair at the table and ran his free hand through his short
hair. "Emmett, thank God. What's going on over there?"

"I'd like to ask you the same thing. What the hell do
you think you're doing? You've put yourself right in the
middle of a murder investigation."

"Bellamy needs my help. Our help."

An exasperated sigh. "What is it with you and this girl?
It's been ten years. You need to move on with your life."

"Her best friend was murdered, Emmett. If she was any
other client, you would already be investigating."

"She's not any other client. She's not a client at all.
You're jumping into this headfirst without gathering any
information, and you're pulling ESI with you. We don't know
anything about her or this situation."

Chance gritted his teeth, resisting the urge to slam the
phone back down. He usually prided himself on his level
head in these types of situations, so it was no surprise that
Emmett was pumping the brakes. This behavior was so out
of character for Chance, but he couldn't explain it even if he
wanted to. He just knew that Bellamy needed his help, and
come hell or high water, he'd do anything in his power to
help her.

There was a sudden shuffling on the other end of the

line, and Sarah's voice came on. "Chance, is Bellamy okay?"

"She's in shock."

A burst of static that sounded like a snort echoed in Chance's ear. "No wonder. She found the body, didn't she?"

Chance thought back to the moment they'd found Sam's body and Bellamy's bizarre reaction to it. The normal reaction would've been to freeze up, cry, faint… Instead, she seemed like she'd expected it. The venom he'd seen in her expression was unlike anything he'd ever seen there before. She looked like a totally different person than the one he grew up with. "Yeah," he said heavily. "She did. But how did you know that?"

In the background, Chance could hear Emmett grumbling about Sarah intruding in his office. There was another scuffle, then Emmett's voice was closer, back on the line. "I don't like this," he said.

"I don't either. Something shady is going on here. This isn't the time to discuss it, but I've been sending Owen the details. He can brief you, if he hasn't already. Sam's murder is proof that there's danger here, and I won't leave Bellamy without getting to the bottom of it. I can't really explain it, but I need you to back me on this."

There was a brief pause. "I'll get the rest of the team on it." Emmett's tone was grudging. He didn't want to get involved, but he was loyal to his bones and he wouldn't leave Chance high and dry.

"Thanks. I need to find Bellamy. I'll be in touch."

Chance blew out a breath and left the cordless phone on the table. He stepped into the hallway just in time to see Officer Ruiz passing by. "Officer Ruiz," Chance said, careful to keep his tone cordial. "I'm looking for Bellamy Burke. Can you point me in her direction?"

Officer Ruiz didn't even slow his stride. He gestured down the hallway with a barely-disguised scowl, bumping Chance's shoulder as he brushed past.

"Thanks so much," Chance called after him. "I look forward to speaking with you soon!"

Satisfied, he turned down the direction the officer had indicated.

Fifteen minutes and one embarrassing conversation later, Chance realized that Officer Ruiz had pointed him in the wrong direction. By the time he finally found someone to escort him to Bellamy, Officer Ruiz had already found her.

She stood behind the front desk, face pale as she listened to Officer Ruiz speak to her in low tones.

Chance didn't like how close the man was standing to her, nor the way he was looking at her like he wanted to eat her alive. He quickened his pace.

"Call me if you think of anything that might help," Officer Ruiz was saying as Chance approached them. He handed Bellamy a business card and turned his cool gaze on Chance. "Mr. Erickson, you finally found us. The same goes to you. Call if you need anything."

"I'm sure that won't be necessary. You've done plenty." Chance took the business card out of Bellamy's hand and smiled coldly at Officer Ruiz as he ripped it in half and tossed it in a nearby trash can.

A muscle ticked in the officer's jaw and he inclined his head before stalking away.

Chance turned his attention to Bellamy. She didn't look

at him, just started walking toward the door. "Let's get out of here," she said.

Chance followed her outside. He was pleased to find that someone had been kind enough to park her car in front of the police station. He'd half expected it to have four slashed tires after his conversations with Officer Ruiz.

Bellamy slid into the passenger's seat and slammed the door.

Chance circled around to the other side. For the first time in his life, he wasn't sure what to say. Words of comfort? Promises of retribution? He suspected she'd appreciate the latter, but he was wading in foreign waters here.

Once he was settled into the driver's seat and he'd started the engine, he glanced at her. "You'll have to direct me to your place."

Bellamy looked up, her eyes distant, and he flashed back to Sam staring at them from the dumpster, the same blankness on her pale face. A shudder ran through him.

"We're not going back to my place. Take me back to the studio."

"What? Why?"

"Ronald Powell killed Sam, and I'm going to make sure he pays for it. I've got a lot of work to do."

Retribution. His guess was correct.

Chance eased the car onto the freeway. By the set of her shoulders, it was obvious she wasn't going to budge on the matter. Despite his better judgement, he knew this was a battle he wouldn't win. "All right," he said. "I have a few ideas. But let's get some rest first. We'll start fresh in the morning."

Bellamy turned to face him. "I don't need your help anymore, Chance. I've dragged you far enough into this. I'll handle it from here."

He drummed his fingers on the steering wheel. Emmett would be tickled pink if he just let the matter drop. He could return home and back to his regularly-scheduled activities. After all, Bellamy had left La Conner - and him - behind a long time ago, so perhaps this wasn't his problem. What did he owe her after ten years apart? They didn't even know each other anymore.

And yet.

Something in him couldn't let it go. He couldn't abandon her now when no one else was on her side. He might be the only person left to look out for her.

The thought conjured a forgotten memory, a weeknight crouching at the top of the staircase. Eavesdropping on his parents' conversation after they thought he was asleep.

His father's words drifted back into his mind. "She's part of this family. We'll protect her, just like we'd protect any of our kids."

That, he realized, was the feeling he couldn't describe. Bellamy was part of his family, ten years apart or not. Secrets or not. Willing or not.

That would never change.

Realizing Bellamy was still waiting for a response, he forced a smile. "Look, Bella, I'm here. I'm in this. If Sam was important to you, she's important to me too."

"You didn't know her. You don't even know me

anymore. It's been a long time, Chance. You don't owe me anything."

The hell he didn't. But he didn't say that. Instead, he took a deep breath and tried a logical approach. "What are you going to do on your own? Whether you like it or not, I have resources that you need. The police have already proved they're not going to help much in this scenario. If you accept my help, you'll have a lot better chance of catching this guy. Let me help you."

She pursed her lips. "All right, fine. But only until we catch this guy. After that, you're out. I don't need you interfering in my life."

"Deal." That was easy.

"And we're playing by my rules."

"All right."

"So. To the studio."

Chance glanced at the clock on the dashboard. Just past midnight.

It was going to be a long night.

"Whatever you say, boss."

Once they arrived, Bellamy led him inside and, without further ado, began digging through debris again. Chance wasn't sure what she was hoping to find - she'd already been through everything once - but he followed suit. Maybe she was looking for some shred of evidence she could use against Powell.

He picked up a drawer that had been discarded on the floor and pulled out a stack of photos still inside. He flipped through them. Most of them were scenery shots, beautifully composed, of all sorts of landscapes. A beach scene with a single palm tree. A rugged mountain with a snow-capped peak. A vast desert covered in sand. On the back of each photograph, a small set of initials was scrawled into the bottom right corner.

BB.

Intrigued, Chance examined them more closely. She hadn't been kidding when she said she traveled the world with Sam. It was amazing what she'd accomplished in the past ten years. Clearly, she'd seen and experienced things that he'd never imagined, and he found himself feeling a bit jealous that he hadn't been there with her. Knowing how shy and timid she'd been when they were younger, he almost couldn't believe how far she'd come.

He glanced over at Bellamy. She was digging through a large basket on the other side of the room. Despite the terrible week she'd had, she was pushing through it. Her expression was calm, set, and determined. She'd grown into a beautiful, strong woman, despite terrible circumstances.

He was so damn proud of her.

At the bottom of the stack, one photo stood out from the rest. It wasn't a landscape. It was a picture of two teenage girls. They looked like they were barely out of high school, standing in front of a rusty Volkswagen van. He recognized Bellamy's long dark hair right away, blowing wildly in the wind. She didn't look much older than she'd been when she disappeared from La Conner. And he guessed it was Sam standing next to her, her arm around Bellamy's shoulders. Sam's hair was longer too, flying in the wind like Bellamy's. She had a huge grin on her face, one arm spread wide as if to welcome the photographer into their lives. Bellamy's expression was more neutral, but there was a sparkle in her eyes even if she wasn't smiling. They both had cameras hanging around their necks.

Chance glanced back at Bellamy again; now she was busy sorting through a box, a look of intense concentration on her face. He looked back at the picture. She was so young there, so thin. How long had she and Sam been friends? He ached to know her story, to know what she'd been through since she'd left La Conner.

He slipped the photo into the pocket of his jeans. It might be helpful in the investigation; at least that's what he told himself.

Moving to another area of the room, he picked up a broken frame. It was a newspaper clipping with a picture attached. The picture looked like it had been taken from some bushes with a long lens. He could see the blurred forms of leaves on the edges of the photo. A group of boys stood in front of the playground of what looked like an elementary school. They couldn't have been older than ten. Three of the boys sneered down at a smaller boy who cowered on the ground at their feet. It was a powerful image, but it was the smaller boy's expression that caught Chance's attention. He looked terrified, shoulders bowed, and his eyes were achingly sad.

"That was my first story."

Chance looked up to see Bellamy standing next to him. He hadn't heard her approach. She nodded at the photo in his hands.

"I was 19. We sent the photo to the newspaper and they ended up writing an entire article on the bullying epidemic at the elementary school. It made the front page."

"What made you choose to photograph this?"

She looked at him. Her blue eyes shone in the dim light. "I didn't choose it. It chose me."

CHAPTER 9

BELLA SPUN IN A SLOW CIRCLE in the middle of her bedroom. She looked at her reflection in the full-length mirror and marveled at the pretty girl staring back at her. She'd never owned a dress so beautiful. It was dark blue, and glittery, and it fell to just above her knees. When she spun, it fanned out in all directions like a princess's dress.

In her reflection, she could see her mother smiling just over her right shoulder. "Do you like it, baby?" her mother asked, voice soft.

"Mama, I love it." Bella grinned. "I feel like a princess."

"You look like a princess." She touched Bella's hair, smoothing the curls that hung down her back. "When is Chance picking you up?"

Bella glanced at the clock on her desk next to her lamp. "Any minute. Is Papa here?"

Her mother shook her head. "Come on, let's put on your sweater." She picked up the white cardigan from its place on the bed and held it out for Bella to slip her arms into.

Bella admired her reflection one more time. "Do I have to wear that? It looks so pretty by itself."

"Yes, baby, or else it's not modest."

Bella scowled. "You don't care if it's modest. You just want me to hide these." She gestured to the dark purple bruises on her arms.

Her mother frowned. She didn't raise her voice - she never did - but her tone had some bite in it when she responded. "Either way, you're not going to that dance without this sweater. And you'll keep it on all night, you understand me? Your father will be at the dance as a chaperone, and don't let him see you without it."

Bella humphed and allowed her mother to pull the sweater over her shoulders. "Fine."

The doorbell rang, and Bella's bad mood dissipated. "There he is," she squealed. She ran past her mother and down the stairs to the front door.

She threw it open to reveal Chance standing on her doorstep. He looked handsome in loose dress pants and a dark blue shirt that matched her dress. He stood with his hands in his pockets and when she opened the door, his eyes widened and his jaw dropped. "Wow, Bella, you look..."

Bella giggled and leaned provocatively against the doorframe. "Like a supermodel?"

"I was going to say you look like a girl, for once." He

grinned at her and winked.

"You're so rude." Bella grabbed her handbag from the chair by the door and cast one last glance at her mother. She stood at the top of the stairs, arms crossed over her middle, and a tear ran down one cheek even though she was smiling. "Bye, Mama. See you later tonight."

"Have fun, baby."

Chance walked her out to the car and opened the back door for her. She slid into the back seat.

"Bellamy, you look beautiful," Mrs. Erickson said from the front seat. "I love your dress."

Bella blushed. "Thanks, Mrs. Erickson."

Mrs. Erickson looked at her with that expression she'd been wearing so much lately, like she was concerned. Bella quickly looked away as Chance slid into the seat next to hers. "Chance, your mama said I look beautiful."

Chance wrinkled his nose. "Well she's a girl. She can say that kind of thing."

Bella laughed as Mrs. Erickson pulled the SUV out of her driveway and they made their way to the high school.

* * * * * *

Bellamy watched the sunrise from the studio's small window. She yawned and stretched, wincing when her muscles screamed in protest. Chance snored softly from the armchair nearby.

Her gaze skimmed over him as he slept. She couldn't help herself. His long legs stretched out in front of him and his head drooped to the side. In sleep, his fierce expression was relaxed.

He wore exhaustion a lot better than she did. She'd caught a glimpse of herself in the mirror earlier that morning. She hadn't gotten more than three or four hours' sleep in the past few days and it showed in the purple bruises under her eyes and the hopeless state of affairs that was her hair.

The problem was, every time she drifted off, she saw Sam's face. Even though her body was exhausted, her mind wouldn't allow her even a brief respite for sleep.

She had to get justice for Sam, and that meant putting Lieutenant Governor Powell behind bars. That was the only way she'd ever be able to sleep again.

Luckily, whoever Powell hired to trash the studio wasn't the brightest bulb in the box. She kept an important key hidden, taped on the bottom of a drawer in one of the cabinets. In the chaos, the key had gotten dislodged; it took her most of the night to find it buried under a pile of debris in the corner.

The key unlocked a locker in Seattle where she kept information on all of her fencing clients. Sure, anonymity was her number one job, but she wasn't the type to blindly trust that her clients wouldn't screw her over.

She made it a priority to investigate and keep a file on each one of her clients' identities. It helped in times of crisis, where she needed some good old blackmail to get the ball rolling.

She had a hefty file on Lieutenant Governor Ronald Powell.

Today would mark the last day of life as Powell knew it.

The sun had risen; there was work to do.

Bellamy picked her way through the debris to where Chance was sprawled and lightly placed her hand on his shoulder. A small thrill went through her at the feel of hard muscle under his t-shirt. At her touch, he came instantly awake.

"Oh, good morning. I must have fallen asleep..."

"You did. At about five o'clock." Bellamy moved away to give him room to stand.

"Did you get any sleep?" he asked, stifling a yawn.

"A little," she lied. "It's time to go. We're going to talk to Mrs. Powell today."

"That's not a bad idea." Chance stretched. "Now that this has turned into a murder investigation, maybe she'll be a little more willing to talk to us."

Bellamy winced. It felt like a knife twisting in her gut, but he was right. As if she could forget that Sam was dead.

Now wasn't the time to grieve, though. She needed to move quickly if she wanted to put her plan into motion before Powell had a chance to move against her.

Chance parked the car just outside the governor's mansion gates and they waited. Bellamy gripped the handle on the car door to keep herself still; she felt jittery just being in the vicinity of Governor Powell's residence.

It was strange that such a beautiful mansion could house so much evil. That a man cruel enough to order the death and dismemberment of Bellamy's best friend could be elected to a government position, and nobody knew his true character.

And worst of all, that such a monster could be married to someone as sweet and timid as Susan Powell.

It echoed Bellamy's childhood.

Bellamy's mother had been a kind person too, and married to a pastor. A man of God who, if no one else, should've been a good person.

Bellamy hadn't been able to do anything about her father, but she could do something about Powell.

And she would.

Bellamy tried to be patient as the car idled outside the gates. It was a Monday, so they assumed that Powell would leave for his office at some point. Since he'd been explicit in his instructions never to return, they could only do so when he wasn't around. And pray that Susan's loyalty didn't run as deep as she showed to the public.

An hour later, they were rewarded by the sight of a black town car leaving the gates. Chance waited a few more minutes, then they eased forward and told the guards they wanted to speak with Mrs. Powell. Bellamy half-expected the governor's wife to deny them entrance, but after a moment, the gates opened.

Bellamy led the way to the front door once they'd parked the car. She knocked and Susan Powell opened the door almost immediately. "I assumed you'd be back," she said. "Come in."

They followed Susan into a large sitting room. Unlike Governor Powell's office, it was open and airy, with light pink carpet and delicate white furniture. It was the governor's wife's version of a study, in the archaic marriage roles from the time when the mansion was originally built.

Bellamy was relieved to see that Chance didn't follow her inside the room. He must have gotten the hint that she wanted to do this alone. So instead, he stood in the doorway and turned his back to them, like he was standing guard.

Susan sat on a plush white couch across from Bellamy. Her gaze strayed back to where Chance stood in the doorway, but she didn't comment.

The way she sat with her hands folded neatly in her lap, back perfectly straight, reminded Bellamy of her mother. The woman looked like she hadn't relaxed a day in her life.

Bellamy took a deep breath. This was just like any other interview for a story. She was an investigative photographer. She'd conducted dozens of interviews just like this, and she was good at it.

Straightening her shoulders, she smiled at Susan.

"Mrs. Powell, my name is Bellamy Burke. We weren't properly introduced yesterday." She extended her hand and Susan shook it.

"It's nice to meet you. If you've come back to see Ron, you just missed him. He left for the office a little bit ago."

"Actually, I'm here to see you."

Susan raised her eyebrows. Her gaze went to Chance again, and she gripped her hands together in her lap. Her knuckles went white. "Why?"

"Mrs. Powell, I'm not with ESI. I'm not with any agency at all. My friend Sam and I are investigative photographers. Chance and I came to see your husband yesterday because my friend was missing. I know she was working on a story about your husband, but I don't know why."

Susan wrung her hands in her lap, but she didn't respond.

"Sam wasn't some sleazy reporter. She was someone who saw the wrongs in the world and tried to make them right. She never took on a story unless there was concrete proof that something was going on, something that could potentially harm innocent people."

Something flickered in Susan's eyes. "I'm sure that's true, but I can't help you."

"Did your husband tell you not to say anything?"

Susan shook her head, lips pursed.

Bellamy leaned forward, her voice soft. "Look, in your position, I understand that appearance is everything. But skeletons tend to come out of the closet, no matter how hard you try to hide them." She took a deep breath, ignoring the dark memories that bubbled to the surface. "I've been where you are. I know what it's like to present a false image to the world and hope they don't see the truth. You may think that what happens behind closed doors isn't anyone's business, but it is. If it's causing you harm... physical, emotional, or otherwise... it needs to stop. I can help you get out, but you have to trust me."

Susan's calm expression crumpled. "He told me not to say anything," she said, her voice breaking on a sob.

"Mrs. Powell, my best friend is dead." Bellamy kept her tone gentle, but firm. She kept a tight lid on the emotions roiling in her stomach, threatening to tear her apart. If she lost her composure now, she had a feeling she'd lose Susan too. "She was murdered. I found her body in a dumpster yesterday. She was mutilated, Susan. And my gut is telling me it has something to do with the story she was working on. The one about your husband."

"W-What? She's dead? Oh, God." Susan hiccupped and grabbed a tissue from the box on the coffee table. She dabbed at her eyes. "I... I saw your friend. She came to me two days ago and told me that Ron is having an affair. She even had pictures to prove it."

"With who?"

Susan shook her head. "I don't... I don't know. She didn't say, and I was too upset to ask. It sounds like it's been going on for a long time, so I don't think it's someone from his office."

"So what did you do?"

"I confronted Ron about it, of course. He got angry and told me that he'd... kill me... if I ever told anyone. I've never been so afraid. Ever since he became governor, he's changed. I don't know who he is anymore."

Bellamy leaned forward. "Has he hurt you, Susan?"

Susan blinked. "What? I don't - "

"It's okay if you don't want to tell me right now. But I can help you."

She bit her lip, looking everywhere in the room but at Bellamy. The words tumbled out of her. "He's been going to so many meetings. Gone so many nights. The stress involved with this job... It wears on him. When he comes home, he's always so angry. Sometimes... Sometimes he can be violent."

Bellamy took her hand and squeezed. She stared into the other woman's eyes, urging her to listen, to believe what she was about to say. Wishing that she'd had the power to say these exact words to her mother ten years ago. "Thank you for telling me. It's going to be okay. I'll make sure your husband won't lay a hand on you ever again."

Tears streamed down Susan's cheeks. She swiped at them with her tissue, and her shoulders finally relaxed.

"Mrs. Powell." Chance stepped forward, his voice quiet but full of authority.

Bellamy jumped. She'd forgotten he was there. She felt her face warm and prayed that he hadn't been listening to their entire conversation. But who was she kidding? Of course he had been.

"I can make sure you're safe." Chance pulled a card out of his pocket and handed it to her. "There's a phone number on here for a man named Roman. He works with me at ESI. He can help you get packed and we'll get you out of here."

"But he'll know I ran away. He'll come after me."

"My team is good at what they do. We'll get you somewhere safe. He can try, but he won't find you, I promise."

Susan stood. Her face was blotchy, but she threw her arms around Chance's shoulders. Another sob escaped her. "Thank you. Thank you so much."

Bellamy let out a breath of relief. Phase one of her plan couldn't have gone more smoothly. Now she hoped she could pull off the rest.

They said their goodbyes. Susan hugged Bellamy as well and thanked her for everything, promising to call Roman as soon as they left.

As the door to the mansion closed behind them,

Chance led the way back to the car. Bellamy grabbed his elbow and pulled him to a stop. She met his questioning eyes and hoped the look on her face expressed the gratitude she felt deep in her bones, because she wasn't sure she could say it out loud.

He got the message. Smiling, he touched his fingertips to the side of her face, then moved them up to her hair. "You're welcome."

* * * * * *

Later that day, Chance and Bellamy stood in the studio, which had become their makeshift base of operations. Chance's phone rang and he picked it up, smiling at the voice on the other end of the line. "Roman. What's the status?"

"I've got Mrs. Powell set up in the safe house. My contact is assisting with her relocation. She'll soon have a new identity on the east coast," Roman reported. "She left before the governor even got home. He won't find her any time soon."

"Good work. Thanks."

Chance hung up and grinned at Bellamy. "Susan Powell is safe." Relief lit up her face and robbed him of his breath. He gawked at her for a second, unable to get past how beautiful she looked.

Bellamy rubbed her hands together and opened her laptop on the nearby counter. "Now that she's safe, it's time to initiate phase two."

Chance went around behind her to peer at the screen.

"What's phase two?"

"Mrs. Powell emailed over the picture that Sam gave her. Now we send it to my contact over at the news station. They'll report the governor's infidelity, it'll be breaking news, and Governor Powell's stellar reputation will be ruined. That should cast enough doubt on him to keep those around him safe. And hopefully, he'll be too busy dealing with the paparazzi to retaliate."

They both stared at the photo on the screen. It was a lengthy shot of an open hotel room window. The governor was lying on his back on the bed, and a woman who was clearly not his wife sat on top of him. They couldn't see the woman's face, but it didn't matter; Ronald Powell's face was clear as day.

Satisfaction lit Bellamy's face as she hit the 'send' button.

"Do you know who the woman is that he's having the affair with?"

Bellamy shook her head. "No, but it doesn't matter. The point is that he's not the golden boy that Oregon thinks he is. With his reputation ruined, the dominos should start to tumble one by one."

Chance stepped back as she closed the laptop and hopped down from the barstool she'd been perched on. She stretched her arms above her head with a sigh.

"If Governor Powell is as powerful as you said, don't you think he'll retaliate? The danger's not over."

Bellamy smiled. "Probably not, but I can take care of myself."

He didn't doubt it. Clearly she was used to handling

things on her own. "But we still need to find evidence that he killed Sam."

"Yeah, and I'm sure your team will. That's why I hired you." Bellamy led the way to the door, pulling her phone out of her pocket. "I'll call a taxi for you. We'll have you home in time for dinner."

Chance followed her. "I don't think it's wise for me to leave yet."

Bellamy shot him a look over her shoulder. "Remember our deal? When I say we're done, you're out."

Damn. He had agreed to that.

She dialed a few numbers on her phone. Before she could raise it to her ear, he placed his hand over it.

"All right, I promised. I'll go. At least let me take you home first. Once I know you're safe there, I'll call a cab and head straight for the airport. I swear."

She eyed him for a moment, clearly debating whether she should allow it. Finally, she nodded. "Okay, fine. But straight to the airport after that."

"Deal."

The drive to her apartment was silent except for her quietly issued directions. Her building was in an even scarier neighborhood than Sam's. It was surrounded by warehouses on all sides, and the building itself looked like it was about to fall down.

When Chance pulled to a stop at the curb, Bellamy turned to look at him. "Thanks for everything," she said.

Chance looked from her to the building. This place was a mugging waiting to happen. There was no way he could leave her there, but what choice did he have? The past ten years had turned them into strangers; he had no right to question her living accommodations.

"Let me at least walk you to your door," he said finally.

"Chance..."

"Then I'm out. I swear."

She frowned, but opened her door and let him follow her inside the building.

Her apartment was on the third floor. They took a rickety elevator and she led him down a narrow hallway.

"How long have you lived here?"

"A few years now." Stubborn pride colored her voice. "It's not much, but it's home."

Chance's gaze landed on the last door at the end of the hall. It hung wide open. Stepping in front of her, he pulled his gun and trained it on the doorway. "Bellamy. Is that your apartment?"

"Yeah." Her voice turned to steel. "The door shouldn't be open. I always lock it."

"Stay here. Don't move." He kept his gun trained on the door and approached slowly. No sound came from inside, but experience told him that didn't mean a thing. He took a step through the doorway and swung the Glock in a wide arc, taking in all exits and potential hiding places. The apartment was tiny, and it was trashed just like the studio. Couch cushions were strewn all over the floor, their fabric shredded, and the kitchen table rested on its side.

Chance cleared the apartment room by room, checked closets and the bathroom until he was sure there was nobody inside. When he returned to the living room, Bellamy stood framed in the doorway, staring at the destruction.

"Powell," she said through clenched teeth.

Chance toed a broken lamp. Thank God he'd insisted on taking her home. What if she'd arrived and the guy was still here?

The thought made his stomach sink to his toes.

Bellamy picked up an overturned chair and slid it under the table, then paused, her eyes on a piece of paper resting on the wood surface.

Chance stepped up next to her and read the words scrawled in red ink.

You know who to call.

Bellamy picked up the paper, crumpled it into a ball, and threw it at the wall. It bounced off and rolled back toward them. "I knew he was behind this," she seethed.

"Who?"

"Ruiz."

Chance gaped at her. "Officer Ruiz?" But then he remembered the man's parting words to them at the police station. "You think he did this?"

"I know he did. He's been in Powell's pocket for a while now."

"How do you know?"

"I just do." Bellamy scowled at the mess around them. "How did the bastard know where I live, though? I've always been careful to keep that private."

"It's probably on public record somewhere."

"It's not. I use the studio address for all of my public information. This apartment isn't even in my name."

Chance raised an eyebrow. "Seems like you've gone to

a lot of trouble. Why?"

"I'm a private person."

Right. And he was the queen of England. "Well, clearly it's not safe for you to stay here."

"I know. I'll get a hotel for tonight."

"No, I mean, it's not safe for you in Portland."

Bellamy's gaze didn't leave the destruction of her apartment, and she didn't answer. Instead, she crouched and picked up a miraculously intact picture frame. It was the same photo she'd shown the bank teller, the one of her and Sam. She stared hard at it, like it had the answers to all of her questions.

She reared her arm back and threw the frame at the wall. Glass shattered, deafening in the quiet room.

Chance grabbed her arm and pulled her back a few steps so she wouldn't be hurt by the flying glass. Her chest heaved, and she turned away from him, hands clenched into fists at her sides.

"Dammit, Sam, you sure know how to make a mess." Her breath hitched. "You should have left it alone."

Chance shoved his hands into his pockets. He wanted to pull her into his arms and tell her everything would be okay, but he couldn't make a promise like that. And even if he did, she wouldn't accept it.

"I'm not leaving."

"Bellamy, you're not safe here. You're coming home with me."

"The hell I am."

Chance shoved a hand through his hair and took a deep breath. "Bella, look at me." He waited until she turned to face him. "You have a murderer after you. Do you understand that? Your life is in danger."

She scowled. "You think I don't know that? The last person I care about was just murdered by this bastard. I won't be next. I'm going to nail this guy and make sure he never sees the light of day again."

"This isn't some random stalker, Bella. This is a powerful man with connections. You can't go against him by yourself."

"I've gone up against plenty of powerful men in my time. I'm still here, and this guy won't be any different."

The reference to her father sent a chill down Chance's spine. It was the first time she'd mentioned him since they'd reconnected. The truth was, she hadn't won against him, had barely survived, but Chance couldn't tell her that.

"Baby, let me help you. This is what I do. I can keep you safe until we find some evidence to link Lieutenant Governor Powell to Sam's murder. I can help you put him in prison where he belongs." Pausing, he took a deep breath. "Please. Let me be the one to keep you safe this time."

Her expression hardened even further. "I can take care of myself."

"I know, but I need to do this. If you won't do it for yourself, do it for me. I won't be able to go back to La Conner knowing you're here, in danger. And I need to be there to work with my team so we can put Powell in prison."

After a moment of aching silence, she reluctantly nodded. "Fine. But I'm not staying there for long. Your team has a few days, then I'm moving on."

Chance's knees turned to jello with relief. "A few days

is all I need."

Chance pulled his phone out of his pocket and made a quick call while Bellamy wandered into the bedroom to pack a bag.

This time he wouldn't fail her.

CHAPTER 10

CHANCE COULDN'T BELIEVE that the girl dancing next to him was Bella Burke. That dress looked great on her; he wished she'd dress like that more often. It was way better than the baggy clothes she usually wore. Her dark hair was pulled away from her face, and he couldn't be sure, but he thought she might be wearing makeup too.

He'd asked her to the dance because his parents suggested it. And also because he couldn't find anyone else to take. But now that he was here, he was glad that he'd asked. She seemed so happy, opposite of the Bella he'd seen lately.

They danced until they were both laughing and breathing so hard Chance thought he was going to pass out. He dragged Bella over to the refreshment table for some punch. She stood next to him while he grabbed their drinks, fanning herself with her hand.

"It's so hot in here."

"Take your sweater off, then."

She laughed nervously and glanced over her shoulder. "I can't."

"Why?"

"Because... it wouldn't be modest."

Chance raised his eyebrows. "You're kidding, right? Who's gonna know?"

Bella swallowed hard. Her gaze drifted around the room again. "Have you seen my dad around here? He's supposed to be chaperoning."

"Nope. Haven't seen him."

Her shoulders relaxed a little. "Why don't we get some air instead? It's nice and cool outside."

Chance shrugged. "Okay."

He handed her a cup and grabbed her other hand to lead the way outside.

She let out a breath once they were out in the cool night air. "That feels nice."

Chance leaned against the wall of the high school and looked up at the night sky. It was clear tonight; stars twinkled above them like they, too, were dancing.

Bella leaned next to him, her shoulder brushing his, and took a sip of her drink. "Nice and quiet out here," she murmured.

"Mm," Chance replied. He glanced down at her. She looked completely content, eyes closed as she tipped her face up to the sky. "Hey, I've got an idea. Come on." He reached down to grab her hand, but it was holding her drink, so he grabbed her arm instead.

Bella winced and jerked away from him with a sharp gasp.

Chance yanked his hand away as if he'd been burned. "What? Did I hurt you?"

She laughed awkwardly, rubbing her arm with her other hand. "No, you just surprised me."

"Are you sure?"

"Yep. What was your idea?"

"Oh yeah. Come on. Follow me." Chance jogged away from the high school in the direction of the football field. He didn't wait to see if she would follow. She always did.

He unhooked the chain that held the gate closed and they slipped inside. All the lights were off, but he didn't need them. He'd spent so many hours practicing here that he could walk it in his sleep. It didn't take long for him to lead the way to the center of the field. The bleachers on each side blocked the lights from the parking lot, enshrouding them in an oasis of darkness.

Bella looked up at the sky, her expression awed. "That's..."

"Beautiful," he finished for her. When she looked at him, he didn't take his eyes away from her face. "You, I mean. You're beautiful."

She looked away, smiling shyly. "Thanks, Chance. You don't look so bad yourself."

He grinned back. "You can take your sweater off if you want. No one will see you."

Bella froze. "Um, I think I'm okay."

"Are you hiding something?"

"What?"

"With your sweater."

"N-No."

"Are you sure? We're friends, you know. You can talk to me."

Bella hesitated, biting her lip. "I'm not supposed to take it off."

"Do you always do what you're told?"

"Yes."

Slowly, Chance moved his hands to the edges of the sweater, near her collar. He kept his eyes on her face, watching for any sign of discomfort, as he slid the fabric down her arms. Bella didn't move, but her eyes were wide.

Once the sweater was off, he stepped back. Even in the darkness, he could see the deep bruises marring her light skin. "What are those?" he asked softly, but he already knew the answer.

Bella ran her hands up her arms, covering the discolored skin with her palms. "Nothing. I fell."

"Come on. Those are hand-shaped bruises, Bella. Who did that to you?"

"No one."

"Your dad?"

"Chance, stop." She looked at him, her voice pleading. "Don't."

Chance took her face in his hands and leaned forward until they were nose to nose. "Tell me."

"I can't."

They stared at each other, a breath apart. She didn't look like the little girl who'd always followed him around. Her blue eyes were wide, locked to his. He could feel her *body shaking under his hands. Chance's eyes dropped to her lips. "If you can't tell me, you can do something else for me instead."*

"What?"

"Let me kiss you."

Bella's eyes widened. Her lips parted. Finally, she smiled and said, "I can do that, cowboy."

Her eyes fell closed and she leaned forward a fraction.

No way was Chance going to let this go. He'd just found the evidence his parents had been looking for. They hadn't explicitly said anything to him about it, and they didn't know he'd eavesdropped on their conversation a week before. But this was what they needed to get the police involved. Physical evidence.

Chance leaned forward, heart racing, and touched his lips to Bellamy's.

* * * * * *

Bellamy stared out the small oval window as they landed in Seattle. She hadn't been back home in ten years, and now she was here twice in one week.

Just being in the vicinity of La Conner made her want to crawl in a hole and hide until the danger passed.

That attitude was the old Bellamy, though. The child Bellamy had been before she left, a terrified little girl who didn't have any power to change her circumstances. She tried to claw her way out, sensing her proximity to her childhood home, but Adult Bellamy shoved her back down.

Paralyzing fear was not how she functioned anymore.

She was not going to imagine her father standing around every corner, holding a belt, waiting to make her life hell again. He had disappeared years ago, probably long dead, and she wouldn't let him haunt her nightmares now.

Nor would she picture her mother's face on the night she dropped Bellamy off at the Greyhound station and told her to never come back.

Adult Bellamy was past those things. They were in the rearview mirror, and they would stay there forever.

It was a long hour and a half drive from Seattle to La Conner. Chance was silent for most of the ride, apart from intermittent phone calls between him and his brothers. From the snippets Bellamy caught, it sounded like they were busy investigating Sam's murder already. Part of her was grateful, but a larger part was pissed off that nobody thought to involve her. Sam was her best friend; she would never badger Bellamy about men, or enthuse over her latest story, and Bellamy would never get the chance to yell at her for leaving the studio a mess again.

She'd never get the chance to repay Sam for saving her life.

As Chance navigated his black truck off the exit for La Conner, he said, "I called an emergency meeting at ESI H.Q. with the team. I know you're tired, but we need to stop at the office before we head home. Okay?"

"An emergency meeting for what?"

"The guys want to debrief you so we can make sure we have all the facts straight. They only know part of the story, but if they're going to take over the case, they need to know everything."

"Are they? Going to take over the case?"

Chance glanced at her. "Well, that's the idea. Many hands make light work, right?"

"Sure. As long as I get to be involved in the work. Don't forget that this is my investigation, cowboy. I'm the one that hired you, so that means I hired your team. I'm not some damsel in distress that you can hide away in a tower and expect me to stay put. That's not how this works."

Chance let out a startled laugh. "I keep forgetting how much you've changed."

Bellamy folded her arms. "I'm not sure that's a compliment, but I'll take it as one."

"That's the only way I meant it." Chance smiled. "All right, I'll keep that in mind. You're the boss."

She settled back in her seat. Good. That was just the way she liked it.

A few minutes later, they parked in front of a red brick building in downtown La Conner. Chance got out and came around to open the door for Bellamy. As she climbed out, a dark green Jeep pulled up next to them. It was old, maybe a 90's model, and it had fresh mud on its tires. Bellamy caught a glimpse of a bouncy blonde ponytail as the driver's side door slammed opposite them.

"Sarah, what are you doing here?" Chance demanded as she came around the front of the vehicle to meet them.

It was two in the morning, but Sarah looked bright-eyed and wide awake. "I'm going to be part of the ESI team soon, and Bellamy is important to me. So I'm here for the emergency meeting, obviously."

"How did you even know about it? I didn't call you."

Sarah gave him an exasperated look.

"It was Owen, wasn't it? Emmett isn't going to like this."

"Emmett can shove it." Sarah put her arm around Bellamy's shoulders and steered her toward the door. "Come on, Bellamy, let's get you some coffee or something. You look dead on your feet."

Chance rushed ahead of them and opened the door to the building. They entered the main office area. "Sorry it's a little bare," he said to Bellamy. "ESI has only been open a year and clients don't typically come into the office."

Despite his words, Bellamy was impressed. The entrance opened to a wide area, with a small reception desk facing the doorway. The top of the desk was bare, but Bellamy assumed a receptionist would sit there at some point. Beyond that, she could see black leather chairs and couches gathered around a large projection screen on the other side of the room. Chance was right; there wasn't much in the way of furniture, but everything was clean and looked comfortable.

Men sprawled in the black leather chairs in the center of the room. All eyes turned to the door as they entered. Emmett stood in front of a projector screen and Bellamy could see Owen sitting in a chair off to the left, a laptop open in his lap. There were three men she didn't recognize in the other chairs. Like Sarah, everyone looked wide awake and ready to go.

Chance took a step forward. His posture had straightened and his tone was professional as he said, "Team, this is Bellamy Burke, our client. And of course, you should all know my sister Sarah by now. Bella, this is the team. You already know Emmett and Owen."

Owen gave her a jaunty wave, but Emmett didn't acknowledge the introduction.

Chance gestured to the man sitting closest to them as they walked past the reception desk and closer to the cluster of chairs. "This is Roman Patrick. He's the team lead aside from Emmett and I. He's an expert in psychology, criminal profiling, and he takes care of everything from medical duties to victims and hostage negotiation."

Even slouched on the couch, Bellamy could tell that the man was tall, well over six feet, with cropped brown hair, strange golden-colored eyes, and a jagged scar across one cheek. His expression wasn't severe, but that scar and his slightly crooked nose made him look almost menacing.

Roman inclined his head to them. His eyes brushed over Bellamy and moved to Sarah. They lingered there a bit longer than necessary before moving on to Chance again.

"And those two over there are Cameron and Dominick, our tactical advisor and sniper, respectively."

Cameron was handsome, with black hair that was a little long and eyes almost as dark. He was fair-skinned, lending a contrast to the black clothing he wore. He kind of looked like a vampire.

Dominick, however, was the complete opposite. His light brown hair was shaggy, long enough to reach past his ears and curl around his nape. Tan-skinned, green eyes, and dressed in jeans and a long-sleeved button-up shirt with an outrageous design printed on it. A cowboy hat sat on his lap and his booted feet were crossed at the ankle, resting on the coffee table in the center of the cluster of chairs.

The men all murmured their hellos. Chance motioned Bellamy toward a chair facing the rest of the team. She sat gratefully; honestly, if she'd stood much longer, she might have fallen over.

"What are you doing here?" Emmett demanded, his stern gaze on Sarah.

Sarah, who had perched on the arm of Bellamy's chair, glared back at him. "I'm here for the meeting, obviously."

Roman spoke up. His voice was deep and smooth, like caramel. "We're dealing with a murder," he said. "We can't bring civilians into this. It's too dangerous."

Sarah's green eyes flashed and her chin notched higher. Bellamy recognized a storm brewing in her expression. "A civilian?" she said sweetly. "I'm a licensed emergency medical technician and trained in both weaponry and self defense. I am no civilian, thank you very much."

"You have no formal military training," Roman said. "No experience in the field. That classifies you as a civilian."

Owen laughed. "You haven't been around long enough to know this, man, but Sarah has a way of getting what she wants around here. You're better off leaving her alone."

Sarah's lips twitched. "Perks of being the only girl."

Roman's expression darkened, but he didn't say anything more. His golden eyes rested on Sarah, though. Dominick and Cameron snickered, earning them a hearty glare from Emmett.

"Quiet," Emmett snapped. "Sarah, you can stay, but be professional. This isn't a family meeting."

Everyone fell silent to the authority in Emmett's voice.

"Bellamy, I'd like to debrief you on a few things." His

tone was brusque. "This is standard procedure when we gain a new client. The more information you give us, the better."

Sarah pressed a cup of coffee into Bellamy's hand and she took a long sip, hoping that the caffeine would give her enough of a boost to get through this. She didn't have the energy or the patience to deal with the unfriendliness in Emmett's expression. He was looking at her like she was the murderer, not the guy they were trying to catch.

"Please tell everyone here who our victim is to you."

"Her name is Samantha Larsen. She was my best friend and business partner."

"How long have you known the victim?"

"Sam," she corrected. "Seven years."

"How did you meet?"

Bellamy's eyes narrowed. "Why does that matter?"

"Because I want everybody up to speed on the situation."

She took another sip of her coffee and met the gazes of Chance's team, one by one. She purposely skipped Emmett. "I'll bring you up to speed. My best friend is dead. She was investigating Lieutenant Governor Ronald Powell. We have a testimony from his wife that he was cheating on her and he threatened to kill her if she told anyone. We have incriminating photographs of the governor's affair. We know he's powerful enough to hire someone to trash our studio and my apartment, and Chance thinks he might be after me for my connection to Sam. Also for releasing said photos to the media, even though they won't hit the news until tomorrow. Sam was investigating him, and she ended up dead just days later. We need to find some evidence to link him to her death and get him thrown in prison for the rest of his miserable life. Any further questions?"

A tense silence followed. She and Emmett glared at each other.

A tic started in his jaw. He was obviously annoyed that she had taken charge of the situation, and that she'd dodged his question about how she and Sam had met. Well, she refused to talk about that time in her life. It wasn't relevant and it threatened to open too many doors that she'd worked hard to keep closed and locked. Even if she was willing to reveal those details to a room full of strangers, she didn't like the distrust in Emmett's eyes. If he didn't trust her, she sure as hell wouldn't trust him with private details of her life either.

"Fine," Emmett snapped. "Everyone got it? We find a link between Sam and Governor Powell. Your assignments are in your folders. Keep me updated." With those words, he left the room and walked down the hallway, his stride clipped.

Clearly dismissed, everyone stood up and got ready to leave. Roman approached Chance and they shook hands. He turned and held his hand out to Bellamy next.

Bellamy stared at his fingers. They were well-manicured and clean. A familiar anxiety fluttered in her chest. It was hard to explain why she didn't like strangers touching her, so she rarely tried. Most of the time, she kept to herself to avoid awkward moments like these.

Roman didn't wait long before he returned his hand to his pocket. To Bellamy's surprise, he smiled at her. His face wasn't so intimidating with such a warm expression. "I'm sorry about your friend," he said. His voice was gentle, and the knot in Bellamy's chest loosened in response. "I promise we'll do everything we can to put her murderer behind bars."

"Thanks. Are you the one who helped Susan get away from the governor?"

Roman nodded. "I was happy to do it. Nobody should have to suffer through treatment like that. If you ever need anything, please don't hesitate to ask. We're all here for you."

Cameron and Dominick murmured their agreement from behind him, their expressions as friendly as his.

A warm feeling spread through her. She was so used to working with shady, violent people, so used to keeping her guard up 24/7. It was strange and… nice… to work with the good guys for a change. "Thank you," she said, looking at all three of them. "All of you."

Roman's gaze moved to Sarah, and his smile disappeared. "Ma'am," he said, and walked toward the front door. Dominick and Cameron fell in behind him with a wave goodbye over their shoulders.

"Come on," Chance said. "Let's get going, too. You need some sleep. It's been a long few days."

Bellamy nodded and followed him to the door. Sarah and Owen exchanged a few muttered words behind her before Sarah jogged to catch up to them, her expression chipper. "I'm going to head home and pack a few things," she said. "I'll meet you at your place."

"Excuse me?" Chance said over his shoulder, raising an eyebrow.

"Oh come on. I'm staying with you until I go back to New York, remember?"

Chance frowned. "You have a bedroom at Mom's."

"Mom's fine. Owen is there if she needs anything. Besides, Bellamy is my friend too. I haven't seen her in a long time, so sue me if I want to catch up. You can't keep her all to yourself."

Bellamy smiled. Obviously Chance wasn't willing to have Sarah stay with him, but Bellamy was. She knew Chance would never do anything to physically hurt her, but emotional harm was another matter. It was best for everyone if Sarah acted as a buffer. Ever since Sam's murder, Bellamy felt like she was walking on a tightrope suspended over a big pit of nothingness. It wouldn't take much to push her over the edge, and one glance from Chance could be her undoing.

She needed Sarah to act as parachute if that happened. Or to prevent it from happening completely. Her metaphor was breaking down, but dammit, she was tired.

Chance opened the front door of the office and allowed the women to walk outside in front of him. "All right," he was saying. "I suppose I have the room, so you can stay with me."

Sarah beamed at Bellamy as they reached their cars. "Perfect. I'll see you in a bit!"

Bellamy shot Sarah a grateful smile as Chance helped her into the passenger seat.

It didn't take long to reach Chance's house - not that it took long to get anywhere in La Conner. It was about the same amount of time that it used to take Bellamy to walk to the Ericksons' house, about fifteen minutes. He turned off the main highway onto an unmarked, narrow dirt lane. Bellamy would never have seen it hidden in the thick trees that lined both sides of the road. An iron gate blocked the drive from any unwanted visitors, and Chance punched a code into a small box on the driver's side. They waited a moment for the gate to slide open.

Bellamy leaned forward as they drove through the winding dirt road and gasped.

The narrow lane widened into a large clearing and a beautiful, brand new house. It was large, two stories, with brown brick walls, dark wood trim and a wrap-around porch.

"This is your house?" she asked. "How can you even afford this?"

Chance smiled as he parked the truck and jogged around to open the door for her. "Business has been good," he said. "Our private cases are good, but our government contracts pay really well. Our team is known to be the best in sticky situations, and those jobs come with higher price tags. I like my privacy, so building a home out here seemed like a good idea. This place was just finished a few months ago and it has top-notch security. You'll be safe here."

Bellamy shook her head as they approached the front door. What kind of 27-year-old could afford a place like this?

Someone who risked his life daily, that's who.

Chance unlocked the front door and led her into an entryway with a tall ceiling and a rustic, wooden chandelier.

"This is beautiful," Bellamy breathed.

"Thanks. It's home. There's a spare bedroom for you upstairs. Can I get you anything first?"

Bellamy glanced down at herself. She would kill for a hot shower, but she was half afraid that she would fall asleep and drown. Perhaps sleep would be the best course of action for the moment. "Thanks," she said. "But I think I'm good."

She paused, meeting his eyes. It was stupid of her to drag him into her problems. Not only was it putting his life in danger, but it put them in close proximity. That was dangerous for her.

She should've taken care of the problem herself. She had plenty of contacts. Most of them were burned now, but she could've made do.

Who was she kidding? She just didn't want to do it herself anymore.

For once, she wanted to rely on someone else. It went against everything she told herself she believed in, but she didn't want to fight it anymore.

"Thanks… for letting me stay here. I appreciate it."

Chance set her bag down on the floor and stepped in close. His eyes scanned her face, searching for answers to a question she didn't know. He seemed to like what he saw there, though, because the lines in his forehead disappeared and his expression softened. "Bella," he murmured in a soft, husky voice. "I'm glad you're here."

The look in his eyes made her stomach do a flip. He'd always been able to see right through her, even when they were young. Sometimes she thought he understood her better than she understood herself. That was a dangerous trait for him to have; she had far too many secrets that would be better off buried, but Chance was like a dog with a bone. Once he sniffed them out, he'd never stop digging until he exposed everything.

She couldn't risk that. Now more than ever, she needed to keep her walls sturdy and reinforced. If she couldn't, it would cost both of them.

"Why wouldn't you answer Emmett's questions?"

Bellamy snapped out of her thoughts and focused on the conversation again. "He was asking questions that weren't relevant to Sam's death."

"He was only trying to give the team an idea of who our vic is. It'll help everyone work the case."

"Sam."

"What?"

"Your 'vic's' name is Sam."

He paused and shoved a hand through his hair. "Damn, I'm sorry. That was insensitive. I'm just trying to understand where your head's at."

"You shouldn't be worrying about that." Bellamy stepped back; she needed distance from his searching eyes, his probing questions, and fast. "I'm the client here, Chance. Your team's job is to put Powell behind bars. My personal life isn't part of that agenda. I'm happy to give you relevant details so you can do your job, but I won't give you any more than that."

A tense silence fell between them. Chance continued to look at her far too intently. It was as if he could see right through her bravado, down to what she was really feeling.

That was unacceptable.

The front door flew open behind them and Sarah made her entrance. If she read the tension in the room, she didn't show it. Instead, she smiled brightly. "Ready for bed? I'm exhausted."

Chance scowled.

Bellamy sighed with relief. "I'm exhausted too. Let's go."

"Well, since you two are buddy-buddy, why don't you show Bellamy to the guest room? I'll be in my office. I need to make a few calls." Chance stalked off. A door slammed in the distance.

Bellamy blew out a breath. "Your timing was perfect. I'm glad you're here."

Sarah grabbed Bellamy's backpack and led the way up the stairs. "I know Chance can be a bit overbearing sometimes. He's a man; it's in the genomes. But I hope you know he acts like that because he cares."

"I don't really need that from him right now," Bellamy muttered.

Sarah paused at the top landing. "Are you really okay? I know how much Sam meant to you."

Bellamy bit her lip. There were few people that she trusted, and over the past few years, Sarah had become one of those people. Because of that, she let her walls drop a little. "I'm... I saw her, Sarah. Her dead body."

"I know. I heard."

"I can't really explain how I feel right now. I need to focus on the task at hand or I won't be able to handle it. Powell needs to pay for what he's done."

Sarah opened the first door on the left and dropped Bellamy's bag on the floor inside. It was a large bedroom, with a king-sized bed taking up most of the square footage. The bedspread was the same tan color as the walls. It screamed "man design," but it looked comfortable. It was a hell of a lot better than most of the beds Bellamy had slept in over the years.

Sarah threw her arms around Bellamy and gave her a tight squeeze. "If there's anything I can do to help you, I'm here. You don't even have to ask. Just look at me and I'll jump to attention."

"I just wish I knew what happened. I mean, I have an idea of what happened to her." Bellamy shuddered. "Even if we find enough evidence to put the governor away for good, we'll probably never know the truth."

"I know. I felt the same way when Dad died." Sarah led Bellamy over to the mattress and urged her to sit, then settled beside her. "Not that I'm comparing that to Sam's death, of course, but that's the thing about death. There's always something left unsaid."

Bellamy nodded. "You never realize what you have until it's gone, right?"

"I know this is hard, Bells. Not just this, but you being here in La Conner again. But try not to worry. If my brothers are on the case, you can bet it'll be solved. They'll make sure that guy never hurts anyone again. I promise."

Bellamy sighed and looked down at her hands. She didn't acknowledge Sarah's comment about La Conner. Sarah, more than anyone, knew how hard it was for her to be around the Ericksons. Chance in particular. "I hope so."

Sarah brightened. "Hey, by the way. Mom wanted me to ask you to come to dinner tomorrow. I know it might be a little weird, but she was bummed that she didn't get to talk with you during the funeral."

Bellamy was already shaking her head.

"She said she'll make those potatoes you use to love," Sarah added in a sing-song voice, raising her eyebrows.

Bellamy paused. Just the thought of it made her stomach grumble. It didn't matter how many years passed; a person's palate could never forget Mary Erickson's cooking. As much as she didn't want to deal with awkward questions, the thought of an old-fashioned family dinner sounded... nice.

A bit of normalcy she hadn't experienced since she was a teenager.

It didn't mean she had to spill all her secrets to the family, and it didn't mean she had to stick around La Conner once this matter was taken care of.

"Okay. I think I can handle that."

"It's a plan, then." Sarah grinned, and bounced toward the door. "You get some rest; you look beat. Sleep in tomorrow and we'll have something really good for breakfast."

"Thanks, Sarah."

"I know this isn't the best of circumstances, but... I'm glad you're here. I've really missed you."

Bellamy smiled as Sarah closed the door behind her. She had to agree.

Sleep had been elusive in recent days, but Bellamy's exhaustion finally caught up to her. She was asleep before she even crawled under the comforter.

* * * * * *

"Is Bellamy resting?" Roman asked.

Chance stood in his office, leaning against his desk, and stared at the phone. He was on a conference call with Emmett, Owen, and Roman. It was three o'clock in the morning, but none of them were the type to sleep when there was a job to discuss.

"Yeah, I think so. I don't think she's slept in a week, so it will be good for her."

"I could tell. She looked dead on her feet."

Chance winced at the reference.

"Owen, what do you have on Governor Powell?" Emmett asked.

"Phone records haven't given me anything promising so far. I'm working on getting access to his email and computer files, but that's going to take a little time."

"So the governor was cheating on his wife," Roman mused. "And Sam, our victim, was a reporter who found out about it and threatened to expose him."

"We're not even sure that she threatened him," Chance pointed out. "She went to Mrs. Powell to warn her about the affair, but we don't know if she ever met with the governor personally."

"Then where's his motive for murder?" Emmett asked.

"Not just murder, but brutal murder," Roman said. "He killed her slowly. The marks on her body are consistent with torture."

"She must have had something more than just an affair," Emmett said.

"Powell has a lot of power in the city. At least some of the police department is in his pocket, which tells me he's probably involved in illegal activities that would need a cover-up." Chance sat back in his desk chair, staring hard at the ceiling. "Sam could've gotten evidence to that. Maybe she had that evidence in her safe deposit box. That's where she was right before she was murdered. Whatever was inside, it must have been something good enough to kill for."

"We need to find out what Sam knew." Emmett paused. "I think you're right. Powell is probably in deeper than he looks. My gut is telling me there's something more going on here. I think Bellamy knows more than she's saying."

"What makes you think so?" Owen asked.

The door to Chance's office opened and he looked up to see Sarah slip inside. She put a finger to her lips, winked at him, and sat down in the chair across from his desk.

Chance frowned at her, but turned his attention back to the phone.

"I can't explain it yet. She seems very informed about Powell and his activities. Why would she warn Sam away from investigating him? That's her job as a reporter," Emmett was saying. "Also, she was very evasive when I started asking her questions. They weren't difficult ones. Any innocent person should have been able to answer them."

"Isn't it possible that she's just exhausted?" Owen asked. "It's not like she's had a homicidal maniac after her while she searched for her murdered best friend, or anything."

"No, I don't think that's it. I think she's more involved than she's letting on. Something tells me she's the key to all of this. I don't like an unreliable client."

"She's not unreliable," Chance said. "She's been through a lot. She's relying on us to help her put that maniac behind bars."

"You don't know anything about her, Chance," Emmett said. "She's been missing for ten years, doing God knows what. We can't be sure that she's innocent in all of this, just because she flashed some doe eyes at you."

"Roman," Owen said. "You're a good judge of character. What do you think?"

There was a long pause while Roman gathered his thoughts. He sounded reluctant when he said, "I will agree that something seems odd. She seems very distrustful of us, even though she hired ESI to help her. Beyond that, her body language - the way she angled her body away from us. Her facial expressions were practiced rather than genuine. There may be more going on than what she's saying, but I can't say if that means she's involved with Sam's murder."

Sarah leaned forward, her voice loud in the quiet office. "Listen, you idiots. I'm hearing a lot of judging and not a lot of productive conversation. I'd expect that from the new guy" - her words dripped venom as she referenced Roman - "but the rest of you know better. Bellamy has a complicated past, and you guys don't even know the full story. Sure, she's been gone a long time, but she's our client and she's clearly in danger. Her best friend is dead and someone ransacked her place. Are you guys going to catch the perpetrator or stand around arguing about her integrity? As our client, she's innocent until proven guilty. Now get off your asses and get some actual work done, will you?"

Shocked silence.

"All right," Emmett said finally. "I hate to say this - and Sarah, you're not even involved in this conversation - but she's right. Let's focus on the task at hand and we'll worry about the rest later."

"Thank you," Chance said, half to the team and half to Sarah. "Keep me updated on what you find."

They said their goodbyes and Chance ended the call. Sarah gave him a satisfied look and stood to leave.

"Sarah."

She stopped at the door and looked over her shoulder at him.

"What's going on with you? Why are you suddenly so determined to be involved with ESI?"

Sarah returned and jumped up to sit on his desk, swinging her legs. "Bellamy's resting. Figured we could let her sleep in tomorrow, make breakfast, maybe get her to relax a bit so she'll open up to us about Sam."

He crossed his arms over his chest and leveled a serious look at her. "What aren't you telling me?"

She fidgeted a bit and wouldn't meet his eyes. "What are you talking about?"

"You haven't seen her in ten years either, but you're acting like you're best friends again with no questions asked. Do you know something that you're not saying?"

"Oh. That." She blew out a breath. "Look, bro, it's not really my place to tell you anything. Bellamy doesn't want her past advertised to everyone, you know?"

"I'm not everyone. How do you know anything? We haven't seen or heard from her since she disappeared, and you barely spoke to her at the funeral."

She bit her lip. "Well... that's not exactly true."

"Excuse me?" Chance thought back to all their conversations about Bellamy. Sarah had seemed so knowledgeable about her and sympathetic to her cause. He'd assumed it was because they'd been close when they were young, but the sudden churning in his gut told him otherwise.

Sarah fidgeted some more before she looked him in the eye. "I wanted to tell you, Chance. I did. But Bellamy asked me not to."

"Asked you not to tell me what?"

"Where she's been all this time."

Chance turned away from her. The air in the room suddenly seemed too thin. He gripped the edge of the desk hard, fighting the simultaneous urge to punch the wall and throttle his sister.

"You've known where Bellamy was all this time and you never told me?" His voice was deadly calm.

"I didn't always know. It wasn't until three years after she left, after... after she was on her own. She wrote a letter to tell you that she was okay, but you had just left for the Marines. I wrote her back, told her I would tell you next time you called, but she asked me not to. She - She wasn't in a good place, Chance. She didn't want to get you involved. I honored that as her friend, because she wanted you to move on. And it seemed like you finally had. We've been writing letters on and off since then. I'm sorry, I've wanted to tell you for so long but I didn't know how."

Chance swallowed hard. Turning around, he saw that Sarah's eyes were bright with tears. She looked as miserable as he felt, and he immediately realized he was a jerk. Sarah had a huge heart, and she would do anything for a friend. He couldn't fault her for that. In fact, it was one of the things he loved about his sister.

He gathered her into a gentle hug.

"It's okay," he murmured. "You were just trying to help. I respect that."

Anger at her would be misplaced.

It was Bellamy that he was angry at. He'd thought they were close when they were young. Maybe they hadn't been best friends like she and Sarah, but there had been something there, something deeper. They'd shared things that she probably never told Sarah about, especially the night she'd disappeared.

Why didn't she tell him what happened? Why did she wait three years before writing to let him know she was okay?

Obviously he didn't know what happened during those three years, but she seemed fine now. She'd built a life for herself; a stable job, her own apartment, even friends.

There had been plenty of chances for her to reach out.

Sarah pulled back and stared hard at him. "You can't be angry with her either. You don't know what she's been through. I'm not even sure I know what she's been through."

"She could have contacted me sooner."

"Yeah, she could have. But come on, Chance. You know Bellamy. Even when she was little, did she ever really ask for our help? No. Mom and Dad eventually just took matters into their own hands, remember?"

He did remember. It had been partly his fault.

"I know you're still dealing with a lot of unresolved issues from back then," Sarah said, and patted his arm. "But I think there's a reason she came back into your life like this. Maybe it's time for you two to make amends."

What did he have to make amends for? He only ever wanted to help, and everything he did was with the best intentions.

He sighed. "Thanks for telling me."

"Glad to get that off my chest." She swiped at her eyes and flashed him a smile. "Let's hit the hay. It's been a long day for everyone."

Chance followed her out of the office.

Sleep wouldn't happen for him tonight - or, now, this morning. Not with this new information. But he did take some small comfort in the fact that he knew enough to confront Bellamy now. It was about time she gave him some answers.

CHAPTER 11

CHANCE SNAPPED AWAKE.

He blinked at the ceiling for a moment, wondering what had woken him. His bedroom was still dark. Rain pattered against the roof, but normally he could sleep through anything. Especially a Washington rainstorm. They were a common occurrence, after all.

It was a strange sound that had woken him. At first he thought it was just a tree branch scraping against the side of the house, but then it happened again.

He sat up, his gaze scanning the room until it fell upon the girl crouched on the branch just outside his window.

"What the - ?"

He would have screamed, but he recognized her pink pajamas.

Scrambling out of bed, he unlocked the latch. "Bella?"

He slid the window open and pulled her inside. They'd

used that particular tree branch many times to sneak in and out of the house unnoticed, but even he wouldn't have dared try to climb it in a storm like this.

Bella was shaking, soaking wet, and dressed in only a thin pair of pink silk pajama pants and a tank top. Once she was inside, she threw her arms around him and buried her face in his neck, her breaths coming out in ragged sobs.

Chance drew her further into the room and closed the window against the storm outside. He didn't know what else to do, so he eased down on the bed and drew her into his lap. Her wet clothes soaked into his pajamas and her cold skin was a shock against his warm chest. He instantly regretted sleeping without a shirt on.

Rubbing his hands up and down her back, he tried to generate some warmth.

"Bella, what's wrong? What happened?"

She shook her head hard, her face tucked under his chin as she hiccupped and tried to steady her breathing.

Okay, Chance was starting to freak out. He'd never seen her like this and he didn't know how to react. Should he run down the hall and wake his parents? The thought of leaving her alone made him nervous, and he didn't think she'd let go of him if he tried.

Chance peeled her away from him and bent to look her in the eye. A flash of lightning illuminated her face, and he gasped. Leaning over, he turned on his bedside lamp.

The right side of her face was swollen and already turning an angry red color. Her right eye was almost swollen shut.

Shock rendered him mute for a moment. She stared at

him, her left eye wide and frightened.

"Bella, what happened to you?"

She shook her head, biting her lip. "Please," she said. "Just let me stay here for a while."

Chance swallowed hard. He wanted to ask her a million questions, but that's not how Bellamy worked. If he pushed her, she would probably run away from him too. "Of course. Of course you can. Come here." He pulled back his covers and slid underneath them, waiting for her to do the same.

She hesitated. Her eyes flashed to his face.

For a moment he thought she would run away, but then she crawled in next to him. He pulled her close to his side and wrapped an arm around her. Her breath hitched on another sob.

"Shh, you're okay. You're safe now."

He continued to murmur soft things to her until her breathing evened out and she fell asleep. After that, he lay awake for a long time, staring at the ceiling and wondering what had happened to her and what to do now.

* * * * * *

Ronald slammed the front door behind him, his irritation evident on his face as he entered the mansion. "Susan," he roared to the empty house.

No answer.

Ronald scowled. Where was the woman when he needed her? She always came when he called.

"Susan!"

Silence pressed in on him from all sides.

He yanked his cell phone out of his pocket and dialed her phone number. It rang once and went straight to voicemail.

"Dammit," he yelled, and stormed into his office.

It had been a day from hell. His underground contacts were trying to blackmail him for more money and the picketing outside the government building had made him late for an important meeting with a senator. As a result, the senator had left without paying for his bill at the restaurant, leaving Ronald to cover it.

And now Susan was nowhere to be found. The stupid woman was probably off shopping and blowing his hard-earned money. She had no respect for how hard he worked to provide for her.

The phone on his desk rang, its shrill bell loud in the silence. Ronald grumbled under his breath and dropped into his office chair, pulling the phone off its hook and up to his ear.

"Governor Powell," he growled.

"Ronald." The voice on the other end was smooth and dark and full of authority. Just the sound of it made Ronald's back snap straight.

"What can I do for you?" Ronald struggled to keep his voice polite. This was another man who wanted to blackmail him. If he'd known how many sleazy characters would come out of the woodwork to attack him, he wouldn't have taken this godforsaken job. It was hard enough to keep the police force and the public away from his private dealings. He was sick and tired of everyone trying to leverage him to do what they wanted.

But there were some battles he could fight, and some he couldn't.

This man was one of the latter.

"Where's your wife, Governor?"

Ronald scowled again. "Are you spying on me?"

"Always. Your wife left this morning with another man. It appears she has deserted you."

A red haze descended over Ronald's vision. That bitch. He'd known it was a matter of time. She had never respected him or his authority. She didn't deserve him.

He just hadn't expected her to do it without confronting him first. She wasn't the type to act on her own.

"How do you know?"

"I have eyes everywhere. But that's not important now. If you help me with a problem of mine, I'll help you with that problem of yours."

And there it was.

Ronald gritted his teeth. Everyone always wanted something from him.

"And what problem would that be?"

"Don't ask questions you already know the answers to, Ronald. I've already taken care of the pest that threatened you with that photo, and I know where your dear wife is. You owe me twofold."

Ronald let out a frustrated breath.

Once again, he was backed into a corner with no choice but to follow this man's directions.

"Tell me what you need me to do."

* * * * * *

The smell of cinnamon lured Bellamy downstairs the next morning. She crept down the staircase and followed the sound of muffled conversation past the entryway and into the kitchen. It was beautiful, with tall ceilings and granite countertops. The cabinets were a rich dark wood and a double oven nestled into one wall.

It reminded her of one of the chef's kitchens on the food channel. Just the sight of it made her mouth water imagining all sorts of delectable foods that Chance might cook there. Had he inherited his mother's talent for cooking?

Sarah and Chance sat on stools at the kitchen island with a heaping plate of french toast between them. Sarah threw her head back and laughed at something Chance said. She wore a pair of worn blue jeans and a white t-shirt and her blonde hair was pulled into her signature tight ponytail. Chance sat next to her, looking handsome in a pair of dark washed jeans and a black shirt. He grinned, his dark brown eyes sparkling at his sister.

Bellamy hesitated in the doorway. Her heart ached at the sight.

Memories from her childhood came rushing back: the Erickson kitchen with its scuffed cabinets, the smell of home-cooked meals, laughter and arguments equally loud at the dinner table. A sense of family so strong that nothing could break it.

Bellamy wanted that. She wanted it so badly that it made her dizzy.

But she'd decided a long time ago that it wasn't her lot in life; it never had been. Her past was too messed up; she'd done too many things that she couldn't come back from. The grown woman she'd always imagined - the one who cooked dinner for her husband and ran the kids to soccer practice - just wasn't in the cards for her.

She was far too damaged for that.

Bellamy's right hand clutched the doorframe, her knuckles turning white. Who was she kidding? She couldn't stay here with Chance like everything was normal; she was a fraud. Soon Chance would realize it and dump her like everyone else had.

It would be better if she left first.

Bellamy stepped back from the doorway, breathing harshly, and did what she did best; she left.

Chance and Sarah hadn't seen her yet. She turned the deadbolt on the front door and pulled it open - she had the presence of mind to close it quietly behind her - and cut across the lawn and into the trees.

The terrible tightness in her chest didn't ease until she was out of view of the house.

Bellamy stopped with her back against the trunk of a nearby tree and bent over, hands on her thighs. She took a few deep breaths around the lump in her throat and waited for the stitch in her side to recede.

The sound of crashing footsteps sent her heart back into overdrive.

Chance thundered into the forest. He ran right past her and stopped a few yards away, his head swinging in a wide circle. When his gaze landed on her, all the tension left his body.

"Bella, you scared the hell out of me. What are you

doing? What's wrong?"

Bellamy stared at him, frozen.

What could she possibly say? That the vision of him and Sarah in the kitchen was too close to normal, too close to everything Bellamy had ever wanted? There was a reason she had never settled down, a reason she lived a nomadic lifestyle with Sam. A family system wasn't something she could handle. The Ericksons reminded her of a family that could've been hers if God hadn't dealt her such a shitty hand.

"I changed my mind," she said, straightening. "I don't need your help. I'm leaving."

Chance stepped closer to her, his eyes searching her face. He raised both hands in a placating gesture. "Hey, if you wanted to take a walk, you could've just let me know."

"I'm not taking a walk. I'll handle Powell on my own. Thanks for your help, but I don't need it anymore."

"I hate to tell you this, but ESI has a strict no-refunds policy." Chance shrugged. "Now that you've hired us, we'll see it through to the end, no matter what."

Bellamy backed up against the tree. "I said you're fired."

Chance stepped closer, shaking his head. "No deal."

"Why won't you just leave it alone? You haven't changed a bit since we were kids."

"Nope, I haven't. You haven't either."

Yes, she had. She'd changed more than Chance could ever know. He was just inches from her now, head cocked to the side, confident smile securely in place. He smelled like pine and man and she could feel his body heat seeping into her skin.

Before Bellamy's common sense could stop her, she reached up and pulled his head down, crushing her lips against his.

Chance didn't pull away. His arms went around her waist and yanked her closer to him.

Something dark and cold flared to life in her chest.

His lips were warm and soft and everything she'd ever needed. His hands slid up her back and one tangled in her short hair, tilting her head to the side so he had better access to her mouth.

The man had no idea who he was kissing.

Bellamy shoved him away, breathing hard. He stumbled back a step and let her go, his expression as dazed as she felt.

"What was - ?"

"I'll stay," Bellamy said quickly, smoothing her hair. "You're re-hired."

Chance just stared at her, mouth slightly open. It took him another moment to recover, but he straightened and shoved his hands in his pockets. "Okay then," he said. "Glad we got that... sorted out."

Bellamy looked down. "You don't have any shoes."

Chance glanced down at his bare feet and wiggled his toes. "I guess not. I'm making you responsible for pulling out any thorns embedded in there."

"No way. It's not my fault you came out here barefoot."

Chance shook his head, a small smile tilting his lips. "Come on, let's go back to the house. My toes are freezing."

He held out a hand to her, and she immediately felt stupid. Why was she freaking out? This was Chance. He was the most non-judgemental person she had ever met. If anyone could accept the real Bellamy, it was him.

She didn't quite trust him enough to divulge all of her secrets, but maybe she could relax a little.

She placed her hand in his and allowed him to lead her back to the house.

"Bellamy." Sarah grinned when they entered the kitchen, as if nothing was out of the ordinary. She pulled out a stool next to her and waved Bellamy onto it. "Come have some of this deliciousness."

Chance circled to the other side of the kitchen island and leaned against the opposite counter, facing them. His dark brown eyes studied Bellamy as she sat down, as if he was trying to put a puzzle together but he didn't have all the pieces.

Was he thinking about that kiss?

Did he regret it?

Bellamy's stomach growled in protest at her hesitation, and she gave into the need to eat something. French toast was her favorite. How had they remembered?

Chance set a steaming plate in front of her. "Help yourself. We've got plenty."

Bellamy dipped a bit of french toast in some syrup and took a bite, ignoring Chance's gaze. She could feel him assessing her, wordlessly asking for answers she couldn't give. Things that she'd shoved down so deep that she wasn't sure they'd ever resurface.

The french toast was divine. It was like every happy Saturday morning of her childhood, rolled up into a delicious dough and fried with cinnamon and butter. When she was young, Mary had realized it was Bellamy's favorite meal, so she'd started making it a couple Saturdays a month. Bellamy would sneak over first thing in the morning before her parents woke up and eat breakfast with the Ericksons. She suspected that her mother knew where she was, but Bellamy was always back home and in bed before her father woke up, so he'd never discovered her absence.

"So good," Bellamy mumbled around a second bite.

Sarah laughed. "When was the last time you ate something?"

When was that? Bellamy couldn't remember, so she shrugged and took another bite. Chance looked disapproving, so she said, "I eat plenty, thank you. It's just been a stressful couple of days - not that I need your approval of my eating habits."

"Well, you'd better have seconds then," he said, pushing the plate closer to her. "You've got a lot of calories to make up for."

Bellamy rolled her eyes. "You've been with me for the last couple days, and you haven't eaten either. Where's your plate?"

Chance grabbed a piece and shoved the whole thing in his mouth.

Bellamy stuck her tongue out at him.

"You guys are ridiculous." Sarah hopped down from the barstool. "Well, I need a hot shower. I'll be upstairs if you need me." She gave Bellamy a pointed look as she left.

Bellamy's stomach dropped to her toes. "What's that about?"

"Finish your breakfast." Chance dropped the remaining

pieces of toast into a bag and put them in the fridge. "We need to talk."

She pushed her plate away. "Like I'll be able to eat another bite after a cryptic comment like that. What's going on?"

Chance ran a hand through his hair. "All right, then come with me."

He led her out of the kitchen and into the living room. It was decorated richly, like the rest of the house, with deep leather couches and masculine pillows. A beautiful stone fireplace stood in the center of one wall with a television mounted above it. She could just imagine spending chilly winter afternoons curled on a rug in front of the fire with a cup of hot cocoa.

Chance sat down on a loveseat and patted the cushion next to him. Bellamy's skin tingled at his closeness even as she fought her wariness about the conversation they were about to have.

"Bella." He cleared his throat, looking as uncomfortable as she felt.

She didn't blame him; if she had the choice, she would skip this conversation completely.

But it was ten years overdue.

Instead of asking the questions she knew were on the tip of his tongue, he lowered his head and dug for something in his pocket. Looking up, he said, "After you disappeared, I was frantic. I thought something had happened to you. I looked everywhere, put up flyers, called the police. Nobody took it seriously, but I knew you wouldn't leave unless someone forced you to."

Bellamy swallowed hard. She'd suspected this was where the conversation was going. She opened her mouth to respond, but she couldn't form the words.

"I went to your house whenever your dad wasn't there. I begged your mom to tell me what happened to you." He held out a small blue box, just bigger than the palm of his hand. The color was faded at the edges, as if it had been well-loved over the years. "She never told me anything. But one day, I stopped by and she told me to take care of something for her."

He opened the box and showed her what was inside.

Bellamy's breath caught.

A small silver pendant rested on a dark blue velvet background. It was about the size of her thumb, a crude-looking silver circle with a dove cut out of the middle.

Bellamy's hands flew to her mouth.

Chance's eyes never left her face. "She told me to take care of it, that you would come back someday. She wanted me to give it to you."

A single tear escaped and slid down her cheek. "That's my mom's necklace," she whispered.

She remembered lying in the grass with her mom when she was just ten years old. She'd taken Bellamy on a picnic to get her away from one of her father's drunken stupors. He'd been upset about something, Bellamy couldn't remember what, and he'd started drinking early. It had been a beautiful fall afternoon. Her mom had held the pendant up to the sky and they'd both looked at the clouds through the dove's silhouette.

"Doves symbolize hope, peace, and freedom," her

mother had told her. "When I feel like I can't go on, I look at this pendant. It helps me remember that there's more to life than this. Someday I'll be free."

Bellamy lifted the pendant from the box and held it up in the air. She squinted at the ceiling through the dove's silhouette. "I can't believe you kept it all this time."

A ghost of a smile appeared on Chance's face.

Bellamy reached up and pulled the collar of her shirt over her right shoulder, revealing a small black tattoo of a dove just underneath her collarbone. "Doves meant a lot to Mama," she said. "I left La Conner, but I always tried to keep a piece of her with me."

Chance examined the tattoo, then glanced at her. "It's beautiful."

Bellamy closed her fist tight around her mother's necklace. So many emotions warred for dominance in her heart. She ached with sorrow and missed her mother more than she could express, but it made her happy that her mother had left something for her.

The silence in the room was suddenly too much.

Maybe she couldn't tell Chance everything, but she did owe him an explanation.

"I didn't run away," she said. She couldn't meet his eyes. If she did, she wouldn't be able to say what she was about to say. "Ten years ago, I mean. Sarah told me that's what everyone thought."

"Then... what happened?"

She took a steadying breath and stared down at her mother's pendant. Somehow it gave her the courage to continue. "My father wasn't a kind man."

"I remember. He had the whole town fooled. Everyone thought he was a great man, a leader in our church, but - "

"Nobody knew what he was really like. At home." She swallowed hard. "That's why I spent so much time at your house when we were little. I didn't like to be at home when he was around."

"I know. I remember." Chance took her hand in his. "You were practically a member of our family. That's why my parents fought so hard to find some evidence of abuse, so we could help you. What I don't know, though, is why you disappeared. What happened that night when you showed up at my house?"

Bellamy remembered it. She'd relived it in her nightmares many times. Images half-formed in her mind, memories she didn't want to come to the surface.

"Bella?"

Bellamy shook her head. It was ten years in the past; why did the terror still feel as fresh as if it had just happened?

"Drunken rages were pretty common for my dad," she said. "But that night it was different. He tried to force himself on me."

Chance gripped the pendant's box hard, his knuckles white, but he waited for her to continue.

"I didn't know what to do, so I just ran. Your house was the only place I ever really felt safe, so that's where I went. Mama came for me the next morning. When I heard the engine out front, I knew I had to go. I thought about waking you up, but I figured I would come back and explain everything later. I never got the chance."

"Bella…" Chance's voice was strained. He made a move as if to put his arm around her, but Bellamy scooted away. She needed to finish this, and if he touched her, she would lose it.

"Mama tried to protect me. That's all she ever did. So she packed a bag and put me on a bus to Colorado. To stay with… to stay with my uncle. Her brother."

Uncle David's face sprang to her mind, as clear as if he was standing right next to her. His mocking laugh echoed in her ears. The coppery smell of blood turned her stomach.

She couldn't tell him the rest.

Chance put his hand over hers. "Why didn't you call me?" The pain in his voice matched the pain she felt in her heart. "I looked for you, Bella. Why didn't you let me know you were okay?"

His hand was warm against her clammy skin. She wanted to lace her fingers through his and squeeze tight and never let go. She wanted to grab him and yank his lips down to hers and kiss him until the pain went away.

"I couldn't. My uncle wasn't a good man either. I thought about reaching out to you, but…"

But she hadn't wanted to involve him any further than she already had.

So many nights she had lain awake, wondering what Chance was doing and if he was okay. When her mother had dropped her off at the bus station, she'd told Bellamy not to contact the Ericksons, or her father would find her. The memory of him standing over her bed that night had haunted her for years after, scaring her into obeying her mother's directions.

By the time she left her uncle's house and found the courage to contact Chance, he'd already joined the Marines and moved on. At that point, Bellamy had been living on the streets and had fallen into her career in crime. It started with standing lookout for illegal black market trades, and before she knew it, she was organizing the trades herself.

Then she was in too deep, and she couldn't get out.

All her life, Bellamy had felt helpless, powerless to protect herself against those that were more powerful than she was. So many years she had spent feeling afraid.

And angry.

She'd been so angry; angry at the hand the universe had dealt her, angry that she couldn't do anything to help herself, angry that the people she cared about kept getting hurt because of her.

Questions and accusations that she'd never been able to voice came bubbling to the surface, like acid that refused to stay down.

"Someone called the police, Chance," she said, meeting his gaze. "That's what set Papa off that night. Someone called in a tip that he was abusive, and Papa thought it was me."

Chance froze.

"I know it was your parents. Sarah told me. Why, though? Was it because of the bruises you saw when you took me to prom?"

The expression on Chance's face confirmed her suspicions. She'd always figured that was the case, but imagining it was one thing. Seeing proof was another.

"If you had left it alone, everything would have been

fine."

"Everything wasn't fine, Bella. He was beating you. Someone had to stop him, or both of you were going to end up dead. You weren't doing anything to help yourselves."

Bellamy flinched as if he had slapped her. "You don't know anything about my situation," she said through gritted teeth. "Don't pretend to know what it was like. If you had left it alone, at least I could have stayed here. Instead I was sent away, and I was on my own for years."

"I tried to get your mom to tell me where you were. I asked so many times. Then she was just gone, and your father disappeared too."

Bellamy slid her hand away from his. Despite everything she'd suffered during her childhood, she'd always clung to one truth: she'd loved her mother and her mother had loved her. She'd been a weak woman, unable to leave a husband who abused her, but she'd always done the best she could for Bellamy. Even sending her to Uncle David's had been done with the best of intentions. She couldn't have known what would happen to Bellamy there.

Bellamy would always bear the guilt for her mother's death. She knew what kind of person her father became when he was drinking, and Bellamy's disappearance would have driven him mad. Not that he cared about her, but because he didn't like anything that was outside of his control.

In the back of her mind, Bellamy had always wondered…

If she had been brave enough to come back home, to face her father, would her mother still be alive?

Her fingers curled into a tight fist around her mother's pendant.

The past was the past. She'd spent the last seven years making herself strong so it wouldn't have a hold on her anymore.

"I learned to take care of myself," she said, voice finally steady. "So I guess I should thank you for not coming to my rescue."

Chance frowned. "I wish you didn't go through any of that."

"Well, I did. It's done. I'm not the same girl anymore. The one who let her dad beat her is dead and buried, and she's never coming back." Bellamy stood, glad that her resolve was back in place.

Chance stood too. "I couldn't help you back then, but I promise to help you now. I'll never let anything like that happen to you again."

"Look, you were my childhood friend and I'm grateful for everything that you've done for me, but I'm not worth your time. I'm not a good person anymore, Chance. All that stuff from the past... it left scars. I'm damaged now."

"That's not true. You're still the same girl I - "

Bellamy held up a hand. "I'll help you find evidence against Powell, but it doesn't change anything between us. What happened when we were kids is in the past, and I don't need anyone to lean on anymore. I'm strong enough to stand on my own two feet."

"It's not a weakness to ask for help. Let me - "

"I don't expect you to understand." Bellamy turned away. "This was a heavy conversation. Let's stop here for today, okay?"

Pausing at the door, she turned to look back at him. She felt like a jerk for not telling him the whole truth, but she just couldn't. It had taken a long time to build these walls around herself. She needed them to remain standing; without them, she wouldn't survive.

At the pained expression on his face, she softened her voice a little. "Thanks for the necklace. I mean it. I'm going to go take a shower."

She left the room and returned to her bedroom, guilt and sorrow heavy in her heart. She'd left him with more questions than answers, just like she had ten years ago. He was only trying to help, she knew that, but she couldn't afford to let him all the way in.

She wasn't kidding; she was damaged.

If he knew the truth about her time with Uncle David or the illegal activities she orchestrated now, he'd never look at her the same way again.

* * * * * *

Back at ESI headquarters, there was a knock on the door to Emmett's office.

Emmett sighed and pushed his laptop away from him. Staring at the screen all night had left him with a pounding headache, borderline migraine. He blinked at the door on the far side of the room, willing his eyes to focus on faraway objects again.

The door opened and Owen poked his head in. Emmett knew he'd been up all night as well, but that was his normal schedule. His blonde hair was arranged in the bedhead look he always wore, and his eyes were bright and alert - the complete opposite of Emmett's current situation.

"Hey, you called?"

"Come in and close the door."

Owen obeyed and sauntered into the room, leaning against the wall with his hands in the pockets of his jeans. "What's up, boss?"

Emmett scowled. "Don't call me that. I need you to do something for me."

"What?"

"Do some digging. I want everything you can find on where Bellamy has been for the last ten years."

Owen raised an eyebrow. "Seriously? You're gonna go behind Chance's back on this? That's low, even for you."

Emmett leaned back in his chair, allowing his back to relax for just a moment. It popped in several places, eliciting a deep sigh from him. He eyed Owen. "Do you believe that he's in his right mind at the moment?"

"Point taken." Owen shifted his feet. "What do you want to know?"

Emmett knew he felt the same way, even if he couldn't admit it yet. Neither of them felt the empathy for Bellamy that Chance and Sarah did. He and Owen had suffered the most when Bellamy's father came after their family. Owen had been bullied so badly in school that he'd dropped out as a sophomore and finished his GED online. He later moved on to college level classes from the safety of his parents' house.

"I need to know where she's been, who she's been

with, what she's done. Everything you can find. Chance might not be willing to pry into her past, but I am. I need to make sure she's telling the truth before I invest time and resources on her story."

Owen nodded. "To be honest, I've already got a search running as we speak."

"Good." Emmett knew he would. "And not a word to anyone."

"Okay."

"Including Sarah. Especially Sarah."

"All right, all right, I hear you." Owen opened the office door. "I'll let you know what I find."

CHAPTER 12

BELLA WASN'T SURE what woke her out of her deep sleep. Perhaps it was the rain pelting the window or the wind shaking the trees outside. But when she opened her eyes, she blinked at the clock on her bedside table.

2:33 a.m.

With a groan, she flopped onto her back and stared at the ceiling.

A dark figure shifted at the end of her bed.

Bella bit back a scream and scooted up to a sitting position.

"Shh, darlin', iss jus' me."

"Papa?" Her heart banged against her ribcage. She leaned over and flipped on the lamp on her bedside table, bathing her bedroom in a soft yellow glow. "What are you doing?"

Her father wore the same clothes as the day before.

They were wrinkled and smelled like alcohol. A bottle of liquor dangled from the fingers of his right hand. His harsh breathing, fast and shallow, filled the room even over the sounds of the storm outside.

"Shh." Her father took a few stumbling steps closer. "Jus' be quiet."

Bella scooted to the far side of the bed, wedging herself into the corner of the wall as he sat on the edge of the mattress. He reached out a hand, faster than a drunk man should've been able to, and grabbed her ankle in a bruising grip. He dragged her until she was practically on his lap.

"Did you know... I had to talk to the police today?" His eyes struggled to focus on her face. Despite his inebriation, Bella knew from experience that his brain was still working fine.

"N-No, I didn't know, Papa." Bella took a deep breath to stop her voice from shaking. "How come?"

His fist shot out, connecting with her cheekbone faster than she could've reacted. Her head snapped to the side and pain bloomed across her face, white hot.

"Don't lie," he snapped. He grabbed her hair and forced her back to face him. "They said there was a tip. Someone called them. I know it was you."

"It wasn't, I promise." Bella covered his hand with hers, trying to relieve some of the pressure on her scalp. "Mama! - " she started to scream, but his other hand slid over her mouth.

He pushed her back onto the mattress, using the weight of his body to hold her in place. His breath smelled like alcohol. She tried not to gag behind his hand.

"I said be quiet. If you make a sound, I'll beat you until you can't stand." His voice was harsh like gravel in her ear.

She whimpered and closed her eyes tight.

"Don't. Move. You understand?"

The weight lifted off her for a moment. Bella's eyes flew open. He was sitting up, fumbling with the buttons on his shirt.

She looked around, her heartbeat thundering in her ears, and her eyes fell on the lamp on her bedside table. A burst of courage spurred her forward. She lunged for the lamp and swung it in a wide arc.

The sharp edge of it cracked against her father's skull. He was a big man, and he went down hard. His body slumped over and fell to the floor next to her bed with a loud thud.

Tears streamed down Bella's cheeks. She bit back a sob and stumbled off the bed and over her father's body. She didn't know where to go, but she knew she had to get away.

If he woke up, he would kill her.

The back door slammed behind her and she sprinted across the backyard, cowering when a loud crash of thunder sounded right over her head. Her bare feet slipped in the wet grass and she stumbled, but regained her footing as she made it into the thick line of trees. Breathing hard, she picked her way across the path she knew by heart toward the only place she felt truly safe.

* * * * * *

Chance didn't follow Bellamy when she fled from the

living room. He wanted to, but he didn't. His brain was too busy processing all the new information he'd gained from their brief conversation. He paced, eyes on the staircase leading to the second floor. Painful memories from the past plagued him and he re-lived everything from a new perspective. Bellamy's perspective.

He'd spent so much of their childhood friendship feeling helpless, powerless to help his best friend when she clearly needed it.

Just when they had found something, she disappeared.

Chance had been sixteen, old enough to drive but nowhere near an adult. He couldn't accept her disappearance. He hung posters, went door to door, even asked around at local train and bus stations. He had even called the police, though they'd been no help once Bellamy's parents reported that she'd just been transferred to a boarding school.

Chance always assumed that proper procedures had been followed in the investigation, but by the time he was old enough to follow up on that, he was off to the Marines and he'd made the decision to move on.

After a while, he'd wondered if Bellamy really was dead like many had speculated.

Why hadn't he done more? He could have found her and her uncle if he had tried harder.

Chance replayed their conversation in his head, looking for signs that he had missed, clues to help him guess what had happened during her three years with her uncle. Judging from her reaction as she talked about it, it couldn't have been good.

His blood boiled at the thought of her suffering more abuse while she was out of his reach.

And knowing that he was the reason she was there in the first place...

"Hey."

Chance jumped and looked over to see Sarah standing in the doorway. He hadn't heard her come down the stairs. Her hair was wet and pulled back in her usual ponytail. She stood with one hand on the doorframe, looking a little tentative. "How'd it go?"

Chance sighed and rubbed his throbbing temples. "It was fine at first. She started to tell me about what happened. She was sent to live with her uncle."

"I know." Sarah sat on the couch, expression tense.

"Do you know what happened to her there?"

"She won't talk about it. I know he wasn't kind though."

"I got that feeling too." Chance sighed. "Why didn't I do more, Sarah? I could have saved her."

"Chance, she was a kid. You were a kid. What could you have done?" Sarah grabbed a pillow and hugged it to her chest. "You've gotta get over this hero complex of yours."

"I could have done something. Mom and Dad could have gotten custody of her somehow..."

"Yeah, after their call to the police station got her sent away in the first place?" Sarah looked at him like he was an idiot. "Look, it doesn't matter. It's done. Crying about the past isn't going to help anyone. Let's just move forward from here and deal with our current situation."

Chance draped an arm over his little sister's shoulder.

"When did you become so wise?"

Sarah shrugged and looked away. "Life experience does that to you."

"Seems like you've learned a lot from your time in New York." Something in her tone bothered him, and he leaned down to examine her face.

She smiled crookedly. "Sorry, bro, but I'm not a mystery wrapped in an enigma like Bellamy is. Don't start an inquisition on me."

Chance grinned and gave her a squeeze. "We'll pick that up later. For now, you're right. I'm in a situation where I can help her now, and I'm going to do just that."

Sarah shrugged out of his grip and lightly punched him in the shoulder. "There you go. Now you sound like my brother again."

* * * * * *

Bellamy emerged from the shower feeling a little more like herself. She stood in the middle of the bedroom wrapped in only a towel, frowning at the expanse of trees outside her window.

Her conversation with Chance played on a loop in her head.

Had she said too much?

It didn't matter.

She needed to worry about the future now. Powell was still walking around as a free man, and apparently he wanted her head on a silver platter.

There was no way she would sit and wait while ESI

handled the case.

It was about time she moved this process along. She had plenty of evidence that she'd gathered over the years against all of her clients, not just Ronald Powell.

Bellamy pulled out her cell phone.

Most of her contacts were probably burned, but blackmail was a funny thing. If she twisted the arms of enough powerful people in Portland, something would surely shake loose.

She needed her flash drive from her locker in Seattle.

And she knew just the person who could deliver it to her.

All she had to do was escape Chance's watch for a few hours today.

A few minutes later, Bellamy cracked open the bedroom door. Muffled noises sounded from downstairs, but she couldn't distinguish what they were. She fingered her mother's pendant hanging around her neck. It felt heavy and warm against the center of her chest.

Go-time.

Sarah and Chance were in the living room. The television blared in front of them; it looked like an old John Wayne movie.

Chance's love of Westerns hadn't died in the last ten years, apparently. He really was a cowboy at heart.

As Bellamy entered the room, the screen changed to a woman standing in front of a weather radar. She gestured at the swirling green mass behind her. It rotated over the ocean off the west coast.

"A powerful storm system is heading toward the Pacific

Northwest in the next few days," the woman reported. "We're expecting high winds and rainfall with widespread thunderstorms. Stay tuned for continuing coverage as the system approaches the coast."

"They always overestimate this stuff," Sarah said in disgust. "It always looks huge until it hits land. Then it dies and we get a few scattered showers."

"Well, Washington isn't exactly known for its severe weather," Chance pointed out.

"You haven't seen severe weather until you've been to New York. I've seen freezing rain, hurricane-strength wind, insane amounts of snow, and temperatures so cold that your wet hair freezes to your face."

"It sounds like you're speaking from experience. Why would you go outside with wet hair if it's that cold?"

Sarah leveled a look at him. "I'm a college student. Sometimes I'm up all night studying and I sleep in, okay? Would you rather me not shower at all?"

"Sounds irresponsible to me."

"It happened one time!"

Bellamy cleared her throat. Both Chance and Sarah spun to look at her.

Sarah's expression immediately brightened. "Oh, hey girl." She paused, and her gaze swept over Bellamy from head to toe. "Didn't you wear that yesterday?"

Bellamy looked down at herself and blushed. "I packed some extra clothes, but whoever trashed my apartment was a real jerk. They're all shredded."

Sarah smacked her brother in the chest. "You didn't get her any new clothes? What is she supposed to wear while she's here?"

"I didn't know. She didn't tell me," Chance said, rubbing his chest.

"Well," Sarah replied with a huff, "I guess I have to do everything around here. Bellamy, I'll take you shopping."

"Oh, are you sure?" Bellamy forced a bright smile. "Getting out of the house for a while sounds nice, actually."

"Of course. It'll be fun; we can go bum around the mall like we used to. Chance will even let us take his credit card."

Chance raised an eyebrow and looked like he might protest, but Sarah shot him a look, so he shut his mouth and pulled out his wallet. He tossed a gold card in her direction and threw up his hands as he walked out of the room. "Be back at a decent time," he called over his shoulder as he exited.

* * * * * *

The ESI office looked deserted when Chance opened the front door an hour later. Dominick, Roman, and Cameron were nowhere to be found. They were probably off working on their assignments about Governor Powell.

Chance walked down the hallway and found Owen and Emmett in Owen's office, a room that doubled as a computer lab. They huddled in front of Owen's massive, curved computer screen. Owen glanced up at the sound of the door opening and elbowed Emmett.

"What'd you find out on Governor Powell?" Chance asked.

"Owen did some digging," Emmett said.

"Okay. What did he get? Anything actionable?"

Emmett straightened. "I asked him to check into Bellamy."

"Excuse me?" Chance scowled. "I thought I asked you to trust me on this."

"It's not you that I don't trust."

"Our focus should be on the governor, not on this witch hunt you're trying to orchestrate." Chance stalked closer to them.

"She hasn't told us everything."

"And for good reason." Chance glared at Emmett. "We had a good talk this morning. She hasn't told me everything, but I know enough to trust her."

"Do you?"

"Yes. We all have things we don't want to talk about." Chance shot a pointed look at Emmett.

"Did she tell you she has a criminal record?" Owen interrupted.

Chance tore his gaze away from his staring match with Emmett and glanced at his younger brother. "What?"

Emmett jabbed a finger at the computer screen. "Owen found the police report. She was arrested when she was sixteen for aggravated assault. She attacked some kid at school, almost killed him. Drugs were involved."

"Allegedly. There's also a news story," Owen added. He had the grace to cast an apologetic look in Chance's direction. "Her uncle, Governor David Merrell, issued a public apology. He told the press that he had taken Bellamy in as a favor to his sister, and she'd led a troubled life. Even ended up paying all of the hospital bills for the kid she attacked."

Chance's hands clenched into fists. "You can't believe everything you read. She told me her uncle wasn't a good man."

"Governor Merrell had a stellar reputation. Everyone in town loved him and his policies. He did a lot of good things during his time in the office," Owen said.

"Everyone loved Bella's father too. Appearances can be deceiving."

"All right," Emmett said. "I'll give you that. Maybe the guy was an asshole. But the fact remains that Bellamy attacked that kid. There were two witnesses. She would have killed him if they hadn't pulled her off at the last minute."

"I don't think that's the whole story. I think you're looking for reasons to believe she's the villain here. Why won't you trust my judgment on this?"

"I don't think you're thinking with your head," Emmett countered. "At least not the head you should be using."

"Excuse me?" Chance stepped closer so he was right in Emmett's face. "Try saying that again."

Owen stepped between them, using his elbows to shove them apart. "Everyone calm down," he said. He turned his back on Emmett and faced Chance. "I'll do some more digging on her uncle, just to be sure. If he wronged her, I'll find evidence. But she's had a hard life, Chance, and that can change a person. We don't know where she's been since she left. She could've gotten involved in all sorts of things she hasn't told you about. Just try to remember that and be careful. Okay?"

Chance jerked his glare away from Emmett and focused on Owen. "She's not the villain here," he said again, but he felt a little less sure of that.

CHAPTER 13

THE SHOPPING DISTRICT DOWNTOWN hadn't changed in the ten years since Bellamy and Sarah frequented the trendy shops. They took Sarah's Jeep and spent the afternoon wandering. Sarah picked a few new outfits for Bellamy and spent way more money than Bellamy would have, if given the choice. She was bright and cheerful as she dragged Bellamy all over town.

A few hours after their excursion began, they decided to stop for lunch.

"Why don't you grab a table? I'm going to use the bathroom," Bellamy said.

Sarah waved a hand in acknowledgement, eyes on her phone, and continued toward the restaurant.

Bellamy waited a moment to make sure Sarah wouldn't follow her, then set off at a brisk walk toward the other end of the mall. It didn't take her long to find bright turquoise hair she was looking for in the crowd.

Jessi sat on a bench in front of a children's toy store. Her bright hair always drew attention, but otherwise she was dressed in jeans and a long brown duster. When she saw Bellamy, she waved a hand enthusiastically.

"Jessi," Bellamy said, dropping onto the bench next to her. "Let's make this quick. I don't have long."

"Sure," Jessi said brightly. "I brought what you asked for. Just so you know, though, Powell's got a bounty on your head. You're lucky you called me; pretty much everyone else in Portland would deliver you on a silver platter at this point."

"Why do you think I called you?" Bellamy held out a hand expectantly.

Jessi grinned and pulled a manilla envelope out of her inner jacket pocket. "Everything's there. For the record, I hope you nail the guy to the wall. I think he's a sleaze-bag."

"That's the plan. And the other thing I asked for?"

She handed over a brown paper bag. Bellamy hefted it in her palm; it was heavy, about the right weight. Glancing around, she opened the top wide enough to peek inside.

A sleek black Sig Sauer winked out at her from the bottom of the bag.

"Loaded?" she asked Jessi.

"Yes, ma'am. High-impact rounds, just like you like."

"Good." Bellamy stood. "I'll make sure payment is delivered promptly. Obviously I don't have the cash on me right now."

"Don't worry, I trust you." Jessi blew a bubble with her bubblegum. "Watch your back, 'kay? See you around."

Bellamy waved goodbye and hurried into the nearest bathroom. Once her folder was settled in her backpack and the gun was tucked safely into her jeans, she returned to the restaurant.

The weight of the gun at her back made her feel much safer. She doubted Powell would find her here in La Conner, but it never hurt to take precautions. Crap would hit the fan as soon as she released these files, so she wanted to be prepared.

Jessi was the most honest contact she had in the Portland underworld; she only hoped she'd made the right decision to trust her.

"Oh, I have missed you," Sarah gushed a little while later, as they ate lunch. "It doesn't feel like it's been ten years since we've hung out. I'm so glad you're back."

Bellamy smiled at her. She didn't have the heart to tell her that she didn't plan on staying. La Conner wasn't her home anymore. Once she released the info she had on Powell, it would only be a matter of time until he was arrested. With the danger over, Bellamy would leave La Conner again, this time for good.

But she had to admit, it was nice to spend time with Sarah again. She reminded Bellamy so much of Sam that it made her heart hurt sometimes.

Sarah sighed and rested her chin on her hand, staring at the crowd rushing past outside the large window. "I bet Chance is glad you're back, too."

Bellamy's mouth twisted into a frown. "I'm not so sure about that."

"What makes you say that?"

Bellamy shrugged. "We talked this morning. I told him about the night I left La Conner. He still sees me as that scared little girl. I tried to tell him I'm not the same anymore. All the stuff I've experienced has changed me. But he doesn't believe it."

"I told him he needs to get over his hero complex. For whatever reason, he still thinks he needs to save you." She rolled her eyes. "Men."

Bellamy snorted. "Joke's on him. I moved beyond saving a long time ago."

"I don't know about that. I still kinda like ya."

"That makes one of you."

Sarah laughed. "Don't let the haters bother you. I'm glad you're here. Besides, maybe this is a second chance for you and him."

Bellamy speared a potato with her fork and waved it at Sarah. "I hired him. This is a professional relationship, that's all. Besides, a romantic relationship isn't in the cards for me. I'm too... damaged."

"We're all a little damaged." A shadow fell over Sarah's expression and she seemed to be looking at something far away. "Love is about finding someone who will accept our damaged parts."

Bellamy cleared her throat. Sure, that sounded nice, but it wasn't very realistic. "So why aren't you going back to New York?"

Sarah sat back in her chair. "I liked living on my own, but I'm not sure being a doctor is for me. I want to help people before they end up in the hospital, instead of trying to save them after. And I just feel like I should be here," she said. "You know, with Dad and you and ESI and everything."

Bellamy's eyes narrowed. "Why do I feel like you're not telling me everything?"

Sarah called for the check and smiled at Bellamy. "Says the woman of many secrets."

Bellamy stared at her in silence. She wasn't letting her off that easily.

"All right, fine, jeez. The truth is, I lost a friend in New York recently. Right before Dad."

"What?" That wasn't what Bellamy had expected. "Why didn't you say anything? What happened?"

Sarah shrugged. "He was mugged. It's not uncommon there. I haven't said anything because it's been so crazy here with Dad's death." She paused, her green eyes sad. "I just keep thinking that maybe I could have done something to save him, you know? Doctors couldn't help him. He was dead before he made it to the hospital."

"I'm sorry," Bellamy said. She was so wrapped up in her own drama that she hadn't even noticed Sarah's suffering. "I didn't know. Was he...?"

"No, he wasn't my boyfriend." Sarah's lips turned up in a half-hearted smile. "Just a really good friend."

"Well, how are things going? You know... romantically?"

"They're not." Sarah paused and her expression darkened. "But speaking of that, you know Roman?"

"Uh-huh."

"I was at ESI this morning, looking for Owen, and I ran into him. He started going off about a civilian being on the team - he's such an asshole - and, you know me, I started yelling right back at him. And he just grabbed me and kissed me. Out of nowhere. No warning. Can you believe that?" Her cheeks flushed.

"And how did you feel about that?"

"W-Well, it was disgusting," Sarah blustered. "Too much teeth. And I was so angry that I couldn't enjoy it anyway. As a matter of fact, I slapped him. Serves him right, right? This is the 21st century. You can't just go around manhandling women like that."

Bellamy just smiled. All the girl talk made her feel almost normal.

* * * * * *

The sun had set by the time Sarah and Bellamy finished their shopping. They hauled huge armfuls of bags to the Jeep and stuffed them in the back, laughing and congratulating each other on their retail prowess. It felt good to relax. It had been too long since Bellamy could do that.

"You get the car started," she told Sarah. "I'm going to run inside and use the bathroom before we make the drive home."

As she jogged back into the store and did her business, she shook her head at herself. Home. She'd called Chance's house home.

One afternoon with Sarah and her walls were already crumbling down around her. All the normalcy almost made her believe this could be her life.

But when all this was over, she'd return to her real home. To Portland.

To a life of crime and solitude and danger.

That was where she belonged; not here, playing "house" with Sarah and Chance.

Bellamy shivered as she left the building. The early fall air had cooled since the sun set. She took a deep breath, savoring the fresh smell of pine. That was her favorite thing about La Conner.

A strong arm locked around Bellamy's waist, pinning her arms to her sides. Bellamy tried to scream, but another hand slapped over her mouth. Her eyes shot across the parking lot to the Jeep, where Sarah was lounging in the front seat, eyes down as she looked at something on her phone.

The rest of the parking lot was empty. There was no one around to help her.

Bellamy's assailant dragged her around a corner and into a nearby alley. She struggled, but the arms around her were like iron vices.

Somehow, Powell had found her.

"Quiet," a voice barked into her ear. It was low, raspy. She didn't recognize it. She turned her head to see that her attacker wore a black ski mask to cover his face. He was tall, at least as tall as Chance, and he was fit. The muscles in his arms proved that.

Definitely not Ronald Powell. Not that she'd expected him to do the job himself. He wasn't the type.

A hired hand, then.

That was just fine. He wasn't getting paid enough for the hell Bellamy was about to unleash on him.

She wasn't the same scared little girl who left La

Conner ten years ago.

The man dragged her back a few more steps and turned her toward the other end of the alley. A black van loomed a short distance away. If he got her into that vehicle, no one would ever see her again.

Bellamy went limp, hoping that her body weight would throw the man off balance, but he was strong. He hauled her back up and continued dragging her. She whipped her head back hard and her skull connected with his nose in a satisfying crunch.

He let out a low curse, but his hand didn't leave her mouth. He gave her a hard shake that made her brain rattle.

"Keep struggling and I'll kill you right now," he hissed.

As if she would obey that kind of command.

She whipped her head back again, harder this time, and stomped on the man's foot as hard as she could. It was a solid hit this time.

The man stumbled back. His arms loosened around her for an instant.

Bellamy let out a short scream before he was on her again. He grabbed her arm and threw her against a nearby wall. The side of her head hit the brick with a sick thud and pain spasmed through her whole body. Her vision went dark for a moment, but instinct kept her fighting.

Before his hands could grab her again, she pulled the Sig Sauer from her pants. Leaning one shoulder against the wall for support, she leveled the gun at the man's chest.

"Take another step and I'll kill you," she snapped.

Her heartbeat was in her head, pounding fast against her skull.

Her hands shook. The barrel of the gun shook with them.

The man continued to advance on her. He was only feet away.

Bellamy pulled the trigger.

Her unsteady hands made the shot go high. Stone exploded on the other side of the alleyway.

The man ducked, his hands covering his face, and let out a low curse.

"This isn't over," he said.

Then he turned and ran, scooping up her backpack - when had that fallen off her shoulder? - as he went.

Bellamy fired another shot at his retreating back. He jerked to the left, his hand coming up to cradle his right bicep, and dove into the van.

"Bellamy!"

Bellamy let out the breath she hadn't realized she'd been holding and watched the vehicle speed away in the other direction. She slid down to the ground as the adrenaline sucked the strength from her body.

The gun slipped from her hands and clattered to the ground. By some miracle, it didn't go off a third time.

The pounding in her head intensified.

She lifted her hand and felt something warm and sticky above her left ear.

"Bellamy, honey, are you all right?"

A fuzzy shape came down in front of her. Bellamy scrabbled for the gun again. She couldn't allow herself to be taken. She wasn't getting in that van.

Strong hands grabbed her wrists.

"Bellamy, it's Chance. Baby, look at me."

The voice penetrated the fog in her mind. She blinked at the shape, willing her eyes to bring him into focus. Chance? Chance was a friend. He could help her. "Chance," she whispered.

"Yeah, baby, I'm here." His voice was gruff. He let out a long string of muttered curses and raised his voice. "She hit her head. Call 911."

Hands reached out to her. Touched her arms, her shoulders, her face. Bellamy shrugged them off, concerned that her body wasn't moving as well as it should. "I told you I'm not the same girl anymore," she murmured.

"I know, baby, you did so good. Hey, Bella, look at me. Don't close your eyes, okay? You hit your head. We need to get you to the hospital."

Bellamy struggled to keep her eyes open, but they felt like they weighed a hundred pounds each. Sirens sounded in the distance.

"Bella, does anything else hurt?"

"No… just my head." She gestured in the general direction.

"Okay. Hold on, okay? I'm going to pick you up. We're going to get you some help." Arms went around her and she felt herself being lifted, cradled against Chance's chest. He was warm and hard and gentle. She snuggled into him and let her eyes fall closed, just for a moment.

"Bellamy Burke." His voice was sharp in her ear. "Don't go to sleep, you hear me? Open your eyes and look at me."

Bellamy shook her head. Even though her eyes were closed, she could see the flashing red lights through her eyelids. The ambulance had arrived. She let out a sigh and relaxed, letting the darkness take her.

CHAPTER 14

EMMETT PARKED NEXT TO the sheriff's SUV. The flashing lights of the other police vehicles nearby cast red and blue shadows on the brick facade of the building.

A small crowd had gathered around the yellow police tape blocking off the alley where Bellamy had been attacked. Emmett recognized most of the curious faces; no doubt word had already spread through town about the incident. Nothing was secret in La Conner.

The crowd parted like the Red Sea as Emmett and Owen approached. They ducked under the yellow police tape and approached Sheriff McCauley, who was standing at the end of the alley with Officer Tom Hansen and a crime scene investigator.

Over the past year, Emmett had worked closely with Sheriff McCauley for ESI's few local clients. Officer Tom Hansen had been friends with Sarah since they were kids and he was a trusted friend in the police department. The crime scene investigator, however, Emmett didn't recognize.

"Emmett," Sheriff McCauley said in greeting. "Figured I'd be seeing you."

"Thanks for holding the scene for us." Emmett shook the sheriff's hand. "We'll be quick."

The crime scene investigator stepped forward. "You know it's against protocol to wait to process a crime scene. Evidence could be compromised."

Ah. He must be from Seattle. La Conner wasn't large enough to staff its own CSI unit, so when events like this occurred, they requested help from other jurisdictions.

Emmett stretched his lips in some semblance of a smile. "I apologize for our tardiness. Owen will just take a quick look and we'll be out of your hair."

"You're not authorized - "

"Keith, I told you already." Sheriff McCauley's voice barely masked his annoyance. "You can wait fifteen minutes. ESI has a vested interest in this case, and they can process this evidence a lot faster than you. You can even go along with Owen if you want, to make sure he doesn't tamper with anything. I'm sure he won't mind."

"Someone looking over my shoulder while I work?" Owen shot a pointed grin at Emmett. "Happens every day at the office. Come on, Keith-meister. Let's get this done."

Keith looked like he wanted to argue, but when Owen strolled away from the group, whistling a merry tune, he shut his mouth and followed.

Sheriff McCauley shook his head. "He's from the city. Doesn't quite understand how we do things here."

Tom laughed. "Not sure anyone does. Even I don't, some days."

Sheriff McCauley shot him a dirty look. "Don't you have some witnesses to interview?"

"Yes sir. I'll head over to the hospital now." Tom looked at Emmett. "Your family's there?"

"Should be. Chance and Sarah rode in the ambulance with Bellamy."

"Good. Haven't seen Sarah in a while. I didn't want to catch up like this, but shit happens."

"That it does." Emmett sighed.

Tom nodded to both of them and strode away.

"Quite the mess we've got here," Sheriff McCauley commented, eyeing Owen and the CSI on the other end of the alley. "Haven't had this much excitement in years."

"Tell me about it. I prefer when it's quiet."

"Any idea who this guy is?"

Emmett crossed his arms over his chest. "We have a suspect, but I need to do some digging first."

"If you need any help, you let me know."

Emmett smiled at the man. "Thanks, Sheriff. I appreciate that."

Owen approached them, followed closely by the CSI. Owen carried a small piece of paper in one hand. "I found a partial print on the gun," Owen said. "Luckily, I always carry lift tape with me. If I can get this back to the office, I should be able to run it and see if we can find a match before we head to the hospital."

"That's not possible," Keith blustered from behind Owen's shoulder. "You don't have access to a database like that, and Seattle PD has a large backlog. It could take weeks to process."

"Whoops, I guess you're right." Owen shrugged. "I'd never hack into a system like that, so we'll have to wait. Oh well."

Keith's jaw dropped. He looked at the sheriff as if to say, 'Are you going to do anything about this?'

"He's joking," Sheriff McCauley said flatly. "But Mr. Erickson does have contacts at the police department, so he'll be able to escalate the process. Don't worry. It's all by the book."

"By the book," Owen repeated with a cheerful nod. "That's my middle name."

"Let's go," Emmett interrupted. "We have work to do. Thanks, gentlemen. Have a good afternoon."

They headed back to the truck, leaving Sheriff McCauley to explain the situation to the good CSI.

* * * * * *

Chance paced back and forth in the hospital waiting room, his fingers clasped too tight behind his back. Sarah sprawled in a chair nearby, her eyes red-rimmed.

The door opened and Emmett, Owen, and his mother rushed in. Mary sank down into the seat next to Sarah and gathered her close. Her hand made soothing motions in Sarah's blonde hair.

Owen approached Chance and clapped him on the back. "I'm sure she'll be okay," he said in a low voice. "You can't keep a girl like that down."

"Did you find anything at the crime scene?" Chance looked between his brothers. "Any evidence that Powell was involved?"

Emmett stood a few paces away with his arms folded over his chest. His expression was inscrutable. "No. But we did find something else."

"What?"

"First, tell me what you saw."

Chance jerked a shaking hand over his hair. "The girls went shopping. They took forever, so I went to check on them. Sarah was waiting for Bellamy in the parking lot. We heard her scream." He took a deep breath as fresh rage swept through his body, leaving him trembling. "Some masked asshole attacked her. It had to be a thug hired by Powell. I didn't get a good look at him. By the time I got there, he was fleeing the scene. I got part of the license plate though." He looked to Owen. "Will you run it for me?"

Owen nodded. "Yeah, of course."

Sarah looked up from her perch, her eyes stricken. "I didn't even notice," she murmured. "I didn't even see him grab her."

Mary hugged her again, muttering nonsensical words of comfort, but her eyes were hard as she looked over her daughter's head at Chance. "We need to find out who did this," she said. "Have you heard anything on Bellamy?"

Chance rolled his shoulders, trying to ease some of the tension in his muscles. "She was unconscious when the ambulance got there. They took her back to run some tests. She took a hard hit to the head."

Mary nodded. "She'll be all right. And we'll be here when she wakes up."

Emmett jerked his head toward the hallway outside the waiting room, his eyes on Chance. "Let's grab some drinks. We might be here a while."

Chance followed him out into the hallway. If he didn't want to talk about the evidence they'd found in front of their mother, it couldn't be good. "What's going on? What did you find?" he demanded.

Emmett glanced back to make sure they were out of earshot and frowned when Owen ambled up behind them.

Owen just raised his eyebrows.

"We found fingerprints on the gun. Owen ran them through the computer system. They're Bellamy's."

"So? She shot the perp as he ran away. Of course her prints are going to be on the gun."

"Chance, her prints are the only ones on the gun," Owen said. "That gun wasn't the perp's. It was Bellamy's."

"That's ridiculous. We just flew from Portland. She couldn't have gotten a gun through security."

"There's more. The gun doesn't have a serial number." Emmett's expression darkened. "It's a black market weapon."

"That's... impossible," Chance said slowly. "How could she have gotten a black market handgun?"

"That's what I'd like to know."

"Maybe our little Bellamy is a black market weapons dealer now," Owen said, straight-faced.

Chance punched him in the arm. "Don't be ridiculous. There has to be an explanation."

"I thought that was a pretty good one."

"Regardless, we need to find evidence that Powell was involved in this. She's not safe, even here." Chance paced away from them. He couldn't think about the gun right now. Guilt was eating him from the inside out. He should have protected her. He was arrogant to think that because he'd taken her from Portland, she would be safe. The blame for her attack rested squarely on his shoulders.

Owen put a hand on his shoulder, his expression serious for once. "You couldn't have known she'd be attacked here."

"She warned me. I arrogantly believed there wouldn't be a threat this far from Portland. I underestimated him."

"I don't buy it," Emmett said. "Some blackmail that Sam may or may not have had against him isn't a strong enough motive to hire a hitman to follow Bellamy here. There has to be something we're missing, and I think Bellamy knows what it is."

"I can't speak to that," Owen said, "but I can tell you how he thought to look here."

Both Chance and Emmett looked at him, eyebrows raised.

"I tracked Sam's movements in the months before she died," Owen said, "and I found something interesting. She booked a flight to La Conner two months before she disappeared."

"What?" Emmett and Chance yelled at the same time.

Mary and Sarah looked up from where they sat on the

other side of the waiting room.

Chance resumed his pacing, his mind working to connect the dots. "Sam's story, or the blackmail she has against Powell, has something to do with La Conner. Do we know what she did while she was here?"

"Here's where it gets interesting," Owen replied. "I tracked her movements on local security cameras. Don't ask me how. We're a small town, so there's not a lot of coverage, but I do know that she spent several hours on the east end. Over by the old Burke house."

Chance's head spun. "Bellamy's old house." His eyes went from Owen's face to Emmett's. "Maybe this isn't just about the story of Governor Powell's infidelity. She was working on the story of Bellamy's past."

"And whatever she found," Emmett continued, "got her killed."

CHAPTER 15

THE FIRST THING BELLAMY HEARD when she fought her way back to consciousness was the beeping of hospital machines. The antibacterial smell in the air made her head spin, even with her eyes closed.

The next thing she noticed was the pleasant floating sensation of pain medication. Even through that, though, she could sense the distant pain in her head.

Her eyes blinked open. It took her a moment to focus on the hospital room. It was dim, with only the glow from the monitors lighting the small area. Chance slouched in the chair next to the bed. Sarah curled up into a chair next to his, fast asleep.

Chance yawned and looked up. His eyes widened when they met hers.

"Thank God," he whispered. He leaned forward and took her hand in his. "How are you feeling?"

"Fine." She coughed. Her throat felt like sandpaper.

Chance handed her a small cup of water. Her hands shook as she lifted it, so he took it from her and held it to her lips. The cool water felt like heaven.

"Pain medication?" she asked after she had taken a few sips.

He nodded. "You have a concussion. You scared the hell out of me. God, I'm sorry I wasn't there, Bella."

Bellamy shook her head and grimaced when her head throbbed. "Wasn't your fault."

"I should have been there to protect you."

"Told you I don't need protection. I can protect myself."

"Yeah, you did. And you did a hell of a job."

Sarah stirred and sat up. "Bellamy!"

She threw herself onto the bed and wrapped Bellamy in a fierce embrace.

Pain made her dizzy, but at that moment, Bellamy didn't care. She smiled and patted Sarah's back with the hand that wasn't attached to the bed by an IV.

"Careful, Sarah," Chance chided.

Sarah sat back. She looked so sad that Bellamy reached out a hand to hers and squeezed.

"Don't apologize," she said. "You have nothing to be sorry for."

Sarah bit her lip and tears welled in her eyes. "I'm so glad you're okay."

"Me too."

Chance cleared his throat. "The police need to speak with you about what happened. Tom Hansen, a friend of ours, has been waiting for you to wake up."

"Tom Hansen, as in the one from high school? The one that used to follow Sarah around all the time?"

"The same one. He works for the police department now. The doctors did a CT scan while you were out. Everything looks okay, thank God. You have a concussion, but you can come home with us as soon as Tom gets your statement."

"Did they catch the guy?"

"Not yet." Chance's eyes turned hard. "But we will."

Something about that made the anxiety in her stomach finally settle. Bellamy nodded and struggled to sit up. "Get Tom in here then," she said. "I hate hospitals. I want to go home."

* * * * * *

Sarah flounced into ESI headquarters, her ponytail bouncing behind her. She had a bone to pick with Emmett, and nobody was going to stop her this time. Roman and the other team members looked up when the front door opened. The other two - she couldn't remember their names, nor did she care at the moment - didn't look concerned, but Roman shot her a disapproving look. She stuck her tongue out at him as she marched by.

He looked like he might retaliate, but a melodic ring sounded from his pocket and he turned away from her, holding his cell phone to his ear.

It was just as well. Sarah didn't know how to act around him since he'd kissed her.

That spine-tingling, toe-curling kiss.

She couldn't get it out of her mind, and she hated it. He had been nothing but rude to her since she'd met him a few days before. Men like him weren't her type - chauvinistic, rude, and condescending - and she wanted nothing to do with him.

But damn, that kiss.

Sarah shook her head at herself and stomped down the hall to Emmett's office. The door was closed, and she didn't knock before she flung it open.

Emmett and Owen both looked up in surprise at her entrance. She waggled a couple fingers in Owen's direction and he raised an eyebrow in response. But his expression was nothing compared to the irritation in Emmett's.

"I've got a bone to pick with you," Sarah huffed.

"Don't you ever knock?" Emmett sat back down in his chair, his back as straight as the stick he had shoved up his ass.

"What's up, sis?" Owen drawled. "Are you here on official business?"

"Yeah, I'm here to kick Emmett's ass into gear."

Emmett sighed impatiently. "For what reason?"

"Mom asked you to mow the lawn last week. Now it's all overgrown and there's weeds everywhere and Bellamy is coming over for dinner. It looks horrible. So get your butt out of that chair and go do some work."

Owen guffawed, then shut up when Emmett shot him a scathing look. "Sorry, bro," he said, "but you've had me so busy with all this research on Bellamy. I haven't had time."

Emmett scowled. "If I remember correctly, you're the one who's unemployed at the moment. Do it yourself."

Sarah opened her mouth to tell him exactly why she had no time for such things, but the door slammed open again. It almost hit her in the back, but she jumped out of the way just in time.

Roman stormed into the room.

"What's the matter?" Emmett demanded.

Roman cast a glance in Sarah's direction. The condescension in his eyes made her want to slap him. Instead, she felt her face flush. Before she could comment on his rudeness, though, he turned his attention back to Emmett.

"I've just heard from the team in charge of Susan Powell's protection."

"The governor's wife?" Sarah asked with interest. "Did she make it to the east coast?"

"No." Roman's jaw tightened. "She's dead."

Emmett pounded a fist on the table. Sarah jumped. "How?"

"I'm not sure yet. She was in a safe location, a hotel room, and she was supposed to board a plane to New York tonight. But she never showed. The security detail assigned to her didn't check in, so my contact went to the hotel to find them. They were all dead."

"How is that possible?" Owen demanded. "We've had eyes on Governor Powell all day. He hasn't made any suspicious contact with anyone. He hasn't even left his office."

Roman shook his head.

Sarah collapsed into one of the armchairs in front of Emmett's desk. "Bellamy is going to be devastated."

Emmett sat back in his chair. "This isn't right. Nothing about this case is right."

"Yeah, nothing makes sense. It's weird that we don't have much of a motive for this. How did Governor Powell kill Susan if he hasn't left his office all day? We're monitoring all his calls and emails. He couldn't have contacted anyone to order a hit without us knowing."

"It's about time we get some answers." Emmett stood up. "Sarah, go home and help Mom."

"What are you going to do?"

"Bellamy's at the center of this. It's about time she answers our questions." Emmett gestured at Roman and Owen to follow him and stormed out of the room.

Owen winked at Sarah as he passed by. "This ought to be a barrel of fun. Enjoy mowing the lawn!"

* * * * * *

"I don't think it's a good idea, Mom," Chance said. "Bellamy just got home from the hospital. She's not feeling up to eating right now."

His mother's sigh crackled through the phone. "The poor thing has been through a lot," she fretted. "She needs a good meal and family around her right now."

"I'm fine," Bellamy said irritably.

Chance raised his eyebrows. She was curled up on the couch, hair sticking up in all directions, face pale, a dark bruise forming on her cheek.

Yeah. Clearly fine.

"I am," she insisted. "How about tomorrow?"

"Did she say tomorrow?" Mary said in Chance's ear. "Tomorrow would be perfect! Be here by six."

"Mom, I don't - "

Mary hung up.

Chance sighed and shoved the phone into his pocket. "I thought you didn't want to associate with your old life while you're here."

Bellamy shrugged. "Mary's cooking sounds pretty good right about now. A near-death experience will do that to you."

Her flippant tone pissed him off. "You're right; you came damn close to death today. I covered our tracks, so I'd really like to know how Powell tracked you here."

"How should I know? He's a man with many resources, I guess."

Right. And Chance was an incompetent idiot.

He gritted his teeth. Emmett's accusations niggled his way back into his mind. There were so many threads unraveling this mystery, and Bellamy seemed to be in the center of all of them. The more she resisted his help, the more he wondered if this case wasn't so much about Sam as it was about Bellamy herself.

One thing hadn't changed in the past ten years, though.

Despite Bellamy's bravado, Chance could tell when she was in pain.

He didn't know the cause; Sam's death, the attack, her injuries, or life in general.

The haunted look in her eyes was still there, no matter how thick she built the walls around herself.

Now wasn't the time to ask all the questions burning in

his gut.

Chance cleared his throat and crossed the room to grab a blanket from the closet. He tucked it around her, careful not to jostle her too much.

"I'm fine, Chance." Her voice was still sharp, but she didn't bat him away.

"Are you hungry? You haven't eaten since breakfast."

Bellamy wrinkled her nose. "I'm not sure I'll be able to keep anything down."

"Chicken noodle soup," Chance said. "That'll be easy to keep down."

When he returned a few minutes later, her eyes were closed. Panic gripped him for a moment, but he took a breath and reminded himself that the doctors said she should be fine to rest. He just had to wake her every two hours to make sure no other symptoms presented.

Between Emmett's football career and his time in the military, he was plenty familiar with concussion care, but the fact that it was Bellamy suffering set him on edge.

He set the bowl of soup on the coffee table and settled into his armchair to watch her sleep.

Two hours later, he woke her and warmed up the soup. This time she ate without protest, eyes heavy-lidded. When she was finished, she settled back against the pillow. "Thank you."

"For what?"

"Taking care of me. Haven't had someone do that in a long time."

Chance's gut twisted, but he forced a smile. "I'm happy to do it."

If he had anything to say about it, she wouldn't have to worry about that ever again.

Bellamy's expression softened. She must've had some pain medication in her system still, because she looked more relaxed than he had ever seen her.

"Tell me about you," she said softly. "Tell me about all the things I've missed."

Chance settled onto the couch and lifted her legs so they rested on his lap. She shifted a little, her body warm against his. "Where to begin," he said. "You know I was in the Marines."

"Yeah, tell me about that. Did you like it?"

"It was the hardest five years of my life, but I'm glad I joined. We helped a lot of people. I saw - and did - a lot of things I'll never forget. But because of that, I had the knowledge and connections to create ESI. Now I get to choose our missions, and I love it. I love that we get to help so many people. People like you."

Bellamy smiled a little, her eyelids drooping. "I like that. You would make a good Marine. I always thought that."

Chance took her hand and rubbed his thumb over her palm. She didn't pull away. "I joined because of you. Every person I helped, I saw your face."

"I always knew you would join a profession like that. You're just that kind of person. You didn't need me to motivate you."

"I think you made me that kind of person, Bella."

She shook her head, eyes closed. "No, I didn't. It's just who you are."

Chance would've argued the point further, but her

hand relaxed in his. Just like that, she was asleep again.

A little while later, a knock on the door had him rising to his feet. Bellamy stirred and opened her eyes. "What is it?" she asked.

"Someone's here. Stay put. I'll go see who it is."

Chance hit the button on the panel next to the door to see Emmett, Owen, and Roman standing on the front porch. As usual, Emmett looked like he'd swallowed a lemon, but even Owen and Roman looked grave.

Chance buzzed them in and opened the front door.

"What are you doing here?" he asked in a low voice.

"We need to talk about what happened today," Emmett said. "There's some new information on the case."

"She's been through enough today, don't you think?"

"We need to get to the bottom of this."

"Now's not the time."

Emmett glared. "If this was any other victim, you wouldn't pussy-foot around it."

"This isn't just any victim," Chance said. "This is Bellamy, and she's been through enough."

Emmett ignored him and shoved past and into the living room. Chance hurried after him, wondering if he could get a good right hook in before Owen separated them.

Bellamy looked up when they entered. She didn't look surprised. "Emmett. What did you find out?"

Roman slipped in behind Emmett and cleared his throat. "Since we didn't have any luck with phone records, I had a friend in Seattle tail Governor Powell. He's had meetings with some shady people, and thanks to Owen's computer hacking skills, we ID'd them. They're involved in a crime ring that's been smuggling weapons in through Portland."

"Weapons. Right."

Chance stepped into the room. Her voice was a little too high-pitched to mimic true surprise.

"Apparently the FBI has been tracking the ring for a while. Governor Powell was arrested this afternoon, and we're working with the FBI to build their case against him."

"About time," Bellamy said, sagging against the pillows. She didn't meet Chance's gaze.

"There's something else," Emmett said. "About Susan Powell."

Chance's gaze flashed to Owen, who confirmed his fears with a slight nod. He stepped in front of Bellamy as if to shield her. "I don't think now's the time for this," he muttered to Emmett.

"There's not going to be a better time."

"What?" Bellamy demanded. All sleepiness was gone from her expression. "What happened to Susan?"

"Susan never got on the plane to the east coast," Owen said. "She had a ticket, but she never went to the airport."

Bellamy's face drained of all color.

Chance muttered a curse and sank down next to her on the couch, taking her hand. It was shaking.

"Where is she?"

"Her body was found by police when they arrested Governor Powell." Emmett's tone was clinical. "He'll be charged with murder in addition to his other charges."

"Oh God," Bellamy breathed. She gripped Chance's hand like it was her last lifeline to sanity. "I guess that's it, then. Thank you for everything you've done. I'll never be able to repay you."

"Not so fast," Emmett interrupted. "I don't think this case is closed."

"W-What? Why not?"

"Like I've been saying from the beginning, there's more to the story here."

Bellamy's skin was devoid of all color. She didn't respond, just stared at Emmett, waiting for him to explain.

"We need you to tell us what happened tonight."

Bellamy looked from Emmett to Chance and back again. "You're not going to give me an explanation?"

Emmett didn't respond.

Owen gave a resigned sigh and sank into the armchair in the corner.

Chance clenched his fists. As much as he wanted to throw Emmett out and go back to the cozy moment he'd been enjoying with Bellamy, it was too late for that now. Emmett was like a dog with a bone, and he wouldn't leave until Bellamy answered his questions.

And damn it, even though he didn't want to hurt her, Chance wanted those questions answered too.

"Owen examined the alley where you were attacked," he said quietly. "He found fingerprints on the gun. They match yours."

"Well, yeah. I shot the bastard."

"Only your prints," Emmett said. "That gun wasn't the attacker's, was it? It was yours."

Bellamy's jaw set. She stared at them all for a long moment, expression hard. "So what if it was?"

"It's a black market weapon," Emmett said sharply. "There's no serial number on it. How did you get it?"

Bellamy shook off Chance's hand and stood, circling around the back of the couch so she could face all of them.

Chance slowly stood as well. He hated feeling like they were ganging up on her, but the avalanche had already begun. He couldn't stop it now even if he tried.

"Bellamy, it's okay. We just want to understand," he said.

"Understand?" she snorted. "All you've done since the beginning is suspect me. Believe it or not, I'm the innocent one here."

"If you were innocent in this mess, you wouldn't have a problem answering our questions."

"Emmett," Chance snapped.

"No," Bellamy said, crossing her arms over her chest. "Let him finish."

Chance gritted his teeth and the look he gave Emmett would have withered any other man. Owen leaned forward in his chair, his gaze intent on the drama unfolding. Roman stood aloof, his expression unreadable as he watched the exchange.

"You may have been one of the family when we were young," Emmett said, voice hard, "but that was ten years ago. You left. I watched my brother go through hell trying to find you. He hasn't been the same since."

Bellamy shifted, but she didn't say anything.

"Now you waltz back into his life ten years later, you come to my father's funeral like you actually cared about him. Now that you've got a psychopathic killer on your tail, you ask for my brother's help. We know nothing about where you've been or what you were doing. I'm not going to stand around while you take advantage of Chance and my family again. If you're truly innocent, then you have a hell of a way of showing it."

"Emmett. That's enough." Chance spoke the words through clenched teeth, and finally Emmett went silent.

Bellamy's face was expressionless as she looked Emmett up and down. "I don't expect you to understand my situation," she said. Her voice was devoid of anything except cold regard for Emmett. "You have no idea what I've done to survive this long, and I don't feel like sharing that with you. For your information, I have a lot of contacts in Portland and Seattle. I got that gun so I could protect myself. If there's one thing I've learned in the last ten years, it's that I can't rely on anyone to save me - including you and your team. If I want to stay alive, that's my responsibility and mine alone. So yeah, I carry a gun. If I didn't, I would be dead right now.

"As for you, Emmett, you've been so busy suspecting me that you've been looking in all the wrong places. Powell won't stay in jail long, and you're too busy chasing me to find the proper evidence you'll need to get him convicted. Since I'm feeling charitable, I'll help you out."

Bellamy looked at Owen. "Use your fancy computer and look up Northeast Marx Street. About, say, 2 nights ago. Three o'clock in the morning. If you look at the traffic cameras in the area, you'll find all the evidence you need to get Powell locked somewhere he'll never get out of."

Owen pulled out his phone and started typing

something on the screen.

Emmett raised an eyebrow. "And how would you know that?"

"I have my sources. If you want me to trust you, that road goes both ways. The truth is," she continued, looking down her nose at Emmett, "you aren't the same Emmett that I remember. You were always the big brother type, protective and overbearing. You were the one who protected me from those bullies in third grade; the one who taught me to swing a baseball bat. I went to you for advice when I wanted to try out for the soccer team. I looked up to you, but the man I'm looking at right now doesn't even deserve an explanation. You're hard now, and not the older brother I remember. I don't need your help. I'll take care of this on my own, just like I always do."

With those words, she turned on her heel and left the living room. They listened to her slow footsteps climbing the stairs, the only sound in the house, followed by a door slamming in the distance.

"Well done," Chance snapped.

Emmett's eyes remained on the doorway where Bellamy had disappeared. He didn't respond to Chance's jab.

Owen stood and cleared his throat. "That didn't go according to plan," he muttered. "Sorry, Chance."

"It was a conversation that needed to happen." Emmett's words were low, rough. "Check out that address she mentioned, Owen. See if there's anything there."

"Already on it."

Emmett sighed and rolled his shoulders. His expression was pained; it was the first emotion Chance had seen from him since they'd showed up on his doorstep. "She's right; I'm not the same man I used to be."

Chance sighed. He wanted to be angry at Emmett for upsetting Bellamy, but he couldn't help feeling a pang of sympathy for his brother. Nobody in the family knew what happened on Emmett's last mission with the SEALs. Whatever it was, it had changed him forever. After a month in the hospital, Emmett was released and he'd refused to talk about it since.

Sometimes, though, Chance caught him staring off into the distance, and the pain in his eyes was a punch to the gut.

"We've all changed," Owen said. He rested a hand on Emmett's shoulder. "Not just you."

Roman nodded his agreement, his own expression tight.

Chance rubbed a hand through his hair. The whole situation was a mess and he didn't know how to proceed. "Look, why don't you guys just head home for the night?" He sighed. "I know you're worried about me, but you can't attack her like that, Emmett. She's been through a lot. We might not know what all of it is, but she won't ever trust us if we treat her like a criminal."

A muscle worked in Emmett's jaw, but he didn't answer. Instead he gave a terse nod.

Owen clapped Emmett on the shoulder and led him toward the front door. He turned at the last moment and inclined his head to Chance. "See you for dinner tomorrow night."

Chance's stomach knotted with dread.

Right. Family dinner tomorrow.

He was looking forward to that about as much as getting kicked in the junk.

CHAPTER 16

*"**COME ON, BABY**, we have to go."*

Her mother's words were fierce. Bella shook herself out of her reverie. She stood frozen in the doorway of her bedroom as her mother threw a bunch of clothes into a small suitcase. She couldn't force herself to step inside. Flashes of the night before kept coming to mind. A shudder ran through her body.

"Where are we going?" She rubbed her hands up and down her arms and glanced down the hallway for the millionth time. "Where's Papa?"

"I don't know. He left this morning." Her mother hauled the suitcase over her shoulder and pushed past Bella to continue down the hall toward the stairs leading to the front

of the house. "We need to go before he gets back."

"But where are we going?"

Her mother huffed out a breath. Her damp hair was falling out of its bun. She pushed the loose strands out of her face and tucked them behind her ears. "The bus station. Put this in the car, please."

Bella grabbed the suitcase and hurried out to the waiting car in the driveway. It was a beat-up old Honda, the same one her mother had been driving around for as long as Bella could remember. The engine was still warm from the trip home from Chance's house.

Bella slid the suitcase into the backseat and took one last look at her house. She wasn't sad that they were leaving, but she did regret not saying goodbye to Chance. She'd left so early this morning that Chance had still been asleep. Bella had heard the telltale sound of the Honda's sputtery, clacking engine and had known it was time to go.

She climbed into the passenger's seat and took a deep breath. She would reach out to him once they were settled and let him know she was okay. He'd be glad, she was sure of it.

A few minutes later, they pulled up to the Greyhound bus station at the end of town. It consisted of a one-man ticket booth and a small bench next to the road. It was a miracle that La Conner even had a bus station. Bella hadn't known about it until just then.

She followed her mother to the ticket counter and stood by while she bought tickets.

"One ticket for Denver, please."

Bella jerked her head toward her mother's voice and

took a step closer. "Why only one?" she whispered. "Aren't you coming with me?"

Bella's mother shook her head. Her eyes were sad. "I can't leave your papa here."

"Who cares about him? Come with me," Bella pleaded.

Her mother smiled and enfolded Bella in a warm hug. "I can't," she repeated. "But you have to go."

"I'm not going without you."

"You have to. You can't stay here, baby."

"What about you? What are you going to do if I'm not around?"

Her mother smiled and pushed Bella's hair behind one ear with shaking fingers. "I'll be fine. Your uncle David will take good care of you."

Bella shook her head, tears swimming in her vision. "I'm not going. I won't."

The dove pendant around her mother's neck glinted in the early morning sunlight as she bent down to retrieve Bella's forgotten suitcase. She pushed the bag into Bella's arms and handed her the bus ticket. "Please, baby. Just do this for me." She nodded toward the bus that had just pulled into the station. "Your freedom is on that bus. I may not have the luxury of leaving, but you do."

Bella shook her head again, but she knew her mother wouldn't take no for an answer this time. She sobbed and threw her arms around her.

Bella's mother squeezed her back, hard, and Bella could feel her body shaking. When she pulled away, her eyes were bright. "I love you."

"I love you too." Bella wiped her eyes on her sleeve and

squared her shoulders. "I'll call you every day."

"I know."

Bella carried her bag over to the bus and put it in the storage compartment. She handed the bus driver her ticket and hurried to a seat near the back so she could look out the window one last time.

Her mother stood alone at the bus station as Bella pulled away. She looked sad and alone, but she smiled and waved until the bus turned the corner and she disappeared from Bella's sight.

* * * * * *

"Bella!" Chance's voice was loud in her ears. "Wake up. Baby, wake up."

Bella snapped to consciousness. Loud screaming echoed in her bedroom. Annoyed, she opened her eyes to tell Chance to knock it off, but quickly realized the screaming was coming from her.

Chance sat on the bed next to her and drew her close so she was almost on his lap. He held her head to his chest. She could hear his rapid heartbeat against her cheek.

"It's okay," he murmured. "I've got you. You're fine."

Bellamy took a ragged breath and tried to quell her panic. She counted backwards from twenty in her head and forced herself to inventory the things around her.

Heavy cotton comforter. Light blue paint on the walls. The smell of Chance's shampoo.

She took another deep breath and felt a little more grounded. She reminded herself again that the past was behind her and forced herself to believe it.

"S-Sorry," she said. "I'm fine now."

Chance didn't move. His hand remained in her hair, holding her head to his chest. "Nightmare?"

Bellamy nodded.

"You get those often?"

"Depends on the week."

He took a deep, shuddering breath and released her. She leaned back, but she didn't move away from him. His eyes were dark in the dim light emanating from the open doorway. "I get them sometimes, too."

"You do?"

"Mm."

His chest was warm under her hands. His heartbeat had returned to a normal rhythm, steady and strong. She would give anything to feel that way.

Strong. Steady.

No longer afraid.

"... Thanks," she muttered softly, lifting her hands away from the warmth.

He nodded. "How's your head?"

"It hurts."

"Okay. Here's some tylenol. Take this and try to get some more sleep." He handed her the pills and a glass of water and watched her take them. "I'll see you in the morning."

He stood to leave, but Bellamy grabbed his hand. The thought of being alone in the dark made her skin crawl. Her whole life, she was always alone in the dark.

She was tired of it.

Chance looked down at her, wordlessly asking what she needed, and she showed him.

She yanked hard on his hand, pulling him toward her, and let go to throw both of her arms around his neck. Their lips crashed together without a sound.

Warmth flooded through her, washing away the fear and the dark and the cold. For once, she could only focus on one thing; Chance, and the way he felt against her.

He was what she needed. If she could feel like this every day, maybe the darkness wouldn't swallow her.

Maybe...

Chance's hands settled on her shoulders. Instead of pulling her closer, though, he gently pushed her away.

Their lips separated.

The only sound in the room was their ragged breathing.

Chance looked down at her. His expression wasn't angry like she'd expected. Instead, he looked sad.

"Bella," he whispered. "As much as I'd like to kiss you senseless, I'm not going to do it right now."

"Why?" Bellamy tugged on his shirt again, urging him closer. Needing his warmth.

"Because," he said, capturing her hands in his and moving them to her lap, "I'm not a medication to make you feel better."

Bellamy gritted her teeth, feeling stupid. Of course he didn't want her. She was an idiot -

Chance dropped a kiss on her forehead and straightened, leaving her sitting on the edge of the mattress. "Don't overthink it. When you want to kiss me for the right reason, trust me, I'll be a willing participant. But for now, you need to get some rest."

After a long moment, she nodded and slid back under the blanket.

Chance stood next to the bed for a moment like he wanted to say something more, but he nodded at her again and left the room. He left the door open a crack, probably so he could hear her if she called out again. Despite her embarrassment, the gesture warmed her heart.

She sank down onto the pillow and closed her eyes, but she knew sleep wouldn't come easily now. Her lips still tingled from Chance's kiss.

It was going to be a long night.

* * * * * *

Owen snapped awake when the soft "ding" from his computer alerted him to a new hit. He squinted at the smart watch on his wrist and groaned.

Ten a.m. He'd been up all night again.

What was that now? His fourth in a row?

His brothers (a.k.a slave drivers) seemed to think that he just pushed a button and sat back to relax while his computer did all the work on these cases.

Ha. If only that was so.

Someone had to program the search algorithm and monitor the results. It was an around-the-clock kind of job.

Not that he didn't love it. He really did.

Computers spoke a language he understood. Simple ones and zeroes, strung together in a logical pattern anyone who knew the language could follow.

People, on the other hand? Not so logical, and definitely not simple.

The mess from the night before was still fresh in Owen's mind. He and Bellamy had never been close, but something about the argument with Emmett had set Owen on edge. He didn't claim to know people, but he felt the same gut feeling that Emmett did. Bellamy was hiding something.

On the other hand, though, weren't they all?

It's not like it was his business what she did in her free time.

Owen's job was simple; use the tech to catch the bad guy. That's all he wanted to focus on.

As soon as they returned from Chance's house, Owen had gotten to work. His computer system had been running a dual search all night long; namely, on the address that Bellamy had given him.

But that wasn't the search that had yielded a hit.

Owen clicked a few buttons on his keyboard and squinted at the too-bright screen. He'd been running facial and license plate recognition on the traffic cameras surrounding the area of Bellamy's attack - that was the second search his computer had been running all night.

Finally, he'd gotten a hit.

And boy was it a doozy.

One of the cars in the area - a gray Camry - was registered to Jonathan Burke.

Bellamy's father.

Owen's mouth fell open.

"What the..." he breathed.

He pulled out his phone and pressed a button.

The other line answered on the first ring.

"Emmett," he said. "Get down here now. You won't believe what I've found."

* * * * * *

Chance drew both arms above his head in a long stretch. He'd been on the phone all day; he needed a break. Ronald Powell had been booked on suspicion of murder and smuggling charges, his FBI inside man had told him. However, they didn't have any solid evidence to keep him there for long. He'd already called for a lawyer. Any time now, he would use his money and influence to force the police to release him.

Which meant that Bellamy was safe for now, but it wouldn't last long.

They needed to find some evidence to convict Powell, and fast.

Chance's phone rang again and he pushed the button to answer it on speaker phone. "Erickson," he said.

"Chance." It was Owen's voice.

"What'd you find?"

"Emmett's here too. I was following up on the attack and I found something pretty interesting."

Chance waited, but Owen drew the pause out for effect. "Well?"

"I found a vehicle - not the van, a different car - leaving the area after Bellamy's attack. It was registered to Jonathan Burke."

Chance couldn't have been more surprised if the devil himself appeared and danced a jig on top of his desk. "Excuse me?"

"You heard right, bro. Bellamy's dad is in town."

Chance leaned back in his chair and stared at the ceiling. "What does that mean?"

"It means this case has more twists and turns than a bent corkscrew."

"There's more," Emmett added.

"Yeah, I started doing some digging into Burke's accounts - Bellamy's dad, not Bellamy herself - and found something crazy." Owen's words came faster with excitement. He lived for this kind of thing.

"Can it get any crazier than the fact that he's back in town?"

"Oh yes it can. I retraced his steps from the time he disappeared seven years ago. It wasn't easy; there's not a lot of surveillance footage still around from back then. Luckily, you've employed the real-life technological Sherlock Holmes." Owen paused again, as if he was waiting for Chance to sing his praises.

He didn't.

"I tracked the money trail and it looks like he headed southeast."

"Okay. To where?"

"It seemed random at first, but get this. Remember the story in the paper about Bellamy when she was arrested? Right around the same time that story broke, the trail leads to Colorado. The last transaction on his bank account was at a gas station about 30 miles outside of Denver."

An empty hole opened in the pit of his stomach. "Wasn't Bellamy in Denver?"

"Yeah. He found her."

Chance had been pacing behind his desk, but at this news he sat down hard in his office chair. "She hasn't mentioned anything about seeing him again."

"I don't think it's a coincidence," Emmett said. "She had to have known he was there."

"Where did he go after that?"

"Nowhere," Owen replied. "The trail stops after that. No financial activity, no parking tickets, nothing. It's like he disappeared."

"Is it possible he dropped off the radar to avoid being followed?"

"Come on, Chance, you're not stupid," Emmett said. "The timing is too eerie. He showed up just days after that story hit the news. Why would he make the trip all the way there and then go off the grid?"

"I don't know." Chance took a deep breath in an attempt to calm himself. "But if she'd seen him, why wouldn't she say anything?"

"Maybe she killed him."

"Now you're just being ridiculous," Chance snapped. "Bellamy was terrified of her father. If she saw him, she would run the other way, not attack him. And besides, that license plate Owen found puts him back in town this week. The question is, why?"

"And did he have something to do with Bellamy's attack?" Emmett sighed. "None of this is adding up. We've got Powell up in Seattle who wants Bellamy dead, and now apparently we've got her missing father returned from purgatory or wherever the hell he was, and he wants her dead too. A lot of people seem to be after her, and she's still refusing to give us any information so we can help her."

"Don't you think it's possible that she doesn't have any information to give?"

"Can you guys focus on the case at hand instead of attacking each other all the time?" Owen interrupted. "You're acting like two teenage girls fighting over the last tampon. How about we all calm down and act like professionals?"

Chance would have laughed at Owen's analogy, but he had too many troubling thoughts swirling around in his head. Emmett was also silent.

"Everyone is coming over to Mom's for dinner tonight," Owen continued. "She's really looking forward to it. I think everyone needs a quiet night at home with family. I shouldn't have to tell my two older brothers to act their age, but I'll bite the bullet on this one. Grow the eff up. Got it?"

Chance and Emmett remained silent.

"Thank you. I'll keep digging into this and see what else I can find. In the meantime, act like adults. See you tonight."

CHAPTER 17

"BELLAMY," MARY EXCLAIMED as she threw open the front door. "Oh, my, come inside. You're soaked." She enfolded Bellamy in a warm hug and Bellamy blinked away the tears that sprang to her eyes. She was suddenly twelve again, running through the halls with Chance and Sarah, giggling and shrieking with laughter. Back when the only worry she had was whether Papa would be drinking that night.

Mary pulled back, tut-tutting over their rain-soaked appearance. "Chance, the least you could do was give the poor girl an umbrella. It's not like it was a surprise that it would rain today. They've been talking about it on the news for a week. It's so good to see you, sweetheart."

Bellamy smiled back at her. To her surprise, it was an

easy thing to do.

"Go help Owen and Emmett with the grill," Mary continued, shooing Chance toward the back door. "Lord knows they could use your assistance with the steaks."

Chance squeezed Bellamy's shoulder once, a gesture of comfort, and followed his mother's directions. Mary took Bellamy's hand and led her into the kitchen. It looked the same as Bellamy remembered. Tile countertops, worn oak cabinets, and an old wooden table that could seat the whole family.

Sarah stood at the kitchen island, her gaze focused on the small TV that sat in the corner on the counter. She looked up when they entered and smiled at Bellamy before directing her gaze to her mother. "They said this storm is supposed to be a bad one."

"I heard the reports," Mary replied, bustling to the counter to cut vegetables.

"It's even worse than the initial reports," Sarah insisted. "It's not supposed to stop raining for at least a week. People are saying we'll flood long before that."

"The river has flooded before," Mary replied. "We're a ways back. I'm sure it won't affect us."

Sarah looked doubtful.

Bellamy pulled out a chair from the table and sank into it. The familiar creak was music to her ears. "I missed this kitchen," she said, surprising herself yet again.

Sarah grinned. "Me too. The worst thing about living in New York is missing family dinner every Sunday. And your cooking, of course, Mom."

"I'm glad you're both back," Mary said. "It's nice to

have the whole family together again." Her face fell. "Well, almost the whole family."

Sarah wrapped an arm around her mother's shoulders and squeezed.

"I'm happy to be here," Bellamy said.

Mary cleared her throat and smiled. " I know things must be hard for you right now. With everything going on, I just want you to know that even after all these years, I still consider you my second daughter. And you always will be. Once an Erickson, always an Erickson."

Those words meant more to Bellamy than she would ever admit. She may have resigned herself to a life on her own, but it was nice to know someone still cared. "Thank you. I wish everyone felt that way."

"What do you mean?" Mary looked offended.

"Emmett," Sarah explained, rolling her eyes. "He's got this weird thing about Bellamy being back. He's suspicious."

"I don't blame him," Bellamy said. "I haven't seen you in ten years and now I've shown up out of the blue and brought trouble right to your doorstep. I wouldn't trust me either."

"Nonsense," Mary said. "Family is the same, whether it's been ten years or ten minutes. But you have to understand, Emmett's been through a lot in the last few years too. He was a Navy SEAL. Did you know that?"

"Yeah, Sarah mentioned it to me in her letters."

"He was with the SEALs for a long time. Because of the nature of his missions, we never knew where he was or if he was safe. On his last mission, something went wrong. He was severely wounded and ended up in a military hospital for six weeks. He doesn't talk about what happened, but he's been a changed man ever since he got home. His physical wounds are gone, but I think he's still healing. So be patient with him."

Bellamy looked at her hands clasped on the table in front of her. She thought about her comments the night before and suddenly felt like the biggest jerk. No wonder he'd looked so stricken before she stomped out of the room. "I'm sorry. I didn't know."

Mary smiled kindly. "We all have wounds that we don't want to reopen. Sarah tells me that you're a photographer. How did you come into that?"

Sarah leaned forward, resting her elbows on the island, and looked at Bellamy with interest.

Bellamy usually made it a policy to never disclose anything beyond what was required, but the kindness in Mary's eyes made her reconsider. She hadn't felt like she was part of a family since she'd spent so much time with the Ericksons in her childhood. It made her feel warm and comforted, and even though she knew it wouldn't last forever, she wanted to bask in it while she could.

It's not like they were asking her to relive some of her darkest moments. The least she could do was share what she could.

"It was a happy coincidence," she said. "I was eighteen and I didn't have a job or a place to live, so I was panhandling to get what I could."

The memories were still so vivid. It had been a cold winter day. Bellamy had been standing for hours in a large park in Portland. She had managed to hitchhike that far from Colorado, anything to get away from her uncle.

"A girl came up to me and told me she could give me some money, but only if I helped her in return. She gave me a camera and some hot coffee, and the rest is history."

Bellamy would never know if she'd helped at all with the shoot that day, or if Sam had just taken pity on her and offered her the position as an apprentice. Either way, it had saved her life. Bellamy knew what could have happened to her if she'd stayed on the streets much longer. She would forever be grateful for Sam's kindness that day.

"Sam is the one who got you off the streets?" Mary asked. "I wish I could thank her."

Bellamy smiled sadly. "Me too. I wouldn't be alive today if it wasn't for her. I wish I could've returned the favor, but instead I might have gotten her killed."

"What happened to her isn't your fault."

Bellamy stiffened at the new voice. Mary and Sarah followed her gaze to Emmett, who leaned against the doorjamb with his arms crossed over his chest. His eyes were steady on Bellamy's face.

She hadn't seen him since their confrontation the night before. After the way they had left things, it was a shock he was speaking to her at all.

"Can I talk to you?" he asked.

Bellamy glanced at Mary and Sarah. She didn't really want to get into it with him again today, but they both gave her smiles of encouragement.

Steeling herself, she followed Emmett out of the kitchen.

He led her through the mud room and outside to the

back deck. Chance and Owen stood arguing over the large grill on the right side, so Emmett led her off to the left.

Miraculously, the dark clouds hovering over La Conner all day had dissipated, leaving the backyard rain-soaked and glistening. The sun had barely set, casting an orange glow on the river at the bottom of the hill. The slow-moving water flickered like it was on fire.

Emmett leaned against the railing, his gaze off into the distance.

After a moment's hesitation, Bellamy followed suit and rested her elbows on the wood next to him.

A moment of silence passed.

"I know you don't trust me," Bellamy said. "But I'm not keeping secrets on purpose."

Emmett didn't acknowledge her.

Okay. This was off to a great start. She waited a moment, took a deep breath and continued. "It's not that I don't want to share my story. I just… can't. I've been damaged by a lot of things, Emmett. There's a reason I never came back here, why I never contacted Chance. I'm not the same person I used to be, and I can never go back to that. I hired ESI because I couldn't face Powell without backup. That's all. Once this is over, I won't be sticking around. I know I don't fit here anymore, and that's fine. But I swear I had nothing to do with Sam's death. If you believe anything I've said, believe that."

Emmett turned to her. His expression was fierce. "Our past doesn't have to shape who we are. Bad things happen to good people, but it's what you do with those experiences that matters." He sighed. "You're not the only one who's changed. I've seen a lot of terrible things in the world, Bellamy, and sometimes that influences my point of view. I won't let anyone hurt my family, and you've already hurt Chance once. If you're telling the truth, just know that I'll have your back. All of ESI will."

Bellamy inclined her head. That was probably the closest she'd ever get to an apology from him. Her heart hurt a little, because she wasn't telling the truth. Not entirely.

She'd meant what she said to Mary and Sarah.

Sam's death was her fault. If she hadn't gotten herself associated with Powell and his black market dealings, Sam might still be alive.

Bellamy would have to live with that, and lying to the Ericksons, for the rest of her life.

Dinner with the Ericksons was just like Bellamy remembered it. None of them spoke about their current problems; instead, they spent their time reminiscing about the past and catching up on everything they'd missed.

"Sarah's going to some fancy college to be a doctor," Owen teased, "and I'm stuck here working in the family business with these two idiots." He gestured to Emmett and Chance with a thumb and rolled his eyes theatrically.

"These idiots are paying you more than you're worth," Emmett growled over everyone's laughter.

"And that, big brother, is why I haven't left."

Sarah shook her head, smiling, and exchanged an exasperated look with Chance.

Bellamy stole a glance at her friend. Why hadn't she told her family that she didn't want to be a doctor? The Ericksons were so warm and open; of course they wouldn't judge her for that decision.

Next time Bellamy got Sarah alone, she would ask.

"Chance is the one with all the money here," Owen complained, continuing his tirade. "He's got the biggest house and he does the least work."

"Hey now, that's not fair. I founded the company. I'm entitled to some days off."

"All the days off, apparently," Emmett said, rolling his eyes.

"You wanna go?"

The challenge was all the men needed. They bulldozed out the back door, shoving and punching each other. A wrestling match ensued. The sounds of laughter and yelling carried into the kitchen through the open window.

"Don't they know it's raining?" Mary asked, exasperated. She rose to her feet and grabbed a dish towel off the kitchen island, bustling toward the back door. "They're going to catch cold."

"What's she going to do with the towel?" Bellamy asked Sarah.

"Whip their asses, probably," Sarah replied, eyes twinkling.

The women shared a giggle, and it was like they were fourteen again.

Bellamy wished that it could go on forever.

* * * * * *

After everyone had eaten their fill and helped with the dishes, Chance made their excuses and he and Bellamy ran through the rain to his truck.

As they splashed through the rain-soaked streets, Chance's heart swelled. There was a lightness to Bellamy that hadn't been there when they first saw each other again at his father's funeral. The serious, spunky girl he'd come to know still made her appearance, but her edges were a bit softer lately.

Chance liked to think he had a hand in that.

He made a left turn a few minutes later and grinned when Bellamy turned to frown at him.

"Isn't your house the other way?" she asked.

Her nose did a cute wrinkle thing when she was thinking hard. Chance almost commented on it, but it was likely to get him slapped. So instead, he said, "We're not going home yet. I have a surprise for you."

Her eyebrows rose. He could almost see the gears turning in her head as she turned to look out the window again. It didn't take her long to recognize the scenery. A wide grin split her face. "Are we going where I think we're going?"

"Maybe."

Chance maneuvered the truck onto a muddy road. The trees grew thick here, forming a narrow tunnel that his truck barely fit through. Eventually it opened up again and they emerged into a small clearing.

Chance parked the vehicle and leaned back in his seat, watching Bellamy's reaction.

"It still looks exactly the same," she breathed. Drawing her hood up over her head, she threw open the door and jumped out.

Chance met her in front of his truck. He glanced down. The mud was deep enough to reach his ankles. They'd both need new shoes after this was over, but the delight in her expression was worth it.

They stood in a small clearing next to the river. The water flowed dark and gray in front of them, swollen from the continued rain. An old log bench sat closer to the river than Chance remembered.

Bellamy stepped up to the bench and ran her hand over the aged wood. She grinned when her fingers reached the initials carved into the top: BB and CE.

"I can't believe this is still here," she exclaimed. "Look how high the river has gotten. It's almost reached the bench."

Chance stepped up beside her. There had once been a good fifteen feet between the bench and the river's edge, but now there were only two or three. "I guess the news reports weren't kidding."

Bellamy nodded. Chance watched her expression as her eyes traveled around the clearing. He could tell that the sun was sinking low behind the ever-present gray clouds. He swept some standing water off the bench and sat down, patting the spot next to him. Bellamy hesitated for a moment before settling next to him, their hips less than an inch apart.

The memory of her lips against his flashed across his mind.

"I can't believe it hasn't changed," she murmured.

Chance cleared his throat. "I came here a lot after you disappeared," he admitted. "I would sit on this bench for hours."

"Really?"

"Mm." He chuckled. "My parents and siblings would call and call, but they don't know where this place is. They couldn't come find me and drag me home, even though they threatened to."

Bellamy's smile faded and she turned to look at him. The approaching darkness turned her blue eyes a stark gray, a perfect match to the sky above them. Time stretched into eternity as their gazes locked.

"I'm so sorry, Chance," she said. "For everything I put you through."

Chance shook his head. He'd spent so many years feeling angry; at her, at God, at the world. Now that she was back in his life, though, he couldn't direct that anger at her anymore. "I know it wasn't your fault."

Bellamy shifted so one leg was underneath her, the other hanging off the side of the bench. "No, I don't deserve your forgiveness. I should have called you. I should have called as soon as I was able - "

Chance reached over and covered her icy hands with his. He squeezed gently, but she didn't stop talking.

"I was so selfish. I still am. I only think about myself and my own problems. I've made so many mistakes, Chance. If I had reached out to you sooner - "

"Bellamy."

" - then maybe I could've caught you before you joined

the Marines - "

"Bella."

" - and maybe I could have come back sooner and we could've - "

Chance's hands framed her face and finally, she stopped talking.

"I'm going to kiss you." He kept his voice quiet. "Not like you've kissed me twice now, in the heat of the moment. Although that was nice."

Her eyes were wide on his face.

"No, I'm going to kiss you right now, and I want us both to fully understand what we're doing this time. No running away, no filling any emotional voids. Just you and me, two people who have been waiting too damn long for this moment. Do you understand?"

Bellamy nodded.

"May I kiss you, Bella?"

Swallowing hard, she nodded again.

Finally. Chance pulled her toward him until their lips met. It wasn't as gentle as he intended. Their lips melded in the way that he'd always wanted them to. Rain pelted their hair, dripping down their faces, mingling with their warm skin. The only sound around them was rain hitting grass and the river's rushing water.

It was magic.

When Chance pulled away, they were both breathing hard. Bellamy stared at him, eyes wide, mouth still parted. Her lips were swollen and pink from his kiss. Something innately male in him was very satisfied with that.

After a moment of silence, Chance grinned. "That

wasn't so hard."

Bellamy smiled back. "I never said it was hard, cowboy."

"Then what took us so long?"

"I don't know." Bellamy crawled onto his lap and wrapped her arms around his neck. "But now it's my turn."

CHAPTER 18

THE PHONE RANG SOMETIME around five a.m.

Chance shifted on the bed, gritting his teeth while he fumbled for the phone on his nightstand. He moved carefully so as not to disturb Bellamy, who was still asleep on his chest.

"Yeah," he growled when he put the phone to his ear.

"Chance, it's me." Owen's voice was serious. He didn't sound tired at all, but he'd always kept an odd sleep schedule.

"Owen, do you realize what time it is?"

"What? No... Oh. I didn't wake you, did I?"

Chance sighed and extracted himself from the bed. He slipped a pillow under Bellamy's head and paused to watch her sleep for a moment more. The sight of her dark hair sticking up in all directions, a stark contrast to the white pillowcase, made him smile.

He'd much rather crawl back into bed with her and relive last night over and over again.

But alas, he had work to do.

He pulled the door closed and headed for his office.

"What's up?"

"I may have a lead on Johnathan Burke."

"I'm listening."

"Well, after Mrs. Burke's death, he left town. We tracked him to Colorado before he disappeared. I've been following up on all his phone and financial records. Get this; when he was in Colorado, he made twelve phone calls to this one number."

"Did you track it?"

"Yeah. It belonged to David Merrell."

"Bellamy's uncle?"

"Yeah."

Chance sat in his chair and put his feet up on his desk. "So he did find Bellamy. Why didn't he go get her?"

"I don't know. Maybe David scared him off. His sister had asked him to protect Bellamy, after all. But that's not the only weird thing." A hint of excitement entered Owen's voice. "Remember after that, there were no financial records, no hit on any facial recognition? Until a month ago."

"What happened a month ago?"

"There are credit card transactions all over the place. Restaurants, banks, gas stations. They start on the east coast and make a steady line to Portland."

"Was he in Portland around the time Sam was murdered?"

"He bought a coffee at the gas station right around the

corner from the bank."

Chance leaned forward, his body humming with sudden adrenaline. "When was the last transaction?"

"Two days ago, at a motel right outside of town."

Chance slapped a palm on his desk and stood. "Send me the address."

* * * * * *

Before Bellamy opened her eyes, she stretched. Her muscles felt relaxed and heavy, the way they only felt when she'd had a good, long sleep.

It had been a long time since she'd had one of those.

She arched her back and bumped into something firm. And warm.

Human.

Bellamy's eyes flew open and she flipped around so fast that it made her head spin.

Her gaze landed on Chance's sleeping form and she froze for a moment. She studied him, willing the blood in her veins to slow down from mach speed. Once she was sure that the man next to her was Chance and not a figment of her nightmares, she allowed herself to relax.

As her panic eased, memories from the night before returned.

Now that it was morning, she couldn't help but feel a little embarrassed. She had never acted like that; never let her guard down so completely with another person. Chance had power over her now; he knew her intimately.

But he didn't know her secrets. If he found out now, he

would despise her.

Her mental tirade ground to a halt when Chance stirred. His eyes opened a fraction and he squinted at her, lips quirked into a sleepy smile. "Hey there, gorgeous," he murmured.

Bellamy blinked at him. She wasn't sure how to respond to the warm fuzzies in her stomach at the sound of his voice. "Morning," she squeaked.

She hoped she didn't look as terrified as she felt.

Chance stretched for a long moment, then rolled out of bed and to his feet. He was wearing only boxers. Bellamy couldn't seem to pull her eyes away from his bare, muscular chest. She swallowed hard.

"Hey."

Bellamy yanked her gaze up to his face, flushing. "Yeah?"

"Want some pancakes? Or would you rather sit and stare at my body all day?"

"You're making me choose?"

He sputtered a surprised laugh and went to a dresser. Pulling a t-shirt over his head, he grinned over his shoulder at her. "At least pancakes will satisfy both of us. Want to wear one of my t-shirts?"

Bellamy glanced down at her plain black bra and shivered, aware of the chill in the air. "Yes please. Is it still raining?"

Chance tossed her a gray shirt and pushed aside the blinds on the nearest window. "Yep, even harder than it was yesterday."

Bellamy pulled the shirt on and followed him from the

room. She sat on the kitchen counter while Chance puttered around, preparing breakfast. She swung her legs, amazed at how comfortable she felt around him, despite the terror that he was getting awfully close to her. It was a far cry from what she'd felt when she first saw him again at the funeral.

For the first time, she felt like maybe she had a chance of rebuilding her life. To connect to him again like when they were kids.

She mentally slapped herself on the wrist.

This was an illusion; she knew, even if she didn't want to admit it. She was here playing House with Chance, but it wouldn't last forever.

It didn't matter how much she wished it would.

"Bella," Chance said. He turned to look at her from where he stood in front of the stove.

His serious tone caught her attention, and she forced her focus away from her mental spiral.

"I got some new information on your father last night."

"My... father?" A chill slid down Bellamy's spine. "What are you talking about?"

"Owen has been doing some digging into your attack the other night. He found a car fleeing the scene around the same time, and it was registered to Jonathan Burke."

Bellamy stared at him. "My father has been missing for seven years. This attack was orchestrated by Ronald Powell. You know, the senator down in Portland who wants to kill me?"

"That's what we thought, too, but Owen tracked this lead. Your father resurfaced recently. Credit card transactions put him in the area within the past few days."

Cold dread settled in the pit of her stomach. It had been so long since she'd seen her father. Just the thought of him brought back all the fear he'd instilled in her when she was young.

"I don't know why he would be here," she said slowly, "but I don't care. Your team is barking up the wrong tree, Chance. We need to be looking for evidence against Powell right now, not chasing ghosts."

Chance approached her, resting his hands on her shoulders. "Look, don't worry. Owen is still digging into Powell, too. We know where your father is. I'm going to get to the bottom of this, I promise."

"Where is he?"

"You let me worry about that. Listen, Emmett and his team will be here after breakfast. We're going to check out the place he's been staying. Owen's close with Powell, too. With any luck, this whole thing will be over today."

"How are you so optimistic?"

He pressed a warm kiss to her cheek. "It's a gift. I just have a feeling today will be a good day."

Bellamy forced a smile, wishing she felt the same way.

CHAPTER 19

IT WAS STILL EARLY WHEN the knock sounded at the door.

Chance opened it to reveal Emmett and his team.

Bellamy, who had followed him from the kitchen, drew up short. Her eyes widened at their full tactical gear. Each man was dressed in all black and armed to the teeth. He guessed Emmett had already briefed them on the situation.

Emmett nodded at Bellamy, his expression ever serious.

Bellamy returned his nod with a stoic expression, but her white-knuckled clasped hands betrayed her nerves.

Chance put an arm around her and drew her close to his side. "Where's Sarah?" he asked Emmett.

Emmett scowled. "Home. For now. I convinced her that Mom might need her if the rain keeps up. The roof is leaking all over the place already."

"How did she feel about that assignment?"

"Not happy." Something like satisfaction glinted in

Emmett's eyes. Sarah would have punched him if she'd been there to see it.

Roman stepped forward. "It's just as well. This could get dangerous." He approached Bellamy and smiled at her. "Did Chance already brief you on the situation?"

She nodded.

"Good. If he's there, we'll get him."

"For the record, I think this is a waste of time." Bellamy met each man's eyes in turn, lingering on Emmett's. "My father has nothing to do with this, whether he's in town or not."

"I hope you're right," Emmett said. "I'd prefer if the bastard never showed his face here again. But we wouldn't be doing our job if we didn't check it out."

"He's right." Chance dropped a kiss on her forehead and stepped forward to grab a bulletproof vest from Cameron's outstretched hand. He pulled it over his head and looked at Emmett. "Ready?"

He nodded and made a circle motion with one hand. "Let's move out."

Bellamy followed them out the door. Chance hung back for a moment while everyone else jogged to the waiting Range Rover.

The rain fell steadily around them. Bellamy looked up at him, complicated emotions flashing across her face.

If only he could turn back time. He would go back to the night before, when the only thing on their minds was a kiss. He would replay it over and over again.

"Be safe," Bellamy said finally, her voice soft. "Please, Chance. Be careful."

He smiled. "I always am. Lock the door behind us and don't open it for anyone, you understand? I can't focus unless I know you're safe."

"I will be. Promise."

Chance nodded and gave her another smile before he headed for the Range Rover and hopped inside. Bellamy stood on the porch as they backed up and took off down the drive, and he watched her close the door just before they disappeared from view.

* * * * * *

Bellamy watched the Range Rover disappear into the haze of falling rain, then slammed the front door closed, breathing hard.

This couldn't be happening.

Chance had to be wrong.

Her father was dead. He had to be, after all these years. Why would he show up now?

It was Ronald Powell.

She didn't know what his motive was or how he'd found out about her father, but he was playing them somehow.

It was time to make her move.

Bellamy took the stairs two at a time and found her phone plugged into the charger on the table next to the bed.

Chance's bed.

Her brain skittered away from the memory of the night before. She didn't have time for a meltdown. She'd deal with the emotional hurricane that was her feelings for

Chance later.

Right now, she had work to do.

She returned to the living room and settled onto the couch where she could watch the rain falling outside. Scrolling through her contacts, she debated each codename. Each one represented a contact for someone in the Portland underbelly.

The question was, how could she tell who to trust?

Which ones could she trust to spread the gossip she was about to instigate?

It took an hour before someone finally answered her call. Sheldon, a low-level fence with a big mouth, picked up on her third attempt.

"What do you want?" His voice was irritable, suspicious.

"Is that any way to talk to an old friend?"

Sheldon snorted. "We're hardly friends. I don't talk to snitches."

"I'm not a snitch. In fact, I'm calling to help you out. It's important."

"Bullshit."

Bellamy huffed an irritated breath. "Ignore me if you want, but at least let me tell you. You might find it interesting."

"I'm listening, obviously. I haven't hung up on you yet, although it's tempting."

"Powell is after me. You've probably already guessed it. But I have insider information that the FBI is bearing down on him as we speak. You need to let everyone in the network know. They'll take down anyone with a connection to him. If you want to save your own ass, now is the time to do it."

"How would you know that?"

"Because I've been working with them."

"Snitch."

"Not a snitch," Bellamy snapped. "It's revenge. He killed my best friend."

Silence fell over the line, and Bellamy knew she'd finally caught Sheldon's attention.

"The FBI almost have everything they need. They'll be moving on Powell's network in the next 24 hours. I'm telling you so you can spread the word. Cut all ties with Powell and disappear. That's the only way you'll escape this without prison time."

"... I'll consider it," Sheldon said. "And I'll pass on the word. Not that anyone will believe you."

"Then I won't lose any sleep at night. I did my part."

"Right. I guess I should thank you, then."

"No need." Bellamy paused. "Just keep this in mind next time I call on a favor."

She hung up and dropped the phone onto the couch next to her.

Sheldon was the best person for the job. He had a mouth a mile wide. Soon all of Portland's underground would hear about the pending FBI raid on Powell. Hopefully, that would cut off his ties to anyone in the city. With no contacts, he couldn't move against her.

She hoped.

* * * * * *

"Okay, assholes, this is the real deal," Emmett said over the roar of the rain on the roof. They sat in the Range Rover outside the motel. "There's no security footage in this dump. We have no idea what he's got stashed in that room. We go in prepared for anything."

The men nodded their agreement as they checked and loaded their weapons.

"Dom, we've already got clearance for you to cover us from the gas station roof across the street. Local PD has blocked off the road so we shouldn't have any incoming traffic."

Dominick grinned. "Yes sir."

"Roman and Cam, you'll cover the exits. If anyone gets past Chance and I, you procure them. Got it?"

Roman and Cameron nodded. "Yes sir," they said in unison.

"Chance and I will take point," Emmett continued. His gaze met Chance's. "This one's personal."

Chance nodded, shoving his Sig in the holster at his hip. Adrenaline spiked, just like it always did before a mission, and he took a breath to steady himself.

"Move out."

The men jumped out of the SUV and scattered. Dominick made his way across the street and into the gas station. Roman and Cameron melted into the surroundings to watch the exits.

Chance and Emmett ran toward the motel room in a crouch, hands on their weapons. Owen had already called ahead and got the room number for them. The team moved like a well-oiled machine. They had done many missions like this, but today felt different. Chance knew he wasn't the only one who felt it. Emmett and the others all had a serious air about them. The importance of this task wasn't lost on them.

The brothers took position on either side of the door and Emmett held up a hand.

Three, he mouthed.

Two.

One.

Chance pulled his gun and Emmett used one booted foot to kick the door down. Chance ducked into the motel room and pointed his gun in a long sweep. Emmett entered behind him, his own gun echoing Chance's motion.

The room was trashed. The bed had been ripped apart, furniture overturned. Chance and Emmett did a thorough search, eyes peeled for any sign of Jonathan Burke.

Empty.

Chance cursed and holstered his gun as he stood in the destroyed bathroom.

"Chance."

Emmett's voice summoned him back to the main room. He stood at the dresser, the only piece of furniture that seemed to be in its right place.

As Chance approached, Emmett turned, a manilla folder in his gloved hand.

"What's that?" Chance asked.

Emmett held it out, his expression stony. "Isn't this Officer Ruiz? The one we just found connected to Ronald Powell's arms trading network?"

Chance took the folder from him and flipped it open. A

stack of black-and-white surveillance photos rested inside. The photo on top showed a clear view of Officer Ruiz, standing at the mouth of an alley on a deserted street. A small woman stood in front of him, her side profile visible to the camera. Ruiz was handing her a black duffel bag.

Even though the woman's face was turned away from the camera, the cowlick in her short dark hair was unmistakable.

"What the hell?" Chance breathed.

Emmett touched a finger to his right ear, activating his radio. "This place is blown. Meet back at the car." He lowered his hand. "Let's get back to HQ. We need to talk to Owen."

Chance closed the folder and tucked it in his vest, his mind reeling. He raised his gun and followed Emmett back out into the rain.

How did Bellamy know Ruiz? What was in the bag he gave her?

Did she have a connection to Powell that she hadn't told them about?

It was a long, silent drive back to the ESI office downtown. Several police cars and a fire truck whizzed past them going the other direction. Water sprayed from their tires in a wide arc.

Chance glanced at Emmett. He was grateful his brother had chosen not to push an 'I told you so' on him. This was the perfect opportunity to call Bellamy into question once again. Hell, Chance was reeling himself. He didn't know what to think.

But if Emmett chose to vocalize his thoughts now, it

was likely Chance would snap and they'd have a fight on their hands.

Luckily, Emmett was wiser than he looked.

When they arrived at ESI, Owen waited for them at the door, bouncing back and forth on the balls of his feet. When they pulled into a parking spot in front of the building, Owen scrambled out into the rain to meet them at the curb. "I found something," he said.

"So did we," Emmett said grimly.

Chance, Emmett, and Roman followed Owen down the hall while the others unloaded the Range Rover.

"I examined the photos you found. We'll get to that in a second. My computer has been running a constant search on Bellamy's name," Owen explained. "It's not as easy as a Google search. My program has been hacking into closed court and government documents. It finally picked up on something just now."

He tapped a few keys and what looked like a scanned document popped up on the screen. It looked like a medical chart, filled with the scribbled handwriting of what could only be a doctor. The letterhead at the top read, "Alpine Mental Health Facilities".

"What's this?" Emmett growled.

"It's hard to read," Owen replied. "But it's a medical report. Bellamy was institutionalized when she was seventeen."

"What?" Chance and Emmett demanded simultaneously.

"That's what I said." Owen zoomed in on the document so they could all see it. "She was there for eight months.

Checked in by David Merrell for extreme violence and self-harm. She tried to commit suicide and Governor Merrell walked in on her. He got her to the hospital just in time. Then he had her committed. The record was sealed, so it took quite a bit of digging to find it."

"But in order to be committed, you have to have symptoms of psychosis, right?" Chance asked. "I haven't seen anything to warrant something like this."

"Not necessarily," Roman replied. "People can be committed for all kinds of reasons. But Owen, you should look into this facility and see what their specialty is. Maybe it will give us a clue why she was there."

"I'm on it. As for the photos, they're legitimate. No evidence of tampering. I even found security footage from right around the date stamped on the picture. Bellamy and this officer were definitely there when these were taken."

"The date is just a week before Sam's disappearance," Emmett said quietly.

Chance stepped back, shaking his head. "We have to be missing something. This can't be right."

"Chance..."

"Meet me in the car. I need to get back to the house." Before Emmett could say anything further or the pity in Owen's eyes could skewer him, Chance left the office.

The seed of doubt buried in his gut was starting to grow.

Every time he answered one question about Bellamy's past, ten more replaced it.

It was time to get some true answers.

CHAPTER 20

BELLA FOUGHT THE NURSES when they came for her. They were a nice-looking older woman and a strong man in his thirties. They were dressed in street clothing, but Bella knew who they were. She'd seen enough medical professionals in her lifetime that she could pick them out in the crowd.

"I'm not going," she yelled. She rolled out of bed and put the mattress between them, looking for some way - any way - out.

"Miss Burke, please, you'll hurt yourself," the woman nurse said. She nodded at her counterpart and he advanced around the bed toward her.

"Stay away from me."

"Princess, you need to calm down. You don't want to reopen your wounds," Uncle David pleaded from his spot in the corner.

Bella looked down at the stark white bandages on her

wrists. Her hands shook violently. She didn't remember doing that. Had she?

"Miss Burke, you'll be safe. Just come with us," the male nurse said.

Bella snapped her head from side to side. Her back hit the wall. She had nowhere else to go. No escape.

"Please be careful," Uncle David said, his brow etched with worry. "Don't hurt her. She's been through enough."

"Don't," Bella snapped as the male nurse took another step toward her. She glanced to her left and saw a window. Before she could second-guess herself, she dove for it and threw it open. It was a two-story drop. She could make it.

She leaped. Her head and shoulders made it through the window frame before she was yanked back inside. She screamed and flailed against her attacker. "Let me go."

A slight pain pricked her neck. Bella felt her body go liquid at the same time her mind went blank. The last thing she saw was Uncle David's worried face before oblivion took her.

* * * * * *

Bellamy paced the living room, arms folded across her chest. She couldn't sit still. Not when Chance and Emmett and the others were out putting themselves in harm's way for her.

Dread settled in the pit of her stomach. Too many things were wrong. What if this was Powell's plan all along? What if she didn't cut off his connections in time?

What if someone got hurt? Or... killed?

Bellamy knew fear. It was her constant companion when she was young. After escaping her uncle and meeting Sam, she thought she'd finally conquered it.

But she'd never felt fear like this. It wasn't fear for her own safety. It was fear for someone she cared about, someone she... loved?

No.

Bellamy sat down hard on the couch.

I don't love Chance. I can't.

How could she? She'd lost the ability to love a long time ago. It had been beaten out of her.

But I do. I think I've always loved him.

The revelation startled her, made her sick. But it was true. She'd loved him since she was six years old and he invited her to his house after he found her crying on the playground. She'd loved him for as long as she could remember.

It's not fair to him.

He'd already demonstrated that he felt something for her, but what? He didn't know about her past, the things she'd done just to survive. He could never know. If he saw the real Bellamy Burke, he would run in the opposite direction. Or haul her off to jail.

Bellamy sighed and massaged circles in her aching temples. The constant drone of the rain on the roof was driving her insane.

The phone rang.

She leaped to her feet and grabbed the headset off the coffee table. "Hello?"

"Bellamy."

"Sarah?" Disappointment bloomed in her chest, but she tamped it down. "What is it?"

"Have you seen the news?"

"What? No, I haven't turned on the TV today."

"Ugh, why doesn't anyone ever listen to me?" Sirens sounded in the background, fuzzy through the phone line.

"What's going on?"

"It's the storm." Her voice crackled. "Remnants of some hurricane. They're saying the storm cell is bigger than they projected. And there's another one right behind it. The river is flooding. They're evacuating half the town."

"Are you okay?"

"Yeah, we're fine. The backyard is one giant pond at the moment. Owen's at HQ and Mom and I are loading up the car. Chance's house is higher up, so he should be fine. We're going to head over there as soon as - Mom, leave that here." A scuffle sounded. Mary's voice sounded in the background, but there was too much static to make out her words. "We can't take everything with us. The Jeep is already full. We have to go." Sarah's voice grew louder again. "Bellamy, I've been trying to call the guys, but nobody is answering."

Bellamy glanced out the window. The rain was relentless and the ground was wet, but there was no sign of flooding. "Okay," she said with forced calm. "They probably don't have their phones. I'll tell them as soon as they get back. Just load up everything you can and head over here."

"Okay - Mom, I'm not going to tell you again. Get in the car. We have to go. Bellamy, we'll see you soon." Sarah hung up.

Bellamy returned the phone to its dock. The pounding in her head was getting worse. Chance had given her Tylenol after she returned from the hospital. Maybe she could find where he stashed it.

A car door slammed in the distance.

Bellamy's heart leapt. She ran to the front door and threw it open. Sure enough, Chance and Emmett were climbing out of the Range Rover in front of the house. Relief made her temporarily dizzy.

She ran out to meet them, unconcerned about her bare feet or the rain that quickly soaked her clothes. "Chance!"

Chance turned. His expression didn't light up like it usually did when he saw her.

She slid to a stop in front of him."Did you find anything?"

Chance and Emmett exchanged glances. "Not… what we expected to find," he said finally.

Emmett didn't look at Bellamy as he pulled a duffle bag out of the back seat.

Bellamy frowned. She'd told them they wouldn't find her father there. Why were they acting so strangely? Maybe they hadn't found anything to link Powell to her attack, either.

There were more important things to worry about at the moment.

"Did Sarah get a hold of you?"

"No," Chance said, brows lowering. "Why?"

Bellamy relayed what Sarah had told her. She looked at Emmett. "They might need your help. You should go get

Owen and make sure they're safe."

Emmett glanced at Chance. When Chance nodded, he got back into the Rover and peeled out of the driveway.

Chance slung the duffle bag over his shoulder. "Come on, let's go inside. We need to talk."

"What's going on? What happened?"

Chance didn't answer right away. He slid off his boots and dropped them just inside the front door, then pulled off his shirt as he walked toward the bedroom.

Bellamy followed. She stood in the doorway while Chance changed into a dry shirt, studiously keeping her gaze away from his bare chest. He didn't bother changing his pants.

"Your father wasn't there," he said finally.

"I told you he wouldn't be. Powell was the one behind the attack, not my father."

"I'm not so sure about that, but we did find something else."

"What?"

Chance crossed the room and leaned against the wall next to the door, pulling her toward him. His hands settled like twenty-pound weights on her shoulders. "Bella, I need you to be honest with me."

Bellamy looked up into his eyes. Her stomach dropped to her toes.

He knew.

She didn't know how, and she didn't know exactly what, but he'd learned something about her past. Something she'd never wanted him to know. He was looking at her differently.

It was the kind of look most people gave her. A mixture of wariness, interest, and suspicion. The kind of look you gave a snake you stumbled upon in the wild.

Bellamy drew a deep breath and forced herself to calm.

She'd always known it would come to this. Not this quickly, perhaps, but maybe it was for the best.

"What did you find?" Her voice betrayed none of the anguish she was drowning in. It was her 'underground' voice. Cool, calm, and professional.

Chance hesitated. His eyes probed hers, searching for answers she could never give him. He pulled something out of his pocket and held it out to her.

Bellamy took the piece of paper from him. Swallowing hard, she unfolded it.

The photo of her and Ruiz yawned up at her like the black hole she wanted to crawl into. She recognized it immediately; it was from a job she'd taken shortly before Sam disappeared. A routine handoff. The duffel bag Ruiz gave her had contained an address and enough cash to fund a small country. Her job had been to deliver the package to his contact at Seattle's port of entry, ensuring that the inspection for a certain ship would be "overlooked."

Bellamy had taken the job without a second thought. She'd played a vital role in a massive arms smuggling operation. Any lives lost to those illegal weapons were her responsibility.

"Do you know that man?" Chance asked. His voice wasn't accusatory; it was almost pleading, as if he was wordlessly asking her to say no.

"I do," Bellamy said firmly. "His name is Officer Ruiz."

"Do you know about his connection to Powell?"

"Yes. This photo proves that Powell was behind the attack. He's the only one who knew about this meeting. He hired someone to take this picture so he could blackmail me."

"What's happening in this picture, Bella? What are you doing with Officer Ruiz? Why didn't you tell me you knew him personally?"

Bellamy swallowed hard. This was it.

Once she crossed this line, they'd never be able to go back. Her relationship with Chance - if that's what it was - would be over.

"I need you to tell me the truth. I love you," he whispered, his eyes never leaving hers. "I always have. If you'll just tell me the truth, I can help you."

Bellamy froze. The air came whooshing out of her chest. "You what?"

"I've always loved you. I loved you before you disappeared. I've loved you every day since. I know you went through hell, Bella, and I'll never begin to understand. Whatever happened in the past, though, I need you to know that it's okay. It will be okay."

"You don't love me. You can't."

"Why not? What aren't you telling me?"

"A lot, Chance." Bellamy shook off his hands and backed up a step. She needed some space between them, needed a second to process the fact that her world was crashing down around her ears. "You can't love me without knowing about my past. You can't tell me everything will be okay when you don't even know."

"Then tell me."

"You want to know?" Her voice grew louder. "Fine. You've got this image of me in your head. The scared little girl who was beaten by her father. The scared little girl who crawled through your bedroom window at three in the morning because she didn't know what else to do. I'm not her anymore, Chance. I haven't been for a long time.

"You know who I am now? I'm the girl who suffered for three years at the hands of Governor David Merrell - my uncle. He did things to me that were far worse than Papa ever could. The only difference is, I fought back. One night, I took a knife from the kitchen and I stabbed him in the chest. I left him there to die."

"So it's true," Chance said. "All the stuff Owen found about you."

"Stuff Owen found...? You've been researching me?"

"Apparently for good reason. I know about the institution, Bellamy. Alpine Mental Health Facility. I know you almost killed someone, that you had some mental struggle..."

"Are you kidding me?" Bellamy backed away, shaking her head. The walls around her were spinning, closing in, robbing her of the ability to breathe. "None of that is true, Chance. None of it."

"It's okay," he said, his hands outstretched in a placating gesture. "I know you've been through hell. Nobody comes out of that unscathed."

Bellamy laughed. "That's the first logical thing you've said all day. I told you I'm not the same girl you remember, Chance. I told you that from the very beginning. You want to know what's happening in this picture?" She waved it in front of his face, then shoved it in his chest. "This is me working an arms deal with Ruiz and, by extension, Powell. I've been on his payroll - and a lot of other crime bosses' - for years. I'm not a good person, and I'm not trying to be. Sam didn't know about my association with him. She got too close, and he killed her for it. Now he's punishing me for retaliating against him."

For once, Chance looked speechless.

The look in his eyes told her that he would never see her the same way again.

Shame flared white hot in her chest, but Bellamy shoved it down, notching her chin higher. She'd promised herself the night she killed her uncle that she would never feel shame for doing what she needed to do to stay alive.

Now wasn't any different.

"I'm not a damsel in distress," she said quietly. "And you're not my prince charming. Thanks for everything you've done, but I'll take care of myself from here."

She took a few steps back and, when he didn't follow her, turned and walked down the stairs.

She opened the front door and did what she did best; she fled.

CHAPTER 21

CHANCE STOOD FROZEN.

His mind raced through every conversation they'd ever had, searching for signs of the truth. Now that he knew, he could see them. Bellamy had tried to tell him, but he didn't want to hear it. She had told him there were things in her past that she couldn't talk about yet. She'd hinted that she'd done things she wasn't proud of.

He should have pressed her harder, encouraged her to tell him sooner.

Instead, he'd been a selfish asshole and had assumed that it wasn't important enough to matter. He'd assumed he could fix everything.

The slam of the front door startled him out of his thoughts.

Bellamy was running.

The sound of his truck's engine roaring to life spurred

Chance to action. He sprinted down the stairs and threw open the front door just in time to see Bellamy speeding down the driveway, spitting gravel from his truck's tires.

"Bellamy," he roared, but she either didn't hear him, or didn't care. Chance ran down the driveway after her, but he was no match for his Ram's four wheel drive. The vehicle disappeared from view before he even reached the end of the clearing.

"Damn, damn, damn." Her information bomb had caused a moment's hesitation that he couldn't take back.

Chance ran back into the house. He yanked the phone off of the receiver on the coffee table and tried to dial Emmett's number, but the line was dead. The storm must have knocked out a phone line somewhere. He pulled his cell phone out of his pocket, but he had no service.

"Are you kidding me?"

Chance chucked the phone as hard as he could. The sound of the device shattering against the wall didn't make him feel any better. He stood for a moment, breathing hard, and tried to regain some semblance of control.

Then he remembered. Each of the Erickson brothers kept a radio in each vehicle and in their homes in case of an emergency. Emmett, ever-cautious, always kept his turned on.

The radio still sat in the top drawer of his desk, gathering dust. Chance turned it on, thankful that the batteries still worked, and turned to their designated channel. "Emmett, Owen, come in. This is Chance. Over."

Static crackled through the speaker for a moment. Chance slammed his fist down on his desk.

"Emmett, Owen. This is Chance. Are you there? Over."

Maybe his brothers hadn't realized the cell towers were down yet. Sarah had just called Bellamy before Chance got home, so they hadn't been down long.

"Chance? This is Emmett. Over."

Thank God. Chance snatched the radio back up. "Emmett, Bellamy's gone. Repeat; Bellamy is gone. What's your location?"

Static echoed for a moment. "We're en route. About 5 minutes out. What happened?"

"She took my truck. If you see her, stop her. She's upset."

"Dammit." Emmett's voice was sharp. "Roger. We've got the team. I'll have them sweep the area. We'll be there soon. Over and out."

Chance dropped the radio back onto his desk and dropped into his chair, his head in his hands. He had finally gotten Bellamy back into his life, and he'd failed her again. She'd been keeping such a tremendous secret from everyone. He couldn't imagine the burden she must have felt.

Chance had killed people. During his time with the military, he'd killed more people than he could count. No matter the reason or the number, it never got any easier. He would have to live with the knowledge that he'd ended lives forever.

Bellamy should've never had to bear that burden.

If he had somehow found a way to protect her, she wouldn't have been sent to her uncle's. She wouldn't have suffered at his hands.

But what did she suffer, exactly? Why had she been placed in that institution in the first place? Things didn't add up. From all appearances, David Merrell was a loving uncle who only wanted what was best for her.

There was no motive for her to stab him in the chest and leave him for dead.

And her involvement with Powell? He couldn't even process that yet.

Chance stood. His mind would go round and round for hours if he allowed it to. But he wasn't the philosophical type; he was a man of action.

And lucky for him, he was a man who liked to be prepared.

The most important thing now was finding Bellamy. Whether it was Powell or her father after her, it wasn't safe for her to be alone.

He powered up his laptop and entered a few quick lines of code into a black screen.

The dove pendant had been a heartfelt gift for Bellamy, but Chance had also placed a small tracker into the clasp for a situation just like this. He wasn't taking any chances with her safety. It hadn't been his intention to use it if she decided to run away again, but he was glad for it.

A map of Seattle popped up on the screen. A blinking dot appeared on the map where his house was.

"Shit," he snapped.

The tracker wasn't updating her location. The storm must have messed with his satellite GPS signal.

When construction on the house was finished, he'd commissioned Owen to install a satellite dish on his roof.

The dish provided a backup when his normal internet went down. It was pre-calibrated for the best connection.

Chance frowned when he booted the program and it still didn't work.

"Emmett, is Owen with you?" Chance radioed.

"I'm here," Owen responded.

"My internet isn't working. I can't get a lock on Bella's GPS signal."

"The one you put in her necklace? Have you switched to the satellite?"

Chance gritted his teeth. "Of course I did. It's not working."

"Go outside and check the dish on the roof. Radio me when you've got a visual."

"Roger." Chance stalked out of his office and into the rain outside. It soaked his new shirt immediately, but he didn't care.

He circled to the back of the house and put some distance between him and the building so he could see the roof.

"Shit," he yelled. A large tree branch must have been blown down by the storm. The branch and the dish were both tipped over, lying on their sides on the roof.

"Shit, damn, motherf - "

"Do you have a visual?" Owen's voice on the radio interrupted Chance's tirade.

"Yes. A tree branch knocked the dish over."

There was a long silence. "Stand by. We'll be there soon."

"We can't wait that long," Chance snapped. "Just walk

me through it. I can fix it."

"Don't get your panties in a bunch. It's too complicated to walk you through over radio. I'll make repairs when we get there. Sit tight."

Chance stomped back into the house, already planning where he would spend the next hour pacing.

* * * * * *

Chance paced back and forth in the living room, in front of the fireplace. A loud tone from the front of the house alerted him that Emmett and the rest of his family were pulling through the front gate. Chance opened the front door just as they parked in the driveway. Emmett and Owen were in Emmett's truck and Sarah and his mother climbed out of Sarah's Jeep. Chance held the door open as his family jogged through the rain and into the house.

Once everyone was inside, Mary pulled Chance into a tight hug. Her shoulders shook. Chance shot a questioning look at Sarah over her shoulder. Sarah shrugged, but her expression was somber also.

Mary was a strong woman, but losing her husband earlier that year and now the storm threatening their home was taking its toll on her. Chance knew that she was upset at the possibility of losing a place with so many memories of his dad. He hugged her tightly and kissed the top of her head. "The house will be okay, Mom. I promise."

Mary nodded under his chin. "I know, honey. I'm just glad everyone's all right." Her voice shook a little, but she strengthened it with a smile up at Chance. "Now we need to find Bellamy."

Chance smiled back at her and turned his attention to Emmett. "Any luck?"

"Roman said they haven't seen her. They're sweeping the area now, but no sign of your truck anywhere."

"What happened?" Sarah asked.

Chance relayed his conversation with Bellamy and the revelation about her uncle's murder and her involvement with Ronald Powell.

Emmett's eyes narrowed in thought. "It lines up with a possible psychotic break. Perhaps she'd suffered abuse for so many years that it finally broke her."

"Wait, hold on a minute." Sarah held up a hand, glaring between her three brothers. "You guys were researching Bellamy?"

"It's standard procedure for any new client," Emmett informed her.

"Standard procedure? Bellamy's not some random client. She's a member of this family. That's an invasion of privacy."

"That's what we do." Owen shrugged. "We invade privacy. That's the only way we can have all the facts. Know your enemy and your allies."

"And which one is Bellamy? An ally?" Sarah let out a bitter laugh. "That's not how you're treating her. Just because your research says one thing, doesn't mean it's the truth. There are two sides to every story. Did you even ask Bellamy about hers?"

"I tried," Chance huffed. "She didn't want to talk about it."

"Yeah, and for good reason." Sarah glared at them all. "I'm disappointed in you guys. I've told you many times that everything's not as it seems. Bellamy hasn't told me everything either, and that's okay. There are some things that you just can't talk about, even to those you love." She stared at each one of them until they looked away. "You guys served in the military. I know you saw things and did things that you'll never tell me about. But I don't assume the worst about you. Because I trust you and I know you made the right decision at the time, no matter what you did."

Emmett's jaw clenched tight. He didn't meet Sarah's eyes, but his shoulders slumped.

Chance nodded his agreement. He'd done things in the service that he'd never be able to tell another soul about. Things that, if told, might make him look like the bad guy. His gut churned as he realized what Sarah was saying.

None of them had trusted Bellamy, and this was the outcome.

Even though Chance had argued her innocence since the beginning, he realized now that he hadn't really trusted her either. He hadn't trusted her enough to ask the hard questions, knowing he would accept whatever the answer was.

Mary stepped between all the kids. She was a head shorter than all of them, but her expression was fierce. "Sarah's right. I know your father and I raised you better than that. All of you."

Sarah looked at Owen. "Keep digging. There's more to the story here. In the meantime, what's our next step? We need to find her."

Chance smiled at his little sister. She'd grown up since she moved away from them. He was proud of the woman she'd become, a leader who was steadier than any of them under pressure. "You're right," he said. "Let's find her first. We can worry about the rest later. We need to get her GPS signal running. We can't do that without the satellite dish."

"I can fix that." Owen nodded. "I can't do any further research until I get some internet access anyway. If I can re-calibrate it, I should be able to get us some internet access, and activate Bellamy's tracker."

"Great." Emmett took command again. "You and Mom stay here and work on that. We'll go join the others and sweep the area. Maybe we can find her before she leaves La Conner."

Sarah nodded. "I'm coming with you."

Emmett shot her a look. "I need you to stay here."

"I'm not staying behind on this one. That's my best friend out there." Her voice shook. "She thinks none of us trust her. We're all she has left, Emmett. I'm not going to abandon her when she needs us most."

Chance stepped forward and wrapped one arm around Sarah's shoulders, pulling her into his side in a protective gesture. His strong, rebellious sister seemed fragile and he couldn't understand why. "I agree. We need all hands on deck this time. Let's cover some ground and see if we can spot her. She can't have gone far in this storm."

Emmett scowled, but didn't argue further. He gave a curt nod and stomped from the room.

Sarah sniffed. Her eyes were bright, but she didn't

allow any tears to fall. "Thank you," she whispered to Chance. She straightened her shoulders, a determined expression replacing the vulnerable one. "Let's go get our girl."

* * * * * *

Bellamy pulled the truck off the main road, squinting through the blur of the windshield wipers. The weather was a lot more serious than she'd thought. Half the roads were already flooded. She drove through puddles large enough that she was afraid she would get stuck, but Chance's truck had just enough clearance to make it. Thank God he was the type of man to own an all-terrain vehicle.

She felt terrible for stealing his car, but she didn't have a choice. She had to get away, and she wasn't dumb enough to do it on foot.

Her head was spinning and she had a vicious headache. She couldn't stop her mind from replaying her confrontation with Chance over and over. The condemnation in his eyes when she told him the truth. He'd looked shocked, but he'd been lying to Bellamy all this time. Investigating her.

Bellamy was the one who should feel betrayed, not him. She rubbed at the pain in her chest, her eyes on the road in front of her. Her stomach heaved, threatening to empty its contents. She slammed on the brakes and threw open the driver's side door, leaning over in case she threw up. The rain soaked her hair and the cold returned her sanity a little. It took a few more deep breaths for her to settle down again so she could drive.

Finally she reached her destination and pulled over, resting her forehead against the steering wheel. She took a few more deep breaths, willing herself to be steady, and looked up to take in her surroundings.

She was back at their secret place, the bench on the side of the river. Her body had been on autopilot, and this was where she'd ended up.

The last time she'd been here, Chance had kissed her.

Had that really only been last night?

The memory made her heart feel like it was shattering into a million pieces.

Bellamy got out and wandered in the direction of their bench. She didn't even care that it was pouring. In fact, she took off her leather jacket and laid it over the back of the bench. The water felt good on her flushed skin; maybe the shock would bring her some clarity.

The water had risen even more than the night before. A solid two inches covered the base of the bench. Bellamy sat and dangled her feet in the water, not sure what to do.

Where do I go from here?

She should go return Chance's truck. She knew that much. Maybe she would just leave it on the edge of town so she could catch a bus somewhere. She could call Sarah later and let her know where it was.

Bellamy knew she was being unreasonable. Chance's reaction was understandable, even expected. If their roles had been reversed, she would have felt the same way.

Why should he feel so betrayed? He hadn't trusted her from the beginning. The truth of that hurt more than

Bellamy could admit to herself.

Half of her was tempted to march back over there and demand that he listen so she could tell him the whole story. But that would mean opening a door she'd closed and locked a long time ago. A door to her darkest memories. She wasn't sure she'd survive reliving them. She wasn't even sure how she'd survived the first time.

Bellamy reached up and unhooked her necklace. Holding the chain in front of her, she stared as the dove pendant swung gently back and forth. She thought about her mother. This pendant had been a sign of hope for her, a hope that she would someday have a better life.

But her mother had died, murdered in her own home. She'd never gotten the chance to move on to something better.

Bellamy didn't want to end up like her. She wanted to be free of her past, to have the hope that the dove pendant signified. To live a life free of the misery she'd endured.

Could she do that with Chance? He was so deeply tied to her past. Just his presence was a reminder of the time she'd lost. Every time she looked at him, she felt like she was fifteen again, running through the streets toward his house on lazy summer mornings.

Running away from her father.

Bellamy let her hand with the pendant drop to her lap. The water had risen to her knees now. The pendant slid into the water, sinking silently under the surface.

She needed a fresh start. It was the only way she could be free.

Somewhere away from her crime pals in Portland,

away from the memories of La Conner and Denver. Maybe somewhere on the east coast...

But before she left, there was one thing she had to do.

Bellamy stared out at the dark, churning water of the river and straightened her shoulders. She would tell Chance the truth. As much as she could, anyway. If she was going to move on to a new life, she didn't want to leave any loose ends behind.

Besides, if she tried to leave without saying anything, she was certain he would track her down. They weren't teenagers anymore, and he had a lot more resources now.

She stood, feeling resolute in her decision. But before she could turn around, something cold and hard pressed into the back of her head. She caught a hint of masculine cologne before a voice she often heard in her nightmares spoke into her ear.

"Hello, princess."

CHAPTER 22

CHANCE AND THE OTHERS SPENT HOURS searching the area for Bellamy. Cameron, Roman and Dominick took one truck and went to search the local bus station. Chance, Emmett, and Sarah took Emmett's truck and headed toward town.

Chance insisted on driving. The hands-on requirement prevented him from losing his mind with worry. Sarah took the passenger seat next to him, her expression tense, and Emmett slouched in the back seat.

"Do you have any idea where we should look? Maybe the cemetery, by her mom's grave?" Sarah asked.

Chance shook his head. "I think I know where she might have gone."

It took far longer than usual to cross to the other side of town. The rain was coming down in sheets and most of the roads had at least three inches of standing water already. Policemen went from door to door in the neighborhoods, warning the locals of the evacuation. Chance and his brothers were well-known in town and when the policemen recognized Emmett's truck, no one bothered them.

Sarah leaned forward in her seat when Chance turned off the main road and onto a rutted, muddy path. "Where are we going?"

Chance grunted, but didn't bother with a reply.

Five short minutes later, they emerged into the clearing and Chance let out a sigh of relief when he saw his truck nearby, its headlights still on. He parked a ways away and jumped out, Sarah and Emmett on his heels.

They approached the truck and peered inside, but it was empty. Sarah looked through the other window and shook her head at him. Chance resisted the urge to punch something and scanned the area.

Where are you, Bella?

He approached the wood bench. The river had risen and water now covered the wooden seat.

A black leather jacket lay over the back of the bench. Chance picked it up; it was cold.

"This is Bellamy's," he said.

Sarah stepped up next to him and ran her fingers over the initials etched into the soaked wood. She looked up at Chance. Her expression spoke volumes, but Chance didn't want to get into it with her right now. He just wanted to know where Bellamy was.

"Chance."

Chance and Sarah looked to where Emmett knelt in the middle of the clearing. The ground was wet and muddy. His hand traced the clear indentation of tire tracks.

Chance's stomach dropped to his toes.

Emmett looked up at them and for the first time since they'd broken into that motel room earlier that morning, he looked worried. "Radio Owen," he growled. "We need to get that GPS working."

* * * * * *

"The tracks are consistent with the van we saw in the alley a few days ago," Owen said. His fingers flew across the keys on his laptop and he squinted at his screen. They were all gathered around Chance's kitchen table. They'd been forced to return to the house while Owen and Mary finished the repairs on the satellite dish. The roof was slippery and littered with debris, so it had taken some time for him to get it up and running again. "Same tire tread. I'd bet money that Bellamy's father was in the area."

"And so was Bellamy," Emmett muttered.

Chance clenched his jaw. This was his fault. Because of his idiot reaction to Bellamy's confession, she was in the hands of a murderous psychopath and they had no way to find her. He'd never felt more helpless in his entire life.

He slammed his fist into the wall.

The pain in his knuckles did nothing to alleviate the guilt gnawing at his insides.

"I shouldn't have let her run off," he snarled, shaking his hand in agitation.

"Now's not the time to focus on that," Sarah said. She put a hand on Chance's shoulder. Her gaze was firm. "We just need to find her."

Chance covered his sister's hand with his own, drawing strength from her. He felt a little ashamed that he was losing his mind while his little sister was calm as could be, but he was grateful.

"Guys," Owen piped up, bringing all attention back to him. "I found something else."

The siblings gathered around him, waiting for him to continue.

"Ronald Powell is dead," Owen said, sounding awed. "I hacked into the Portland police database - sorry, Mom - and gained access to Powell's encrypted phone. It turns out, Powell was behind everything... sort of. "

"What are you talking about?" Emmett growled.

"He was the one who hired someone to kill Sam. I finally found evidence of that. But he was also receiving orders from an unknown number. I did some digging while I was waiting for the satellite to re-calibrate," Owen explained. "The phone number links back to a phone registered to Jonathan Burke."

"So?" Emmett prodded. "Bellamy's father was behind everything all along? He was somehow pulling the strings with Powell?"

"In a manner of speaking, yes. Except it wasn't Jonathan Burke. Just someone pretending to be him." Owen tapped a few more keys. An image appeared on his computer screen. It was a still from a security feed, showing a man walking into a gas station. "That's Jonathan Burke."

"No it's not," Chance said slowly. "I remember Pastor Burke. That's not him."

"You're right." Owen tapped a few more keys, and a newspaper article appeared on the screen, next to the grainy gas station image.

The headline read, *Governor David Merrell Pays for Boy's Hospital Stay.*

Just underneath, a handsome middle-aged man smiled at them from a photo.

It was the same man as the gas station photo.

"David Merrell had a Swiss bank account that doesn't show up on any of his accounting records. Because of that, nobody seized those assets when he died in that fire. I stumbled across it, but I didn't think anything of it until now. You know that mental institution Bellamy was booked into when she was seventeen? It was owned by a shell corporation with ties to that Swiss bank account. David Merrell's bank account."

A shocked silence descended over the group.

"Remember that assault charge she was arrested for? A hefty deposit showed up in the guy's account two weeks before she allegedly attacked him. A deposit from that same account. All of it came from David."

Chance gripped the edge of the table. He felt sick. One look at Emmett proved that he was feeling the same way.

"We need to find her."

CHAPTER 23

BELLAMY'S HEAD HURT. Was there ever a time where she didn't have an ache that pervaded every thought? Memory returned in hazy flashes that only half made sense. She tried to shift, but her hands were numb.

Her eyes slid open and she blinked a few times to bring her surroundings into focus. The room was dim. She hung from her wrists, her toes barely brushing the ground. Rough hewn rope dug into her skin, tied in intricate knots to a hook protruding from the ceiling.

A small twin bed sat in the corner of the room, covered with a rumpled blue blanket, as if it had recently been slept in. A small lamp rested on a table next to the bed, its dim light losing the battle with the darkness. The walls were bare, and a thick layer of dust coated everything. It took her a moment to recognize the room, but when she did, her heart sank.

My bedroom.

The bedroom of her childhood, and many of her nightmares since.

Movement drew her gaze to the opposite corner of the room as a dark figure stirred and took a step toward her.

"Ah, princess. Finally awake." The figure took another step forward and his face came into focus in the dim light.

"U-Uncle David?" Terror washed over her like icy water, freezing the blood in her veins.

David smiled, but it wasn't a pleasant one. It was the same smile he'd always had; the smile of a predator closing in on its prey. "So glad you remember me. It's been so long."

He looked the same as in her nightmares, albeit a little older and a lot shabbier. He was still tall. Not muscular, but not thin either. His once-dark hair was graying now, and his face had a sallow, sunken-in look to it. The clothes he wore looked old and seemed to hang on his frame. His eyes raked her body from top to bottom, crazed and intent.

"W-What are y-you doing here?" Bellamy's teeth chattered and she realized that her clothes were still soaked from the rain. How long had she been hanging here?

David circled her. "You know, I took you under my wing when you were so young. Maybe I spoiled you, but I treated you so well, princess. Better than I would have treated my own daughter, even. I just wish you could have seen it that way."

"How-?"

He laughed, low and menacing. "How am I alive? How, indeed. My own niece stabbed me in the back, after all. Literally." He grinned, but it turned into a sneer. "What a nice time you've had since you betrayed me."

He held up her mother's necklace.

Bellamy froze, watching the pendant swing back and forth in front of her.

Bile rose in her throat, acidic and bitter, and she swallowed hard. She tested the bindings on her wrists, but of course they were solid. David was no amateur.

She knew what was coming next.

* * * * * *

"Why isn't it working?" Chance raged. He stalked back and forth across the living room. His jaw was clenched so hard that he was certain it would be stuck that way.

Owen sat on the couch with his laptop on the coffee table in front of him. "Even though we fixed the satellite connection, the storm is still wreaking havoc on the GPS," he replied, frustrated. "I can't get a read on her location. All I know is she's still in town."

"You can't give me anything better than that?" Chance snapped.

"Dude, I'm working on it."

Chance groaned and ran a hand through his hair and over his face. He'd thought he was so brilliant when he put that tracking device in Bellamy's necklace. But what good did it do if he couldn't even use it to find her? He prayed that she still had the necklace on her, and that Owen's calculations were correct and she was indeed still in town. It had been almost twelve hours since she ran out. Her kidnapper could have her miles away by now.

Sarah came up behind him and put a hand on his shoulder. She looked just as tense as he was, but she tried to give him a comforting smile.

"We'll find her. Right, Emmett?"

Emmett stood at the window, arms crossed over his chest. He didn't answer.

Chance dropped onto the couch next to Owen and re-checked the ammo in his gun for the millionth time. This had already been the longest day of his life, and it wasn't going to be over anytime soon. Was it really only that morning that he'd kissed Bellamy goodbye and they'd gone to find her father? It felt like an eternity ago.

* * * * * *

"I was so kind to you, and how did you repay me?"

David's voice was calm, but Bellamy didn't like the crazed look in his eyes. He'd always been cold and calculating, but something was different now. He was breathing hard and his movements were jerky, like he wasn't in full control of himself. Bellamy couldn't reconcile this version of her uncle with the one she'd spent years with. She couldn't predict what he would do, and that scared her more than she would admit.

She again pulled at the rope on her wrists, trying to work it loose without drawing his attention.

"You must get it from your father," David continued. He circled in front of her again and Bellamy's eyes caught the glint of steel in his hands. He was holding a knife, turning it over and over in his fingers.

"I killed him too, you know."

Bellamy's gaze shot up to meet his. Her uncle had always been mentally abusive, intent on showing her his power and control, but he'd never been violent. He'd always preferred mental abuse over physical violence.

"Oh, yes, I never told you." David smiled that terrifying smile again. "He came to me after he killed your mother. That fool thought he could take you from me, but I wouldn't let him near you."

"You killed him?" She didn't really want to hear the details, but she had to keep him talking. It was her only chance of survival. "How?"

David dragged a finger across the blade and rested it on the tip, the sharp point barely poking into his skin. "I shot him in the head." He smiled at the memory. "He begged for his life, but I didn't show him any mercy. I never liked him, you know. Ever since he took your mother from me. I loved her."

Something about the way he said that made chills break out across Bellamy's skin.

"What do you mean?" she asked between chattering teeth.

David smiled like a parent indulging a spoiled child. "Your mother and I were always very close," he said. "I gave her this necklace, you know. She always said she hated me. She threw it back in my face when I gave it to her, but she took it with her when she left, didn't she? When she married your pathetic excuse of a father. I knew she always regretted leaving me."

He paused, and the reality of the situation sank in.

Bellamy thought back to the complicated expression on her mother's face when she told her the meaning behind the necklace. The puzzle pieces fell into place. Her mother had been abused by David too. David wasn't physically abusive, but Bellamy knew from experience that the mental abuse was just as debilitating. Her mother's dream of being free had been a joke; she'd thought she was getting away by marrying Bellamy's father.

But in truth, she'd just traded one monster for another.

Her mother had known. When she sent Bellamy away, she'd known what she was sending her daughter to.

Tears sprang to Bellamy's eyes. Even through everything her mother had allowed her father to do, Bellamy had always held on to the belief that her mother loved her.

She was a fool. No one had ever truly loved her.

Bellamy couldn't hold her head up with the weight of that revelation. She allowed it to hang and looked at the floor, battling not to let the tears show.

"Don't you cry for him." David's voice was sharp. He bounced on the balls of his feet, turning that knife over and over in his hands. "He got your mother, but I would never allow him to get you. I saved you, princess. I shot him in the head. I won. I couldn't allow him to take what's mine again."

"What did you do with him?" Bellamy's voice was quiet. "My father, I mean. What did you do with his body?"

"Oh, I buried him. I threw his body in an old trunk and buried it in the backyard. You know that tree swing you always sat on? Your father was right underneath it."

Bellamy swallowed hard and raised her head. Oddly,

she did feel thankful to him. Jonathan had killed her mother - and if he'd found Bellamy, he would have done the same to her.

But all the abuse she'd received at David's hand could never be forgiven. He had spent years tearing down everything she knew; her confidence, her independence, her sense of self.

She looked at him with all the hatred she'd harbored for so many years.

Nobody would save her. She was on her own, just like she'd always been.

She didn't care if she lived or died. Never would she be a victim again. Never would she cower from anyone who would seek to hurt her. She wasn't going to give her uncle the satisfaction of seeing her fear.

Not this time.

"Is that why you killed Sam?" she demanded. "Did she find out about you?"

"Ah, Samantha," David said. "She was a smart girl, but too nosey for her own good. I had a plan. I assumed your father's identity, biding my time and watching you. Waiting for the right moment to make your world fall apart around you. I've been cultivating Ronald Powell for years, funding his little arms dealings and blackmailing him into doing what I want. I'm the reason you were employed with him in the first place."

Bellamy stared at the ground, her mind reeling as all the pieces fell into place. "You were connected to Powell," she repeated. "That's how Sam found you."

"Yes." He stepped close to her, so they were a breath

apart. "She dug around and found out about me. She cornered me at a gas station, began asking me questions. Questions about you. She was too close. Too close. So I followed her to the bank. I made sure she would never tell a soul what she discovered."

A red haze clouded Bellamy's vision. Her best friend had been murdered by pure bad luck. She investigated the wrong person and stumbled into something much bigger than she could handle.

She'd been murdered all because she had the misfortune of knowing Bellamy.

All those years of working for Powell, the things Bellamy had done to survive, the guilt she'd carried around, the belief that she was just a bad person...

Uncle David was behind all of it.

He had manipulated her, just like he always did.

Bellamy reared her head back and spit in David's face.

CHAPTER 24

"THERE SHE IS!"

Chance's head snapped up from where he'd been poring over a map with Emmett.

Owen leaned back in his chair and stretched his arms over his head. His back popped in at least three places. He winced, brow furrowing as he examined the blinking dot on his screen. "Wait a second," he said. "This can't be right. She's in Mom's neighborhood."

Chance shot to his feet. "Her parents' house."

He started toward the door, but Emmett grabbed his arm and pulled him to a stop.

"Hold on a minute."

Chance yanked his arm free and glared at his older brother. "I'm not waiting another second. She's already been in that psycho's hands for ten hours."

"Chance, listen to him," Sarah said. "You can't go off

half-cocked. This guy has probably killed more than one person. He has Bellamy hostage. We need a plan."

"You don't need a plan," Emmett growled at her. "We need a plan. You're not going."

Sarah put her hands on her hips. "You're going to need me. I hate to say this, but Bellamy could be hurt. I have emergency medical training."

"Roman's our medic."

Sarah turned to glare at Roman. He had been standing against the wall, watching the exchange. He leveled a long, considering look at her, and raised his hands in a placating gesture. "Sorry, boss, but I think I agree with her on this one. It's personal. She needs to go. I'll be there to provide backup."

Sarah looked taken aback at Roman's graceful response. She sent him a brief smile before turning back to look at Emmett.

Emmett glared at the two of them.

"Emmett," Chance snapped. "If we're going to make a plan, let's do it. We don't have time to argue."

After a moment of silence, Emmett nodded and stood to address the team. "Here's how we're going to do this."

* * * * * *

David's fury was like nothing Bellamy had ever seen.

He had told her many times that he didn't like to resort to physical punishments. Instead he would find creative ways to hurt her, like the institution visit or the boy she had "attacked".

She'd quickly learned to stay on his good side. He was vindictive and vicious when it came to punishment.

But now it was as if something in him had snapped. No longer was he controlled and thoughtful; instead he seemed to be the opposite.

Unpredictable. Violent.

He got right in her face until they were nose to nose and grabbed her chin in a bruising grip. "No one speaks to me that way," he said, his voice so low that she could barely hear it.

He released her and slapped her so hard that her ears rang. Bellamy's head snapped to the left. Tears burned her eyes but she bit her lip, refusing to let them fall.

"You betrayed me!" he shouted, all his iron control lost. "I knew you were just like your mother. Just like your father." He fingered the knife, suddenly calm again, and smiled at her. "There's only one fitting punishment. I'm going to cut you like you cut me."

Bellamy shook her hair out of her face, breathing hard. She wasn't sure if she was more terrified when he was yelling or when he was quiet. His years in hiding had changed him into something else; something she'd never seen before.

He was going to kill her.

She closed her eyes and pictured Chance's face. He had done so much for her since they met again. It had been heartless to leave him like that, no matter what his reaction to her confession had been. He probably thought she ran away again.

Would he even look for her this time?

He didn't deserve this. He'd never know what happened to her.

She loved him, and she'd never get the chance to tell him.

Bellamy clenched her teeth as David drew nearer. She thought she'd given up believing in God a long time ago, but she found herself sending a mental prayer to the Big Guy, just in case.

David tapped the knife on his chin. "It's been so long," he mused. "I almost can't remember how it began. Oh, yes."

He touched the blade to her left bicep.

"You tried to get the knife away from me. We fought. You cut me here."

The blade was sharp; it cut through her skin like butter. Bellamy bit her lip to stop the cry that wanted to escape. Warm liquid dripped down her arm, but she was so numb that she almost didn't feel the pain.

Almost.

David smiled and wiped the blood off the blade with his index finger. "Much more satisfying than I remember. Now where was next?"

Bellamy's right thigh.

David cut long and deep. This time Bellamy did cry out as pain lanced through her body. Her vision went dark for a moment. The only sound in the room was the gasping coming from her chest.

"Does that hurt, princess? It's only just the beginning."

* * * * * *

Six inches of water covered the roads. Chance thumped his palm against the dashboard in frustration. The team had taken two vehicles, and even though they were both all-terrain, it was still slow-going.

Chance rode in the first vehicle with his siblings. It was quiet; they were all tense and anxious. He glanced in the backseat to see that Sarah's face was pale, but the set of her shoulders told him that she was determined to help Bellamy however she could.

Owen sat next to her, his eyes glued to the tablet in his lap, watching the flashing dot that indicated Bellamy's location for any sign of movement.

Chance faced front again and looked at Emmett. "Can't you go any faster?"

Emmett glanced at him. Normally he would have responded with an irritated quip, but he was quiet. His brows furrowed, the only indicator that he felt the same urgency Chance did.

Chance slumped back against the seat and checked the magazine in his pistol again. He knew it was full, but he needed something for his hands to do or he was going to lose it.

When Bellamy walked back into his life, he should have recognized that she'd changed. He'd been so stuck on his mental picture of her that he'd never taken the time to get to know the woman in front of him.

And when he was faced with evidence that she wasn't the innocent child he remembered, he'd allowed himself to be suspicious of her. Doubted her. Questioned her.

As if he was the epitome of innocence himself.

Chance gritted his teeth, praying with all his might that she was still alive.

His stomach twisted and he swallowed hard to settle it. He needed to clear his mind; he couldn't go into a hostage situation like this.

Emmett pulled his radio out of its holster on the dash. "We're getting close," he said. "When we get there, fan out. We need all the exits covered. Chance and I are going in first. You guys cover the exits and shoot anyone who's not supposed to leave that building."

"Roger," Roman's voice replied.

Emmett pulled the truck over a few houses down from Bellamy's childhood home. The neighborhood was eerily quiet with everyone evacuated. It was a small relief to the team, though. At least they wouldn't have to worry about innocent people being caught in the crossfire.

Thunder rumbled in the distance and rain splashed around them, but otherwise it was silent. Chance turned off the safety on his Sig Sauer and nodded to Emmett, who had done the same. Every member of the team wore tactical gear and bullet-proof vests over their clothing. Even Sarah had dressed to look the part. Her blonde hair was tucked under a black hat.

"Sarah, you stay behind us. Only come out when we tell you," Chance told her.

Sarah rolled her eyes and showed him the gun she held at her side, as if that was proof enough that she was ready for this. She may not officially be a part of ESI, but she'd had plenty of practice with a weapon - thanks to her brothers.

Chance and Emmett approached the house with Sarah

on their heels. Water leaked into the top of his boots, at least a foot deep. This area was close to the river and it was flooding faster than everywhere else. They had to move at a painstaking pace to avoid loud splashing sounds. Roman and Cameron disappeared around the back of the house. Dominick was already set up somewhere behind them with his rifle aimed at the front door.

Emmett held a finger to his lips when they reached the front door, more for Sarah's benefit than Chance's. He reached out a gloved hand and tried the doorknob. To Chance's surprise, the door opened easily despite the flooding. Only about three inches of water covered the hardwood floor in front of them, thanks to the building's cement foundation. Emmett pointed at himself, then down the main hall. He indicated that Chance should search the upstairs. Chance nodded his acknowledgement and they split up. He watched Sarah creep down the main hallway behind Emmett for a moment before he turned to the stairs.

Chance let out a deep breath and allowed focus to settle over him. He'd done ops like this a hundred times. He knew how to move silently, to sweep every room before entering. Just like any other op, he told himself. That was the only way he'd be able to refrain from charging up the stairs like a madman.

Chance took the stairs one at a time, slower than he thought possible. When he'd almost reached the top, the blood froze in his veins when he heard the scream.

CHAPTER 25

BELLAMY SHRIEKED AS the knife sliced her side.

Her limbs shook. Blood covered her body. She could hear it dripping down onto the floor below her, too loud in the silent house.

She couldn't think past the throbbing from every open wound.

David had stopped smiling. He wore a look of grim determination now.

Every swipe of his knife was calculated to maximize her pain.

"Almost there," he said, his voice almost soothing. "After this, do you remember what happened next?"

Bellamy didn't answer. She used every ounce of

strength she had to hold her head high and meet his gaze.

His face went in and out of focus.

She could feel unconsciousness threatening to pull her under, but she was determined to stare into his eyes until he killed her.

She could only hope that he would be haunted by it for the rest of his miserable life.

David lifted his shirt to reveal an ugly purple scar on his chest.

"It was here," he said. His eyes were wide, his pupils so dilated that she couldn't see the dark brown of his irises.

Bellamy clenched her teeth, drawing on the last reserves of her strength.

All her life, she had been a victim, never fighting back against the people who hurt her. Always playing to their whims, doing whatever she could to stay alive.

Damned if she was going to die the same way.

"Do it," she snarled at him. She hoped her voice sounded as strong as the vehemence in her words, but her strength was flagging.

David's eyebrows lowered and he grabbed her chin in a merciless grasp. "No one defies me."

He raised the knife and the point touched her chest, just over her pounding heart.

Bellamy closed her eyes. This was it.

Chance's face came to her mind again.

The way he'd held her after her nightmare. The look in his eyes when he'd given her the dove pendant. The feel of his lips when he kissed her on their bench in the rain.

She loved him.

If she was honest with herself, she'd loved him since she was five years old and he'd invited her to play with him. He'd had her heart all these years and he didn't even know it.

She hoped someday he would understand why she'd run away. Not because she was afraid of him or angry at him, but because she'd been afraid of her own feelings.

Ever since he'd come back into her life, he had broken down her walls piece by piece, leaving her vulnerable. She'd felt more alive in the last two weeks than she had in the last eight years, and he was to blame.

It was wonderful, and terrifying, and she wished it could have gone on forever.

A loud bang echoed in the room.

Had David decided to shoot her and get it over with? Her pain was already so intense that she hadn't felt the bullet.

Her eyes flew open.

The bedroom door hung open, vibrating from the force of being slammed against the wall. Chance stood in the doorway, as if her thoughts had summoned him there. He was dressed in black. His dark clothes were soaked, sticking to him and showing every muscle in his chest and arms. He was breathing hard, but his gaze was intent and focused on David. Both arms stretched in front of him, steady and strong. A dangerous-looking black pistol pointed right at David's chest.

Chance.

Bellamy wasn't sure if she breathed his name out loud or in her mind. Relief and terror flooded simultaneously through her.

He didn't know David like she did. David would kill him before Chance could -

Chance took the shot.

A loud bang echoed in the room. Then another.

Bellamy squeezed her eyes shut, trying to dispel the ringing in her ears.

The air smelled like gunpowder and blood and death.

David staggered back, away from Bellamy, and his hands went to his chest. Dark stains bloomed on his shirt. He looked down, his mouth opening in a snarl.

His eyes moved back to Chance, and Bellamy's blood froze at the look of retribution in his gaze.

Then his body tipped and he fell to the floor with a loud thump, his head turned away from them.

He didn't move again.

Bellamy stared at his prone body.

Was he dead? Just like that?

He had been torturing her for what felt like a lifetime, and in a matter of seconds, he was gone.

Bellamy tried to feel something; horror, happiness, relief, anything, but instead she just felt empty.

Chance surged toward her. His eyes swept her up and down, taking in her wounds, and his expression darkened.

Without a word, he picked up David's knife from the ground and sliced the ropes that bound her wrists to the ceiling.

Bellamy wasn't ready for the sudden gravity.

Her legs couldn't support her weight and she would have toppled to the ground, but Chance grabbed her around the waist and pulled her against him.

"Chance," she whispered. "How-?"

Pain slammed through her as he jostled her wounds, but she didn't have the energy to protest.

Chance's body trembled against hers.

"I thought I was too late," he said into her hair.

Bellamy felt like she was wading through neck-deep mud. Her body felt heavy, her mind sluggish. She was in shock. She wanted to lift her arms to hug him back, but they hung listless by her side.

Chance lifted his head to look down at her, but sudden movement drew Bellamy's gaze from his.

A dark figure loomed over Chance's shoulder. She opened her mouth to shout a warning, but David crashed her bedside table lamp against the side of Chance's head before she could get a word out.

Chance went down hard. His gun skittered across the floor.

Bellamy was on her own two feet somehow and she couldn't take her eyes off of Chance's body. He didn't move.

Was he dead?

The relief she'd been feeling turned to dread, and then to a fury greater than anything she'd ever known.

Bellamy let out a screech - at least she thought it came from her own mouth - and hurled herself at her uncle.

They both toppled to the floor.

She rained blows down on David's head, to hurt him the way he'd hurt Chance, but she'd lost too much blood. David overpowered her easily, grabbing her wrists and pinning them above her head as he rolled on top of her.

He released them and his hands circled her neck with surprising strength despite the bullet wounds in his chest.

David's eyes were huge, the skin on his face paperwhite. He was fading fast, blood pouring from his chest, but his grip was strong.

Bellamy scrabbled at his hands, but she couldn't loosen them. Panic made her chest heave, desperate to inhale oxygen into her lungs.

Her eyes went to Chance's body again. He still hadn't moved. She couldn't even see his chest rising and falling.

If she died here, David would kill him.

If she lived, at least he stood a chance.

Her scrambling fingers hit the cold butt of a gun. She dragged the weapon toward her, wedging it between their bodies. The barrel pressed into David's neck, just underneath his chin.

David was so intent on choking her that he didn't notice until it was too late.

His dark eyes met hers.

Time slowed. Bellamy remembered every moment that he'd exercised his control over her. Every time he made a snide comment or locked her in her room without food for days. Every time he visited her in the mental hospital and took pleasure in touching her while she was drugged and couldn't move.

Every time her father had hit her mother. Every time she'd tried to stop him, only to become the abused herself. Every time her mother held her while she cried herself to sleep afterwards.

Every time she had been the victim, with no power to

fight back.

Bellamy met David's eyes. "I'm not the same girl... you used to pick on," she choked out.

His grip tightened on her throat in one last desperate attempt at victory.

She pulled the trigger once, twice, three times.

The flash of the gunpowder was bright in the dark room. The light and sound incapacitated her for a moment, and she didn't move as David's body slumped over hers. His grip loosened around her neck and she choked in a breath of precious air.

Her lungs filled again and again, leaving her gasping underneath the weight of her uncle's body.

Bellamy shoved him away with a Herculean effort.

He rolled onto the floor next to her, and this time he was truly dead.

Her strength was gone, her body shaking from cold and blood loss, but she hauled herself across the floor to Chance's prone form and forced herself up to her knees next to him.

"Chance?" she whispered. She reached out a trembling hand and shook his shoulder. "Chance, wake up."

He didn't move.

"Chance. Please. Please don't leave me," she sobbed. "Please, I love you."

Footsteps sounded in the hallway, moving fast in her direction. Bellamy threw herself in front of Chance's body and scrambled to her feet.

Two black figures entered the room. She swung the gun up in their direction. "Don't come any closer," she snapped. "I'll shoot."

"Bellamy?"

She didn't register her name. The barrel of the gun wobbled in her grip and she licked her lips, willing herself to steady it. She wasn't sure how she was still conscious. Everything seemed like it was happening at the other end of a dark tunnel.

"Bellamy, hey, put the gun down. Hey, it's Sarah. Can you hear me?"

Bellamy froze, blinking hard. She tried to bring the figure's face into focus, but she still had spots in her vision from the gun's blasts. She recognized Sarah's voice, though, and allowed the gun to slip from her fingers. She fell to her hands and knees with relief.

"Help him," she said.

Emmett rushed to Chance's side while Sarah kneeled in front of Bellamy. Her face was pale and tense as she looked Bellamy over. "We need to get you to a hospital. Oh, God, Bellamy, I'm so sorry."

"Not me," Bellamy insisted. "Help him."

"He's unconscious. Blow to the head," Emmett reported from Chance's side.

"I'm more worried about you," Sarah said. "Lie down; we need to stop the bleeding."

Bellamy shook her head. "I-I'm fine." Her voice sounded far away to her own ears. "Just... help Chance."

Sarah murmured to Emmett, but Bellamy couldn't make out the words. The dark tunnel she was observing everything through suddenly yawned, growing bigger. Now that she knew Chance would be taken care of, she allowed the darkness to take her.

CHAPTER 26

SARAH WATCHED BELLAMY'S EYES roll back into her head. Her body went boneless and she would have tipped over sideways if Sarah hadn't grabbed onto her shoulders.

Emmett leaned forward and supported Bellamy's back and head as Sarah laid her down on the floor beside Chance.

"Call 911," Sarah said. "We need an ambulance here. Now."

Emmett nodded once and stood to follow her directive. For once, he didn't seem to question her ability.

"Sarah. Emmett." Owen burst into the room. He took in the scene with a quick glance and locked eyes with his twin. "What do you need?"

Sarah looked down at her brother and her best friend. For a moment, panic seized her. What should she do first? Bellamy was covered in blood. She couldn't even tell where she was wounded or how much of it was hers.

Oh God, was she going to be okay?

An image popped into Sarah's head, a memory of another close friend, covered in blood in a dark alley. Sightless eyes staring into hers as he took his last breath.

Owen dropped to his haunches next to her. He put a hand on her shoulder and said, "Focus. What do you need?"

Sarah took a deep breath and closed her eyes. She shoved the mental image into a box and locked it. Now wasn't the time to let her panic take over; instead, she allowed her training to kick in.

"Grab my med kit from my bag. We need to stop this bleeding or she's not going to last long."

"We need an ambulance," she heard Emmett say from the other side of the room. His expression was fierce as he held the radio speaker to his ear. He rattled off the address, pausing as the operator responded. "What do you mean, thirty minutes? We don't have that long. Get me the sheriff. I need to talk to McCauley."

Sarah tuned him out as Owen returned with her kit. She grabbed a pair of scissors and cut away Bellamy's blood-soaked clothing so she could see the damage. She had various cuts on her arms and legs, but the worst was a deep laceration on her right side. It oozed dark liquid. If Sarah didn't stop the bleeding, Bellamy would lose too much and even a transfusion might not save her.

"We need to clean this," Sarah muttered to Owen. "Hand me that bottle of alcohol."

Owen handed her a large brown bottle. "Tell me what I can do to help."

"Hold her down. She's not gonna like this."

Owen grabbed hold of Bellamy's shoulders as Sarah uncapped the bottle. She trickled a bit of the liquid onto the wound.

Bellamy bucked in Owen's grip and let out a hoarse shout.

"Dammit." Owen tried to grab her flailing wrists, but Bellamy jerked away from him, muttering incoherently.

Emmett appeared next to them and grabbed Bellamy's legs. Sarah glanced over to see that his face was pale. "Do it. Hurry up," he said through clenched teeth.

Sarah nodded and poured a generous amount of liquid on the laceration. Bellamy shook her head back and forth, but she couldn't break from her brothers' grip.

"Please, stop," she whispered. "Please."

"Shit," Emmett said. "Hurry up, will you?"

Sarah grabbed a good amount of gauze and padded it over the wound, taping it securely. "Apply pressure to this."

Owen nodded grimly and placed his hands over Bellamy's side.

"How long is that ambulance going to be?" Sarah asked Emmett.

"Fifteen minutes. The roads are flooded but McCauley is sending a chopper."

"Let's hope we can make it that long." Sarah scooted over to Chance and ran deft hands over his body, checking for any other injuries.

"Is Chance all right?" Owen asked.

"I think so." Sarah felt around his head. There was a large lump forming right behind his left ear. "I think it's just a knock on the head."

"He got knocked out? He might lose his man card for that one." A ghost of a smile passed over Owen's face.

Sarah couldn't help but smile back. "Looks like Bellamy's the one who did the saving this time."

Emmett didn't answer. His eyes were still on Bellamy.

"Emmett. What's wrong?" Sarah asked.

"She shouldn't have been in this situation."

"What do you mean?"

"I mean we should have protected her better. I didn't trust her, and because of that she was almost killed."

Sarah reached out to touch his arm. She didn't speak until he looked away from Bellamy and down to her. "The important thing is that she's alive. We need to keep her that way so Chance can say what he needs to say to her. And after he's done, you need to do the same."

Emmett looked at her for a long moment and pulled her into a side hug. "Thanks."

They stood vigil by Bellamy's side until the sound of the helicopter's blades broke the silence, signaling that help had finally arrived.

CHAPTER 27

THE SHARP, TANGY SMELL OF antiseptic penetrated the layers of unconsciousness. Bellamy would recognize it anywhere, and she fought through the darkness to reach awareness. She hated hospitals.

What had she done this time? Her memory was murky at best. Was it her father that put her here? Would she wake up with her mother beside her, smiling even though her eyes were worried?

She awoke slowly, still in a dream-like fog that she recognized as pain medication. Somewhere she knew that something terrible had happened, but she didn't want to try to remember. Instead, she wanted to float here forever, pain-free and carefree.

Before long, though, the memories started to return. Bits and pieces fell into place in the puzzle that was the last seven days.

Paul's funeral. Bellamy didn't want to go, but Sam packed a bag for her and bought a plane ticket. She saw Chance again for the first time in ten years.

Sam's brown eyes staring out at her from the dumpster. No, she didn't want to think about that.

Chance kissing her on the bench by the river. It was just like she remembered from high school. His lips were warm, like a fire on a cold day. Warm tingles spread through her at the thought.

Rain, falling in sheets.

The metal of a blade glinting in a dim room.

Her uncle's dark eyes widening in death on top of her.

Chance lying dead next to her - -

Bellamy's eyes flew open. The rhythmic beeping from the machine next to her went crazy, echoing her panic. The fluorescent lighting blinded her.

"Bella?"

The familiar voice washed over her, leaving a warm feeling in its wake. Bellamy relaxed against the pillow and her gaze swung over to the man standing next to the bed. She blinked a few times until his face came into focus.

"Chance." His name came out barely a whisper and she winced at the pain that lanced through her throat.

"Bella, sweetheart, I'm so glad you're awake." A stark white bandage wrapped around Chance's head and he was a bit pale, but otherwise he looked healthy. He grinned from ear to ear at her.

"What-?" she tried, but no sound came out. She cleared her throat, wincing again.

"Shh," Chance told her. "Your throat is still pretty

bruised. The doctors said you might not have a voice for a while. No permanent damage to your vocal chords though."

The memories came flooding back. Bellamy closed her eyes against the torrent of painful images. It had been David all along. He had tortured her. He had hurt Chance. Bellamy had thought he was dead.

She had killed David.

She killed him.

Bellamy opened her eyes.

Chance pulled a chair up next to the bed. He sank into it, his eyes never leaving her face. He took one of her hands with both of his and raised it to his lips in a gentle kiss.

With her other hand, Bellamy reached up and touched the bandage around his head. She shot him a questioning look.

"Oh, this? I'm fine. Just a minor concussion. I can't believe I let the bastard take me by surprise like that." Chance's expression darkened. "I'm just glad you're okay. Do you remember what happened?"

Bellamy nodded, replaying the scene in her head again. She looked away from him. "I... killed him."

Chance squeezed her hand until her eyes met his. "You were protecting yourself," he told her. "From a monster that doesn't deserve to walk this earth. You shouldn't feel guilty."

She frowned. Guilty didn't describe how she felt. On the contrary, she felt a rush of satisfaction that she'd gotten justice for the wrongs that David had done to her. For Sam's death. For hurting Chance.

No, she didn't feel guilty at all.

The bastard had deserved it.

Her past really had changed her, turned her into a monster. She'd fought it, but Emmett was right all along.

"He killed your father," Chance continued. "The police found his body right where you said it would be."

"I told you that?"

Chance smiled. "You were a little loopy in the ambulance. But Sarah sat with you and she heard you murmuring about it, so we checked it out. I'm sorry."

Bellamy shook her head. "Don't be," she whispered. "I'm not sorry that either of them is dead."

He squeezed her hand tighter. "We also found Sam's research. David had a flash drive on him. He must've stolen it from her. It had everything she discovered about your uncle, and your father. That, along with the evidence Owen found and Powell's murder, should be enough to make sure the world knows the truth."

Bellamy stared at the ceiling. Again she felt a pang of sadness over Sam's death, and more than a pang of guilt. She wasn't sure she'd ever stop blaming herself for her friend's murder. But at least she'd made sure he would never hurt anyone else.

Chance turned her hand over. He reached into his pocket to retrieve something and dropped it into her palm. Bellamy lifted it up so she could see it. For a moment, she was distracted by the IV sticking out of her hand. The clear tube was connected to her skin, held by a piece of white tape. Her hand looked pale and fragile. What did the rest of her look like under these bandages? She shook off the thought and focused on the item in her palm.

It was her mother's pendant.

Bellamy stared hard at it. A dozen memories flooded through her. All the times her mother had told her the meaning behind the pendant, the freedom that she was never able to have. The truth that she'd discovered about her mother's relationship with David. Bellamy's revelation that if she was to gain her own freedom, she needed a fresh start. David's face when he saw the necklace. His satisfied expression as he slashed her skin with his knife.

Bellamy dropped the necklace as if she'd been burned.

Chance's smiled faded and he looked at her with a question in his eyes.

She looked down at the necklace again. That's right; in the moments before her kidnapping, she'd been sitting on the bench in the rain. She'd decided that she needed to leave if she was ever going to be free of her past. But looking at Chance now, could she do that?

Yes. She had to.

Her eyes wandered to the white bandage around his head. He'd gotten off easy this time, but she was dangerous. Uncle David and Ronald Powell might be dead, but Bellamy had many other enemies from her time working as a fence.

She couldn't put Chance and his family at risk. How long would she know happiness before one of them ended up like Sam had?

"Chance," she whispered. She couldn't meet his eyes, so she kept her gaze on the pendant in her lap. "As soon as I get out of this hospital, I'm leaving."

There was a moment of silence. She didn't dare look up to see Chance's expression.

"I'm dangerous." Her voice was still a breathy rasp, but she knew if she didn't say this now, she'd never have the courage again. "Emmett was right. I'm not the same person I used to be. I'm not a good person, like you and your family. I have a lot of enemies and it won't take long for them to find me. I can't stay here. I don't deserve to stay here."

Chance shifted in his seat and leaned forward. "I got something else for you."

Leaning to the left, he reached under his chair and pulled out a white gift bag. He placed it on her lap.

"Chance - "

"Open it."

Bellamy sighed and reached inside the bag. Her fingers brushed against something soft, and she pulled it out.

It was a black leather jacket, soft and supple and brand new.

Chance's large hands dwarfed her small ones. "I don't want you to leave."

Swallowing hard, Bellamy met his eyes. There was no doubt there, only sincerity.

Chance picked up the pendant and pushed it into her palm. "Running isn't the answer. You've been running for too long."

"I can't put you in danger again. You or anyone else." Bellamy met his eyes, silently begging him to understand. "People I love get hurt."

"Hey, do you know who I work for?" Chance smiled. "I should be the one worried about that, not you. I can handle whatever you throw at me. We'll get through it if we stay together."

"Chance..."

He shook his head to stop her protest. "I heard you," he said. "After David hit me. You told me not to leave you, Bella, and I didn't. But it has to work the other way, too. You can't leave me either."

Bellamy looked away, unsure how to respond. She couldn't decipher her own feelings at the moment. But Chance's fingers touched her cheek and directed her gaze back to him.

"I've loved you since I was five years old," he began. "I've loved you like a friend, I've loved you like a sister, and now I love you as the woman who fought through hell to make it here. I understand now that you're not the same girl I loved back then, and that's okay. I accept all of you, Bella. Even the dark and broken parts."

Bellamy's eyes filled with tears. He was the only person she'd ever met who could take her defenses down with one smile. She had never returned during all those years because deep down, she knew it would come to this, and she was scared.

Staying with him meant accepting his feelings and her own. It meant becoming vulnerable and allowing him to see all of her. It meant becoming part of a real family that loved her as much as she loved them.

She was afraid of the future, of putting her soul into someone else's hands. But those words she'd spoken when she thought he was dying were the truth. She loved him, and despite the risks, she wanted to be with him.

"Chance," she sobbed. She grabbed his shoulders and pulled him into an embrace. She didn't care that it pulled the IV out of her hand. She didn't care that the wounds all over her body protested.

She had a long way to go before she would be okay. It would be a lot of hard work, and a lot of learning how to trust again. It wouldn't be easy.

But she knew, without a doubt, that if there was anyone she could trust with her heart, it was Chance Erickson. So she whispered the words she'd been wanting to say since the moment she saw him at his father's funeral.

"I love you."

CHAPTER 28

A WEEK LATER, THE STORM HAD PASSED and cleanup began in La Conner.

Bellamy was released from the hospital with strict orders to take it easy. Chance took her to his parents' house, where the family was trying to pick up the pieces now that the waters had receded.

At the height of the storm, the basement of the house had been ten inches underwater. Chance and his brothers helped haul furniture out onto the back deck where it could dry. Bellamy relaxed in a chair outside and sipped lemonade with Mary.

"How are you feeling?" Mary asked. "Do you need anything?"

Bellamy gave her a small smile and shook her head. "I'm okay, thanks."

Mary sighed and leaned back, watching as Owen and

Chance struggled to fit a huge bookcase through the back door. "I hope we can get the basement cleaned and put back together before Sarah comes back from New York."

"When is she coming back?" Bellamy vaguely remembered Sarah talking to her about it when she came to visit in the hospital, but she'd been in and out of consciousness for the first few days after she woke up.

"Two or three days. She's packing up her apartment. It sounds like she's really moving home."

"How do you feel about that?"

Mary smiled. "I'm always happy to have my babies closer to me. It will be nice to have some company around the house. It's been so quiet since Paul's passing."

Bellamy took a sip of her lemonade, not sure how to respond. She still felt a little awkward and guilty staying with Chance and the rest of the family, but she was trying hard to put it behind her.

"I'm glad you're here too, Bellamy." Mary's voice was quiet. She smiled at Bellamy in the same way she smiled at the rest of her children. "It's been too long since you've been home with your family."

Bellamy smiled and felt her eyes fill with tears. She glanced at the men working and looked around at the house and the yard. There were so many memories here, new and old, good and bad. Despite their differences, the Erickson family had always been there for her. Even when they didn't agree with her and didn't trust her, they had protected her. Mary was right; this was her home and the Ericksons were her family. They always had been.

Chance caught her eye from across the yard and

sauntered over to them. "How's the pain? Need more medicine? More lemonade?"

"I'm fine," Bellamy said. "I promise."

Chance dropped a kiss on her forehead and went back to work.

Mary smiled as Bellamy shook her head in exasperation. "He just worries."

"I know." Bellamy sighed. "I just feel a little smothered."

The older woman laughed. "You can expect to feel that way for a while, my dear. He almost lost you. He doesn't want to let you out of his sight." She winked. "It means he loves you."

Her words caused a warm fuzzy feeling in Bellamy's chest. They slipped into a casual silence, each watching the men work.

An hour later, the neighbors came over and Chance and Mary walked next door to help with their basement. Bellamy took the opportunity to get up and move around. Ever since she'd been released from the hospital, Chance had watched her like a hawk. She couldn't even stand up to go to the restroom without him panicking about overexertion. She appreciated the thought and she knew he was worried, but she was going a little stir-crazy.

Bellamy leaned against the deck railing and looked out over the yard. The river had receded back to where it was supposed to be, but it had left a bunch of garbage strewn all over the grass. She hobbled down the stairs and began picking up the larger pieces that she could reach without bending over too far.

"You should be resting."

Bellamy jumped and turned around to see Emmett leaning against a nearby tree, arms crossed over his chest. He regarded her with a guarded expression.

She swallowed and returned to her work. Things had been strained between her and Emmett since she woke up in the hospital. She had a vague memory of Emmett being there when Sarah came and found her and Chance, but the images were still a little fuzzy in her mind. She had made peace with everyone else in the family since she woke up, but Emmett hadn't come to see her in the hospital, and he hadn't spoken to her since she was released. Chance had told her that everything was good between them now, but she still got the feeling that Emmett didn't trust her. She wasn't sure if he ever would, and she couldn't blame him.

Emmett's gaze was heavy on the back of her neck as she continued to work. She was keenly aware of how slow she was moving. "I'm fine," she said over her shoulder, bending carefully to pick up a soda can. The stitches in her side pulled and she sucked in a sharp breath.

Emmett was by her side in an instant. He grabbed her elbow and helped her back into a standing position. "Careful," he said. "Chance will kill me if he sees you working."

Bellamy sighed and allowed him to steer her back to the deck in defeat. "I just wanted to help."

"You saved Chance's life. I think you've helped enough."

She shot him a look, but his expression wasn't sarcastic. It was sincere. "He saved mine," she corrected him.

Emmett helped her back into her chair and leaned on the deck railing next to her. His broad shoulders hunched up to his neck. "Bellamy, I need to apologize to you."

"Emmett-"

"No, hear me out." He paused as if to gather his thoughts. "You were right, what you said. I've changed since we were young. Trust doesn't come easily to me anymore and I know I made it difficult for you."

"It's not -"

"The truth is," he interrupted again. "You saved Chance's life. Mom said that you've been a part of the family for a long time and she's right. You're more of an Erickson than I am."

Bellamy clasped her hands together in her lap and kept her head down. "Thanks, but I don't feel like I deserve your praise."

"I know how hard it is to escape the past." Emmett waited until she looked up at him before he continued. His green eyes met hers. "But I was wrong. The past doesn't define you. And it only has a hold on you if you let it." He looked away and seemed to be lost in his own thoughts.

"Do you really believe that?"

He looked down at her again. "I have to."

Bellamy stared across the grass at the slow-moving river. "I don't know what happened to you, but I can speak from experience when I say that the past does shape us."

She felt Emmett's gaze shoot to her face, but she didn't look at him.

"The truth is, the past makes us who we are. I wouldn't wish my experiences on anyone else, but they've made me stronger." She looked up and smiled at him. "Because of the things I went through, I'm standing here today. I'm bruised,

I'm broken, but I'm still here. So are you. I get the feeling that we're a lot alike, Emmett. I've always looked up to you. I still do. Whatever you're dealing with, just know that you have to let it go if you're going to move on." Bellamy chuckled under her breath. "I'm trying to take my own advice on that too."

Emmett's jaw set. "I wish I could, but my past isn't something I can let go or walk away from."

"Then face it. Face it head on. If you do that, you'll come out the other side a lot stronger."

He sat in silence for a moment, his eyes stormy as he looked out across the backyard. Bellamy wasn't sure if he would speak to her again, but after a long time, he looked down and smiled at her. "Thanks, Bellamy. I'm glad you're sticking around."

"Me too." Bellamy smiled at him. For the first time in a long time, she felt like she was right where she belonged. "Maybe you haven't changed so much after all."

Emmett smiled back. "You too, kid. You're not so bad yourself."

NEXT IN THE ESI SERIES

Keep reading for a sneak peek at the next book in the ESI series:

COUNTERPLAY

Available now!

https://bit.ly/CounterPlay

PROLOGUE

Five Years Ago...

ROMAN TAPPED THE BOTTOM of the magazine in his M4, ensuring it was firmly in place, and pulled the charging handle toward him. The sound echoed in the jungle around him, but surveillance had already determined that the area was clear.

He released a breath and checked his earpiece. The quiet static assured him it was working properly, even though his team was operating on radio silence.

"We're passing Alpha," a voice spoke into the radio. It was Jeffries, team lead. As usual, he was calm and collected despite the fact that they were about to engage in a firefight with one of the most dangerous drug lords in the world.

They were just outside the Golden Triangle, which meant a firefight here could bring several neighboring cartels down on them before they could make an escape.

But they had the opportunity to cut off the head of the snake, and the United States government wouldn't let that pass them by, no matter the risk.

Roman's intel from two years undercover had gotten them here, and many lives had been lost to find the location of Altez's compound. After today, Roman's cover would be compromised. He could never go back to the cartel again.

It was now or never.

Roman crept through the trees, using the shadows to blend into his surroundings as he approached the main building of the compound. His teammates were doing the same thing on the south, west, and north sides of the structure.

Altez was sure of his safety near the Golden Triangle. He didn't even have a wall surrounding his massive home. No cameras, towers, or guards aside from the two posted just outside his front door.

Roman crouched in a tall bush just outside the radius of light from the door and pulled his night-vision goggles down around his neck. He took aim at the guards and waited.

"Breach," Jeffries ordered over the radio.

Roman's first shot hit the left guard in the forehead. Thanks to the suppressor on the end of Roman's gun, the man dropped before his partner even knew what happened. Before the second guard could react, Roman took a second shot and dropped him too.

Although he couldn't hear accompanying gunfire, Roman knew his team was breaching the house from the other entry points.

"Front door is clear," Roman said. "I'm entering the building."

He kicked open the front door and swung his gun in a wide arc. A man popped out of a side door, assault rifle aimed at Roman, but Roman took him out before he could get off a shot.

One by one, his team cleared the rooms on the lower level. Altez was nowhere to be found, and they only ran into a handful of guards.

"Just passed Charlie," Jeffries said into the comms. "Clear the upper floor. I'll watch for stragglers."

Roman led the way upstairs, moving slow and precise. He could feel more than hear his teammates behind him. It was comforting that he had someone on his six, so he could focus on the area in front of him.

He kicked open the first door on the right. A high-pitched scream split the darkness and Roman ducked away from the light flooding in from the hallway. The loud bang of a gunshot echoed not even a second later, followed by a thud.

"Wilson is down," Martinez said into the comms.

Roman cursed silently and yanked his night-vision goggles back up over his eyes. In the green filter, he saw a woman standing in the corner of the bedroom, a gun shaking in front of her. He couldn't make out many details, but she was blonde and wearing a short nightgown. The covers on the bed were rumpled as if she'd just rolled out of them.

"Put the gun down," Roman yelled.

The woman turned and fired blindly in his direction.

He ducked and trained his gun on her again. "Ma'am, put the gun down or I will shoot you."

She shouted a stream of panicked Spanish, but she didn't lower the weapon.

Roman cursed. "Where is Altez? *¿Dónde está Altez?*"

"Roman. Report," Jeffries said in Roman's earpiece.

The woman shook her head. The barrel of the gun shook harder. She was crying now, shouting in broken Spanish. Roman had five years of Spanish under his belt, but he couldn't understand a word she was saying.

"Put the weapon down," he warned. "I don't want to shoot you."

"Holt. Report," Jeffries said again.

"There's a woman here with a gun," Martinez reported. "I'm pinned down in the hallway with Wilson. I can't get to him."

"I'm coming," Jeffries said. "Holt, don't move. Keep her occupied, but don't shoot her. She may know where Altez is."

Easier said than done.

"I don't want to hurt you," Roman said to the woman in Spanish. "Please, put the gun down."

She shook her head, sobbing, and backed up a few steps until her back hit the wall. Her gun was pointing in his general direction, but it was too dark for her to see him. Luckily, she was smart enough not to shoot blindly again.

Footsteps echoed in the hall.

Jeffries appeared in the doorway just as the woman swung her gun around. The barrel steadied, and she let out a breath as she readied to fire.

Roman shot her before she could pull the trigger. She dropped like a stone.

Jeffries rushed forward and kicked the gun away from her limp hands. Roman dropped to his knees next to her and felt his stomach keep falling.

Blood bloomed from a hole in her chest, right where her heart was.

She didn't have a pulse.

Jeffries cursed and lowered his gun, his expression grim. "That's Maria, Altez's wife."

Roman swallowed hard.

This was their only chance to catch him.

Roman had just killed an innocent woman, and Altez got away.

CHAPTER 1

Three weeks ago...

"SARAH ERICKSON!"

The blaring beauty of 80's rock turned tinny as Sarah's headphones were yanked off her ears. She jerked her head up from the medical textbook she'd been squinting at.

"What the?"

Ryan stood with his hands on his hips, camera swinging from the strap around his neck. "I've been calling you for ten minutes. Would it kill you to turn the music off?"

Sarah stuck her tongue out. "First you tell me to wear headphones because it's *interrupting your concentration*" - she emphasized the phrase with air quotes – "and now you're telling me to turn it off?"

"You can't even retain anything with music that loud."

"Says who?"

"I think your grades speak for themselves."

Sarah glared at Ryan, and he glared right back.

Then they both busted up laughing.

"What do you need?" Sarah asked when they had both calmed down. "I'm trying to get some studying in before my shift starts."

Ryan looked down at her EMT uniform. "Are you on ambulance duty tonight?"

"Yeah, until three a.m. Now, what do you want?"

Ryan made a face and raised his camera, snapping a picture of her before she could duck out of sight. Instead of grinning at her like he usually would, his expression stayed sober. "I'm going out for a while. Just wanted to let you know so you didn't freak out."

"Now?" Sarah touched the screen of her phone, squinting at the date. "But it's Tuesday."

"I know. You're going to have to eat Chinese without me." Ryan backed up a few steps, raising a hand. "I've got something important to do. I'll see you later."

"Wait," Sarah said, following him down the hallway and into the living room. "What's more important than Chinese food?"

Ryan pulled on his jacket, hesitated, and then disappeared into his bedroom. He emerged a moment later without his camera. He gave Sarah a kiss on the cheek as he passed, but his expression was already somewhere else.

"Loveyoubye," he said over his shoulder as he closed the front door behind him.

Sarah frowned at the closed door. "Loveyoubye," she murmured.

She took a few moments to ponder Ryan's strange attitude, but she had a test the next morning and only a limited amount of time before her shift started.

* * * * *

Ambulance duty was Sarah's favorite shift. She thrived on the challenge of each call, and she loved helping people.

That night was a quiet one. Between New York City's astronomical crime rate and the insane amount of people living in a small area, her team was usually pretty busy, but they only had one call during Sarah's shift – a car accident with only minor injuries.

Sarah sat with Jackson and Nora, her partner and driver respectively, and played cards during the downtime. She should have been studying, but her brain was fried. She'd rather be paid to play Texas Hold 'Em than study for her biology test.

It was almost 3 a.m. when the station's alert tone sounded in the speaker above their heads.

"So close," Jackson groaned, getting to his feet. He was an older guy, in his mid-forties. "I was looking forward to going to bed at a decent time tonight."

"Got one more in you?" Nora asked with a smile.

"Ugh, I guess so."

Sarah jumped to her feet and put her ear close to the speaker, listening as the dispatcher rattled off an address. "It's a mugging," she said. "Severe injury, possibly fatal."

Jackson rubbed his neck. "Why do you sound excited about that?"

Sarah grinned. "I love this job."

"Yeah, you love it a little too much."

Nora opened the door to the garage, keys jingling in her hand. "Come on, let's do this. I'd like to get home at a decent time too."

The mugging had occurred in Chelsea. Back in the day, the neighborhood was known for its drug activity, but lately, the crime of choice was theft – larceny, muggings, bank robberies. Sarah had been to the area multiple times in her three years of EMS work.

By the time their ambulance arrived on the scene, it was already roped off and several police cars sat nearby with their lights flashing.

Sarah hopped out, Jackson right behind her, and hurried toward the crowd forming at the entrance to an alley. They parted for her like the Red Sea, and she ducked under the police tape.

A policeman waved her over to where the victim lay, another policeman administering CPR.

Sarah dropped to her knees next to the man, her eyes scanning his body for obvious injuries. A dark stain on his coat was already spreading.

"He's hardly breathing," the policeman next to her said, sounding out of breath. "I've been doing CPR but he needs a doctor. Now."

Sarah nodded and gestured for him to move. "We'll take care of him."

She opened the man's coat and lifted up his shirt, exposing the stab wound in his chest. It was just below his heart, but that didn't mean he was safe. There were plenty of other vital organs in that area that could be affected.

"Sir, I'm going to need you to –"

Sarah froze when she finally looked at the man's face.

"R-Ryan?"

Ryan's face was barely recognizable. His cheeks were swollen, his eyes nearly shut, and blood from his broken nose smeared his skin.

He tried to smile at her, but it looked more like a grimace. "I was hoping you'd come," he said softly.

"Ryan, what..." Sarah looked down at the wound on his chest, horror spreading through her like wildfire. "What happened? What are you doing in Chelsea?"

Ryan wheezed a breath, his eyes fluttering closed.

Jackson kneeled next to her. One glance at the damage and he called over his shoulder for Nora to bring the stretcher. "What are you doing?" he said impatiently. "We need to stop the bleeding."

"This is Ryan, my roommate."

For the first time in her career, she felt completely frozen.

Jackson spared her a pitying look. "Now isn't the time to freeze on me, Erickson. Help Nora with the stretcher. Move!"

Sarah stumbled to her feet and ran to the ambulance. She took one end of the stretcher and they hurried it back to Ryan's side. Jackson was already taping gauze over the wound, muttering soothing words.

Ryan appeared to be unconscious. Sarah dropped to her knees and put a finger to the pulse on his neck. It was weak, barely there at all.

"Ryan," she said urgently. "Ryan, you need to wake up. We're going to help you, but you need to wake up."

Ryan didn't move.

"CPR, Erickson, let's go," Jackson snapped.

Sarah bit back a sob and placed her hands over Ryan's chest. She counted the compressions aloud, anything to keep herself from completely losing it.

"We're losing him," Jackson said. "Nora, grab the defib kit."

Sarah put her mouth over his. His chest rose with the force of her air. "Come on, Ryan," she muttered.

"I think his lung is punctured," Jackson said. "His skin is turning blue. He's not getting enough oxygen."

Ryan's eyelids fluttered open. He focused on her, and his lips twitched in another smile. "Sorry," he said softly.

"Shh," Sarah said. "You're going to be fine. Hang in there, okay?"

His eyes closed again.

Sarah looked up at Jackson. The grim expression on his face told her everything she needed to know.

"No. He's going to be fine, right?"

Jackson placed a silent hand on her shoulder.

Sarah shook it off, turning back to Ryan. She grabbed his hand and squeezed it tight. "Ryan, can you hear me?"

No answer.

She dropped his hand and started doing compressions again. She counted to thirty, gave him three breaths, and started all over again.

"Sarah," Jackson said from beside her, voice gentle.

Sarah shook her head and continued her compressions. She wouldn't give up on him. She'd seen people survive worse.

He was a fighter. He could fight through it.

"Sarah, he's gone, sweetheart."

Sarah opened her eyes, her hands slowing on Ryan's chest. With shaking fingers, she touched his neck.

No pulse.

Nora stepped up next to them, the defib kit in her hands. Jackson shook his head at her, then took Sarah's arm and pulled her to her feet.

He led her back to the ambulance and sat her down on the edge.

Sarah watched as he covered Ryan's body with a black sheet. He conversed with the head policeman, probably ordering a coroner to the scene.

She barely registered when her phone rang. With numb fingers, she pulled it out of her pocket.

"Hello?" Her voice sounded hollow, even to her.

"Sarah." It was Owen, her twin brother. His voice sounded worse than she felt. "Sorry to call you this late, but..."

Sarah swallowed hard. "What's wrong?"

"It's time to come home." A long pause. "It's Dad."

THANKS FOR READING!

Thank you so much for supporting me and my work. Please consider leaving an honest review on either Amazon or GoodReads. They are so important to authors, and I'd love to know what you think! Don't forget to share your review on social media with the hashtag *#esiseries* and recommend this book to your friends!

DON'T FORGET TO SIGN UP FOR MY MONTHLY NEWSLETTER

TO RECEIVE SPECIAL OFFERS, GIVEAWAYS, DISCOUNTS, BONUS CONTENT, UPDATES FROM THE AUTHOR, INFO ON NEW RELEASES AND OTHER GREAT READS:

WWW.CEARANOBLES.COM/SUBSCRIBE

ACKNOWLEDGEMENTS

This book would not be in your hands today without the help of an army of family, friends and acquaintances who encouraged me to keep going, even when I wanted to give up.

First and forever, to my amazing husband Grady, who's always willing to assume whatever role I need him to — creative director, brainstorming partner, beta reader, cheerleader, and silent observer. I love you babe!

Second, to my parents, for allowing me to lock myself in my bedroom for days at a time so I could fuel my love of the written word. Without you, I wouldn't have grown up with the passion to be an author.

Third, to my beta readers — Jolyn, Krissy, Grady, Alicia and Sarah — for taking the time to read this story in ALL its iterations... and for the courage to give me your honest feedback.

And lastly, to you, my readers. THANK YOU for reading this story. I am so grateful for your support, and I hope you'll stick around. I have many more stories to tell! Until next time, happy reading!

Ceara Nobles is a Utah-based author of romantic suspense and fantasy novels. She graduated from the University of Utah in 2011 with a B.A. in Computer Animation, then realized she hated it. So she decided to pursue her true love of writing instead. She spends her days writing sales copy as a copywriter... and her evenings writing exciting stories as an author. And she loves both! When she's not busy writing, you can find her snuggling her new baby girl, road tripping with her hubby, or shooing her cats off her laptop.

CONNECT WITH CEARA ON:
    Website: www.cearanobles.com
    Facebook: @cearanoblesauthor
    Instagram: @cearanoblesbooks
    Twitter: @cearanobles
    GoodReads: Ceara Nobles

Made in United States
North Haven, CT
26 November 2022

27305776R00224